World Fantasy Awa
author of two short story collections, *The Dark Country*
and *Red Dreams*, and a highly acclaimed novel,
Darkside.

He lives in Los Angeles, California.

Also by Dennis Etchison and published by Futura

DARKSIDE
THE DARK COUNTRY
CUTTING EDGE edited by Dennis Etchison

DENNIS ETCHISON

Red Dreams

Futura

A Futura Book

First published in the United States of America in 1984
by Scream Press, Santa Cruz

This edition published in 1988
by Futura Publications, a Division of
Macdonald & Co (Publishers) Ltd
London & Sydney

All characters in this publication are fictitious and any resemblance to real persons, living or dead, is purely coincidental.

ISBN 0 7088 3725 5

Printed and bound in Great Britain by
Collins, Glasgow

Futura Publications
A Division of
Macdonald & Co (Publishers) Ltd
Greater London House
Hampstead Road
London NW1 7QX

A member of Maxwell Pergamon Publishing Corporation plc

ACKNOWLEDGEMENTS

The stories listed below first appeared in slightly different form under the following copyrights:

"TALKING IN THE DARK": © 1984 by Charles L. Grant.
"WET SEASON": © 1965 by Star Press, Inc.
"I CAN HEAR THE DARK": © 1978 by Dennis Etchison.
"THE GRAVEYARD BLUES": © 1973 by Mercury Press, Inc. Copyright assigned to the author.
"ON THE PIKE": © 1977 by Dennis Etchison.
"KEEPER OF THE LIGHT": © 1973 by Phenix Publishers, Ltd.
"BLACK SUN": © 1974 by Damon Knight.
"WHITE MOON RISING": © 1977 by Stuart David Schiff.
"THE CHILL": © 1981 by Dennis Etchison.
"THE SMELL OF DEATH": © 1971 by Mercury Press, Inc. Copyright assigned to the author.
"DROP CITY": © 1974 by Mercury Press, Inc. Copyright assigned to the author.
"THE CHAIR": © 1983 by Dennis Etchison.

The versions included in this volume—and these versions alone—represent the definitive texts.
All stories reprinted by permission of the author and the author's agent, Kirby McCauley.

The following story appears in paperback here for the first time: "NOT FROM AROUND HERE": © 1984 by Dennis Etchison.

to

NORMAN LOWE

1945–1980

We wanted more; we looked to find
An open door, an utter deed of love
Transforming day's evil darkness . . . .

—Kenneth Patchen

TABLE OF CONTENTS

Introduction

by Karl Edward Wagner

Dennis Etchison describes himself as an "overworked, underslept, professional wrestling fan" with the "goal to teach John Studd a thing or two in the squared circle." He has also been described as a blend of James Dean and Dudley Moore with a dash of Woody Allen. Friends would add that Etchison probably passed up a career as a stand-up comedian when he turned to writing his own particular brand of horror fiction.

Etchison has been selling short fiction since 1960, but only in the last few years has he begun to receive deserved acclaim as the finest writer of psychological horror this genre has produced. It is never an easy matter to make a name (or earn a living) solely through short fiction, and Etchison, never very prolific, hasn't helped things with his intensely introspective stories of urban paranoia and personal alienation. The average shock fan, in search of shambling multitentacled horrors, psychotic slashers, or scarlet-fanged vampires, will find Etchison at best incomprehensible. The reader of supermarket-pop horror, accustomed to stock characters, soap-opera situations, menacing and/or menaced children, and reassuring happy endings, will consider Etchison a public menace. Even among serious fans of the horror genre, the elusive, ultimately negativistic nature of Etchison's writing is too subtle for some readers and too downbeat for others.

It would be a pat conclusion to describe Etchison as a "cult writer"—a writer who is not well known to the general readership, but who has gained a small and enthusiastic circle of fans. Unfortunately this has not been the case. Throughout most of his career Etchison has worked in total obscurity—a circumstance that for many years has led each new editor who has encountered an Etchison story lurking somewhere in the slush pile to proclaim Etchison as his or her New Discovery and to characterize him as The Young California Writer. Characteristically, Etchison has taken all this in his usual bitter good humor, and he has been known to don his authentic wrestling mask at conventions and to appear thus as The Unknown Writer.

But no longer The Unknown Writer. Etchison's 1981 story, "The Dark Country," won both the British Fantasy Award and the World Fantasy Award for best short fiction of that year. This was the title story of his first collection of short stories, *The Dark Country*, published by Scream/Press in 1982. It has taken more than twenty years, but at last followers of the fantasy/horror genre have discovered Dennis Etchison. They are not likely to forget him.

And it's high time.

A native Californian, Dennis Etchison was born in Stockton on March 20, 1943. He has lived most of his life in the Los Angeles area, and his present home is on a wooded ravine off North Beverly Glen Boulevard. Not surprisingly, Etchison has a keen interest in films—an interest which seems to be a trait common to writers of fantasy/horror fiction. For Etchison this has been more than just a hobby, as he has done a great deal of screenwriting, including screenplay adaptations of works by Ray Bradbury, Stephen King, Colin Wilson, as well as his own fiction. He has also written the novelizations of several recent horror films: *The Fog, Halloween II, Halloween III*, and *Videodrome* (these last three under his pseudonym, Jack Martin).

Some of Etchison's other interests are less typical of a

fantasy writer. For many years now he has not owned a car—making him the only pedestrian in Los Angeles who is not without a car due to obedience to current fads or to reliance upon chauffeured limos. When his last car broke down one time too many, Etchison simply left it stalled there on the freeway and walked off without a backward glance. This is an attitude toward freeways and things mechanical that shows through in Etchison's writings. These things are impersonal, incomprehensible, and not to be trusted.

When not engaged in the suicidal feat of walking down North Beverly Glen Boulevard (with its absence of sidewalks and abundance of blind downhill curves), Etchison likes to spend his days lounging about his house, chain-smoking and watching television—soaps, game shows, and wrestling matches. For watching films, he much prefers the religious experience of the movie theatre to the home comforts of the tube. A bachelor who loves to eat but cannot cook, Etchison is a connoisseur of junk food, fast fares, and all-nite marts. His is a love-hate relationship with, and a fascination and dependence upon, the drive-thru convenience trappings of modern urban life. I cannot imagine Etchison writing a horror story about a haunted gothic mansion, but I do know that he has discovered unsuspected horrors in game shows, in mass-advertised kitchen appliances, in all-nite convenience stores, in Interstate rest areas, in laundromats, in television laugh-tracks, in hospitals, in class reunions, in fad cults, in amusement parks, in walking. Etchison preys upon all those little insecurities that are the gnawing basis of modern terrors—only a very short reach of the imagination from real fears. Sometimes a very, very short reach—one hopes, nonetheless, a reach.

Etchison is that rarest of genre writers: an original visionary. One cannot describe his work as "in the tradition of" or "a new interpretation of" or even "a bold new departure from." Etchison's nightmares and fears are intensely personal, and his genius is to make us realize that we share them. In a genre plagued with stultifying adjectives and florid fine-writing, Etchison's prose is as clean and precise as a surgeon's scalpel. Etchison does not belong to the pulp tradition of horror fiction, with its slobbering monsters, haunted mansions, and eldritch gods. Nor does he belong to the modern school of mainstream horror, with its recycled formula plots involving trendy middleclass couples threatened by demonic possession and/or psychic powers. Etchison's nightmare visions are those of loneliness—of an individual adrift in a society beyond his control, beyond his comprehension, in which only sheep-like acceptance and robot-like nonawareness permit survival. Underlying it all is a sort of desperate, dark humor—condemned men joking as they are led to the gallows.

Etchison's characters always seem to be striving ineffectually to recall some imperfectly remembered moment, to reach some dimly realized goal. They are uneasy and afraid in commonplace situations because they are outsiders within our superficially safe society. One may point to such influences as Charles Beaumont or Harlan Ellison, similarities of theme with Ramsey Campbell or M. John Harrison, but perhaps the kinship is greater toward such writers as Franz Kafka and Albert Camus. At times Etchison seems very much a product of young California of the 1950s betrayed by the impersonal selfishness of the affluent California of today. In Dennis Etchison's writings, one sees Jim, James Dean's character in *Rebel Without a Cause*, now as a middle-class man who is profoundly discontent with the society he is growing old in, beset by nostalgic memories of a past that failed him, threatened by visions of an inescapable future.

Red Dreams is Etchison's second collection, compiled from over two decades of short fiction work. A number of his earlier stories are collected here, as well as several of his most recent works. Etchison maintains that his early stories are his least favorite, despite a certain fondness for them "because they represent my state of mind at that age." Of "Not From Around Here," one of his most recent works, appearing in this book for the first time,

Etchison states, "This is my favorite piece of short fiction to date, and certainly the most personally meaningful—a kind of summing up of themes and concerns which have obsessed me for years." *Red Dreams* is a good cross-section of Etchison's writing career, and no doubt each reader will form his own opinions as to which stories stand out and for what reasons. These opinions will be personal ones, and validly so—for these are personal visions.

As for myself, I look to the future Etchison collection when he will consider his current works of fiction only of nostalgic interest, and point toward his then-current stories as best expressing his concepts and abilities. A perfectionist is never satisfied with what he has created, and Dennis Etchison is a perfectionist.

But consider: if *Red Dreams* is an example of what Etchison has accomplished in his first twenty years of writing, what does he intend to do to us during the next two decades . . . ?

—Karl Edward Wagner

TALKING IN THE DARK

In the damp bedroom Victor Ripon sat hunched over his desk, making last-minute corrections on the ninth or tenth draft, he couldn't remember which, of a letter to the one person in the world who might be able to help. Outside, puppies with the voices of children struggled against their leashes for a chance to be let in from the cold. He ignored them and bore down. Their efforts at sympathy were wasted on him; he had nothing more to give. After thirty-three years he had finally stepped out of the melodrama.

He clicked the pen against his teeth. Since the letter was to a man he had never met, he had to be certain that his words would not seem naive or foolish.

Dear Sir, he reread, squinting down at the latest version's cramped, meticulously cursive backhand. He lifted the three-hole notebook paper by the edges so as not to risk smearing the ballpoint ink. Dear Sir . . .

> First let me say that I sincerely hope this letter reaches you. I do not have your home address so I have taken the liberty of writing in care of your publisher. If they forward it to you please let me know.
>
> I am not in the habit of writing to authors. This is

the first time. So please bear with me if my letter is not perfect in spelling, etc.

I have been reading your Works for approximately 6 yrs., in other words since shortly after I was married but more about that later. Mr. Christian, Rex if I may call you that and I feel I can, you are my favorite author and greatest fan. Some people say you are too morbid and depressing but I disagree. You do not write for children or women with weak hearts (I am guessing) but in your books people always get what they deserve. No other author I have read teaches this so well. I can see why you are one of the most popular authors in the world. I have all 6 of your books, I hope there are only 6, I wouldn't like to think I missed any! (If so could you send me a list of the titles and where I might obtain them? A S.A.S.E. is enclosed for your convenience. Thank you.)

My favorite is THE SILVERING, I found that to be a very excellent plot, to tell the truth it scared the shit out of me if you know what I mean and I think you do, right? (Wink wink.) MOON OVER THE NEST is right up there, too. My wife introduced me to your novels, my ex-wife I should say and I guess I should thank her for that much. She left me 2½ years ago, took the kids to San Diego first and then to Salt Lake City I found out later. I don't know why, she didn't say. I have tried to track her down but no luck. Twice with my late parents' help I found out where she was staying but too late. So that is the way she wants it, I guess. I miss the kids though, my little boy especially.

In your next book, THE EDGE, I noticed you made one small mistake, I hope you don't mind my pointing it out. In that one you have Moreham killing his old girlfriend by electrocution (before he does other things to her!) while she is setting up their word processor link. Excuse me but this is wrong. I know this because I was employed in the Computer

Field after dropping out of Pre-Med to support my family. The current utilized by a Mark IIIA terminal is not enough to produce a lethal shock, even if the interface circuits were wired in sequence as you describe (which is impossible anyway, sorry, just thought you might like to know). Also the .066 nanosecond figure should be corrected. . . .

And so on in a similar vein. Victor worked his way through three more densely-packed pages of commentary and helpful advice regarding Rex Christian's other best-sellers, including *Jesus Had A Son, The Masked Moon* and the collection of short stories, *Nightmare Territory,* before returning to more personal matters.

If you ever find yourself in my neck of the woods please feel free to drop by. We could have a few beers and sit up talking about the many things we have in common. Like our love of old movies. I can tell you feel the same way about such "classics" (?) as ROBOT INVADERS, MARS VS. EARTH and HOUSE OF BLOOD from the way you wrote about them in your series of articles for TV GUIDE. I subscribed so I wouldn't miss a single installment. There are others we could talk about, even watch if we're lucky. I get Channel 56 here in Gezira, you may have heard about it, they show old chestnuts of that persuasion all night long!!

If you have not guessed by now, I too try my hand at writing occasionally myself. I have been working for the past 1½ years on a story entitled PLEASE, PLEASE, SORRY, THANK YOU. It will be a very important story, I believe. Don't worry, I'm not going to ask you to read it. (You are probably too busy, anyway.) Besides, I read WRITER'S DIGEST so I know where to send it if and when I succeed in bringing it to a satisfactory stage of completion. But you are my inspiration. Without you I would not have the courage to go on with it at all.

He hesitated before the conclusion, as he had when first drafting it four nights ago. On the other side of the window pane the sky was already smoking over with a fine mist, turning rapidly from the color of arterial blood to a dead slate gray. The sea rushed and drubbed at the coastline a mile to the west, shaking and steadily eroding the bedrock upon which his town was built; the vibrations which reached the glass membrane next to him were like the rhythms of a buried human heart.

> There is one more thing. I have a very important question to ask you, I hope you don't mind. It is a simple thing (to you) and I'm sure you could answer it. You might say I should ask someone else but the truth is I don't know anyone else who could help. What I know isn't enough. I thought it would be but it isn't. It seems to me that the things we learned up until now, the really important things, and I can tell we've had many of the same experiences (the Sixties, etc.), when it came time to live them, the system balked. And we're dying. But don't worry, I'm a fighter. I learned a long time ago: never give up.
>
> I live in my parents' old house now, so we could have plenty of privacy. In my opinion we could help each other very much. My number is 474-2841. If I'm not here I'll be at the Blue & White (corner of Rosetta and Damietta), that is where I work, anybody can tell you where to find it. I hope to hear from you at your earliest convenience.
>
> Meanwhile, I'm waiting with bated breath for your book of essays, OTHER CEDENTS, they mentioned it on "Wake Up, America" and I can hardly wait! If you care to let me read the manuscript prior to publication I promise to return it by Express Mail in perfect condition. (Just asking, hint hint.) In any event please come by for a visit on your next trip to the West Coast. I hope you will take me up on it sometime (soon!), I really need the answer. We

Horror Fans have to stick together. As you said in your Introduction to NIGHTMARE TERRITORY, "It may be a long time till morning, but there's no law against talking in the dark."

Faithfully Yours,
VICTOR RIPON

He sat back. He breathed in, out. It was the first breath he had been aware of taking for several minutes. The view from the window was no longer clear. A blanket of fog had descended to shroud all evidence of life outside his room. The puppies next door had quieted, resigned to their fate. Still a hopeful smile played at the corners of his mouth. He stacked and folded the pages to fit the already-stamped envelope. There. Now there wasn't anything to do but wait.

He stretched expansively, hearing his joints pop like dry bones, and his fingernails touched the window. So early, and yet the glass was chillingly brittle, ready to shatter under the slightest provocation.

With any luck he wouldn't have long to wait at all.

The days shrank as the season contracted, drawing inward against the approaching winter. Trees bared stiffening limbs, scraped the sky and etched patterns of stars as sharp and cold as diamond dust above the horizon. Victor got out his old Army jacket. The main house became dank and tomblike, magnifying the creaking of dryrotted timbers. He took to sleeping in the guest cabin, though the portable heater kept him tight and shivering night after night.

He pressed bravely ahead with his story, the outlines and preliminary versions of which by now filled two thick notebooks, reorganizing, redrafting and obsessively repolishing lines and paragraphs with a jeweler's precision.

But it was not good enough.

He wanted the pages to sing with ideas that had once seemed so important to him, all and everything he knew, and yet they did not, and no amount of diligence was able to bring them to life. The story came to be a burden and weighed more heavily in his hands each time he lifted it out of the drawer. After a few weeks he was reluctant to open the desk at all.

He stayed in bed more and slept less, dragging himself up for work each day only at the last possible minute. Nothing except Rex Christian's books held any interest for him now, and he had read them all so many times he believed he knew them by heart, almost as well as his own stillborn effort. Channel 56 exhausted its library of late-night movies and sold out to a fundamentalist religious sect peddling fire and brimstone. The nights lengthened and the long winter closed around him.

Each day, he thought, *I die a little. I must. I get out of bed, don't I?*

Mornings he walked the two miles along the creek into town, re-examining the last few years like beads to be memorized in his pocketed fists before they slipped away forever. He walked faster, but his life only seemed to recede that much more swiftly across the dunes and back to the sea. He could neither hold onto nor completely forget how things had once been. Whether or not they had ever truly been the way he remembered them was not the point. The spell of the past, his past, real or imagined, had settled over him like the shadow of giant wings, and he could not escape.

He submerged himself in his work at the shop, a space he rented for small appliance repair behind the Blue & White Diner, but that was not enough, either. For a time he tried to tell himself that nothing else mattered. But it was an evasion. *You can run,* he thought, *but, you can't hide*. Rex Christian had taught him that.

Some days he would have traded anything he owned and all that he had ever earned to wake up one more time with the special smell of her on his pillow—just that, no matter whether he ever actually set eyes on her again. Other days his old revenge fantasies got the better of him. But all that was real for him now was the numbness of more and more hours at the shop, struggling to penetrate the inner workings of what others paid him to fix, the broken remnants of households which had fallen apart suddenly, without warning or explanation.

When not busy at work, the smallest of rewards kept him going. The weekly changes of program at the local movie theater, diverting but instantly forgettable; the specialties of the house at the Blue & White, prepared for him by the new waitress, whose name turned out to be Jolene; and Jolene herself when business was slow and there was nowhere else to go. She catered to him without complaint, serving something, perhaps, behind his eyes that he thought he had put to rest long ago. He was grateful to her for being there. But he could not repay her in kind. He did not feel it, could not even if he had wanted to.

By late December he had almost given up hope.

The weekends were the worst. He had to get out, buttoned against the cold, though the coffee in town was never hot enough and the talk after the movies was mindless and did not nourish. But he could bear the big house no longer, and even the guest cabin had begun to enclose him like a vault.

This Saturday night, the last week before Christmas, the going was painfully slow. Steam expanded from his mouth like ectoplasm. He turned up his collar against an icy offshore wind. There were sand devils in the road, a halo around the ghost of a moon which hung over his shoulder and paced him relentlessly. At his side, to the north, dark reeds rustled and scratched the old riverbank with a sound of rusted blades. He stuffed his hands deeper into his jacket and trudged on toward the impersonal glow of the business district.

The neon above the Blue & White burned coolly in the darkness.

The nightlife in Gezira, such as it was—Siamese silhouettes of couples cruising for burgers, clutches of frantic teenagers on their way to or from the mall—appeared undiscouraged by the cold. If anything the pedestrians scissoring by seemed less inhibited than ever, pumping reserves of adrenaline and huffing wraiths of steam as if their last-minute shopping mattered more than anything else in this world. The bubble machine atop a police car revolved like a deranged Christmas tree light. Children giggled obscenities and fled as a firecracker resounded between lampposts; it might have been a gunshot. The patrol car spun out, burning rubber, and screeched past in the wrong direction.

He took a breath, opened the door to the diner and ducked inside.

The interior was clean and bright as a hospital cafeteria. A solitary pensioner dawdled at the end of the counter, spilling coffee as he cradled a cup in both hands. Twin milkshake glasses, both empty, balanced near the edge. As Victor entered, jangling the bell, the waitress glanced up. She saw him and beamed.

"Hi!"

"Hi, yourself."

"I'll be a few more minutes. Do you mind? The night girl just called. She's gonna be late." Jolene watched him as she cleaned off the tables, trying to read his face as if it were the first page of a test. Her eyes flicked nervously between his.

"Take your time," he said. He drew off his gloves and shuffled up to the counter. "No hurry."

"The movie—?"

"We won't miss anything."

She blinked at him. "But I thought the last show—"

"It starts," he said, "when we get there."

"Oh." She finished the tables, clearing away the remains of what other people could not finish. "I see," she said. "Are—are you all right?"

"Yes."

"Well, you don't sound like it." She looked at him as if she wanted to smooth his hair, take his temperature, enfold him in her big arms and stroke his head. Instead she wiped her hands and tilted her face quizzically, keeping her distance. "How about something to eat?"

"Just coffee," he said. "My stomach's . . ." He sought

the precise word; it eluded him. He gave up. "It's not right."

"Again?"

"Again." He tried a smile. It came out wrong. "Sorry. Maybe next time."

She considered the plate which she had been keeping warm on the grill. It contained a huge portion of fried shrimp, his favorite. She sighed.

The door jingled and a tall man came in. He was dressed like a logger or survivalist from up north, with plaid shirt, hiking boots, full beard and long hair. Victor decided he had never seen him before, though something about the man was vaguely familiar.

Jolene dealt out another set-up of flatware. He didn't need a menu. He knew what he wanted.

Victor considered the man, remembering the sixties. That could be me, he thought; I could have gone that way, too, if I had had the courage. And look at him. He's better off. He doesn't have any attachments to shake. He opted out a long time ago, and now there's nothing to pull him down.

Jolene set the man's order to cooking and returned to Victor.

"It won't be long," she said. "I promise." She gestured at the old Zenith portable next to the cash register. "You want the TV on?"

She needed to do something for him, Victor realized. She *needed* to. "Sure," he said agreeably. "Why not?"

She flicked a knob.

The nightly episode of a new religious game show, *You Think That's Heavy?* was in progress. In each segment a downtrodden soul from the audience was brought onstage and led up a ramp through a series of possible solutions, including a mock employment bureau, a bank loan office, a dating service, a psychiatric clinic, and, finally, when all else had failed, a preacher with shiny cheeks and an unnatural preoccupation with hair. Invariably this last station of the journey was the one that took. Just now a poor woman with three children and a husband who could not support them was sobbing her way to the top of the hill.

I hope to God she finds what she needs, Victor thought absently. She looks like she deserves it. Of course you can't tell. They're awfully good at getting sympathy. . . .

But someone will come down and set things right for her, sooner or later. She'll get what she deserves, and it will be right as rain. I believe that.

But what about the kids? They're the ones I'm worried about. . . .

At that moment the door to the diner rang open and several small children charged in, fresh from a spree on the mall, clutching a few cheap toys and a bag of McDonald's French fries. They spotted the big man in the red plaid shirt and ran to him, all stumbles and hugs. The man winked at Jolene, shrugged and relocated to a corner booth.

"Whadaya gonna do?" he said helplessly, "I reckon I gotta feed 'em, right?"

"I'll get the children's menus," said Jolene.

"You got any chili dogs?" said the man. "We came a long way. Don't have a whole lot left to spend. Is that okay?"

"Give them the shrimp," suggested Victor. "I can't handle it."

Jolene winked back. "I think we can come up with something," she said.

The pensioner observed the children warily. Who could say what they might have brought in with them? He obviously did not want to find out. His hands shook, spilling more coffee. It ran between his fingers as if his palms had begun to bleed.

Well, thought Victor, maybe I was wrong. Look at the big guy now. He can't run away from it, either. But it could be he doesn't want to. He's got them, and they'll stick by him no matter what. Lucky, I guess. What's his secret?

Out on the sidewalk passers-by hurried on their way, a

look of expectation and dread glazing their eyes. Victor picked up his coffee. It was almost hot enough to taste.

There was another burst of ringing.

He braced himself, not knowing what to expect. He scanned the doorway.

But this time it was not a customer. It was the telephone.

Jolene reached across the counter, pushing dirty dishes out of the way. One of the milkshake glasses teetered and smashed to the floor. At the end of the counter, the pensioner jumped as though the spirit of Christmas past had just lain its withered fingers on the back of his neck.

"What?" Jolene balanced the receiver. "I'm sorry, there's so much—yes. I said yes. Hold on." She passed the phone to Victor. "It's for you," she said.

"It is?"

"Sure is," she said. "I can't tell if it's a—"

"Yes?"

"Victor?"

"Yeah?"

"Vic!" said the reedy voice on the line. "Great to get ahold of you, finally! This is Rex. Rex Christian!"

"Really?" said Victor, stunned.

"Yup. Look, I'll be passing through your town in about, oh, say an hour. I was just wondering. Are you free tonight, by any chance?"

"Uh, sure, Re . . ."

"Don't say my name!"

"Okay," said Victor.

"I'm on my way from a meeting in San Francisco. Traveling incognito, you might say. You don't know how people can be if the word gets out. So I'd appreciate it if, you know, you don't let on who you're talking to. Understand?"

"I understand." It must be hard, he thought, being a celebrity.

"I knew you would."

Victor cupped his hand around the mouthpiece. The old man from the end of the counter fumbled money from his coin purse and staggered out. Victor tried to say the right things. He wasn't ready. However, he remembered how to get to his own house. He gave directions from Highway 1, speaking as clearly and calmly as he could.

"Who was that?" asked Jolene when he had hung up.

"Nobody," said Victor.

"What?"

"A friend, I mean. He . . ."

"He what?"

"I've got to . . . meet him. I forgot."

Her expression, held together until now by nervous anticipation, wilted before his eyes. The tension left her; her posture sagged. Suddenly she looked older, overweight, lumpen. He did not know what to say.

He grabbed his gloves and made ready to leave. She smoothed her apron, head down, hiding a tic, and then made a great effort to face him. The smile was right but the lines were deeper than ever before.

"Call me?" she said. "If you want to. It's up to you. I don't care."

"Jolene . . ."

"No, really! I couldn't take the cold tonight, anyway. I—I hope you have a nice meeting. I can tell it's important."

"Business," he said. "You know."

"I know."

"I'm sorry."

She forced a laugh. "What on earth for? Don't you worry."

He nodded, embarrassed.

"Take care of yourself," she said.

You deserve better, he thought, than me, Jolene.

"You, too," he said. "I didn't plan it this way. Please believe . . ."

"I believe you. Now get going or you'll be late."

He felt relieved. He felt awful. He felt woefully unprepared. But at least he felt something.

All the way home the hidden river ran at his side, muffled by the reeds but no longer distant. This time he noticed that there were secret voices in the waters, talking to themselves and to each other, to the night with the tongues of wild children on their way back to the sea.

Now he considered the possibility that they might be talking to him.

Victor unlocked the old house and fired up the heater. He had little chance to clean. By the time he heard the car he was covered with a cold sweat, and his stomach, which he had neglected to feed, constricted in a hopeless panic.

He parted the bathroom curtains.

The car below was long and sleek. A limousine? No, but it was a late-model sedan, a full-size Detroit tank with foglights.

A man climbed out, lugging a briefcase, and made for the front of the house.

Victor ran downstairs and flung open the door.

He saw a child approaching in the moonlight. It was the same person he had seen leave the shadow of the car. From the upstairs window the figure had appeared deceptively foreshortened.

The boy came into the circle of the porchlight, sticking his chin out and grinning rows of pearly teeth.

"Vic?"

Victor was confused.

Then he saw.

It was not a child, after all.

"I'm Rex Christian," said the dwarf, extending a stubby hand. "Glad to meet you!"

The hand felt cold and compressed as a rubber ball in Victor's grip. He released it with an involuntary shudder. He cleared his throat.

"Come on in. I . . . I've been expecting you."

The visitor wobbled to an overstuffed chair and bounced up onto the cushion. His round-toed shoes jutted out in front of him.

"So! This is where one of my biggest fans lives!"

"I guess so," said Victor. "This is it."

"Great! It's perfect!"

On the stained wall, a grandfather clock sliced at the thick air.

"Can I get you something?" Victor's own voice sounded hollow in his ears. "Like something to drink?"

"I'd settle for a beer. Just one, though. I want to keep a clear head."

Beer, thought Victor. Let me see . . . He couldn't think. He looked away. The small face, the monkey mouth were too much for him. He wanted to laugh and cry at the same time.

"You owe me, remember?"

"What?"

"The beer. In your letter you said—"

"Oh. Oh, yeah. Just a minute."

Victor went to the kitchen. By the time he returned he had replayed his visitor's words in his mind until he recognized the rhythm. Everything the dwarf—midget, whatever he was—had said so far fit the style. There was no doubt about it. For better or worse, the person in the other room was in fact Rex Christian. The enormity of the occasion finally hit him. Setting the bottles on the coffee table between them, he almost knocked one over.

My time has come, he thought. My problems are about to be over. My prayers have been answered.

"This must be pretty far out of the way for you," Victor said.

"Not at all! Thanks for the invitation."

"Yeah," said Victor. "I mean, no. I mean . . ."

And in that instant he saw himself, this house, his life as it really was for the first time. He was overwhelmed with self-consciousness and shame.

"Did . . . did you have any trouble finding the place?"

"Nope. Followed your directions. Perfect!"

Victor studied the virgules in the carpet, trying to find his next words there.

Rex Christian leaned forward in his chair. The effort nearly doubled him over.

"Look, I know what it's like for you."

"You do?"

"Believe me, I do. That's my business, isn't it? I've seen it all before."

Rex sat back and took a long pull from the tall bottle. His Adam's apple rolled like a ball bearing in his throat.

"You must know a lot about people," said Victor.

"Never enough. That's why I take a trip like this, at least once a year." He chortled. "I rent a car, visit folks like you all over the country. It's a way of paying them back. Plus it helps me with my research."

"I see." There was an awkward pause. "You . . . you said you were in San Francisco. On business. Was that part of this year's trip?"

"Right. Nothing beats the old one-on-one, does it?"

So he didn't come all this way just to see me, thought Victor. There were others. "From your writing, well, I thought you'd be a very private person."

"I am! Somebody wants a book, they have to climb the mountain. But when it comes to my fans it's a different story. They're raw material. I go to the source, know what I mean?"

"I used to be a people-person," said Victor, loosening up a bit. He drained his bottle. He thought of going for two more. But the writer had hardly touched his. "Now, well, I don't go out much. I guess you could say I've turned into more of a project-type person."

"Glad to hear it!"

"You are?"

"It just so happens I've got a project you might be interested in. A new book. It's called *A Long Time Till Morning.*"

"I like the title," said Victor. "Excuse me."

He rose unsteadily and made a beeline for the stairs. The beer had gone through his system in record time. When he came out of the bathroom, he gazed down in wonderment from the top of the landing. Rex Christian was still sitting there, stiff and proper as a ventriloquist's dummy. I can't believe this is happening, he thought. Now everything's changed. There he is, sitting in my living room!

His heart pounded with exhilaration.

Let me never forget this. Every minute, every second, every detail. I don't want to miss a thing. This is important; this matters. The most important night of my life.

He bounded down the stairs and snagged two more beers and an opener from the kitchen, then reseated himself on the sofa.

Rex Christian greeted him with a sparkling grin.

"Tell me about your new book," said Victor breathlessly. "I want to hear everything. I guess I'll be the first, won't I?"

"One of the first." The author folded his tiny hands. "It's about an epidemic that's sweeping the country—I don't have the details yet. I'm still roughing it out. All I gave my editor was a two-page outline."

"And he bought it?"

Rex Christian grinned.

"What kind of epidemic?"

"That's where you can help, Vic."

"If it's research you want, well, just tell me what you need. I used to do a lot of that in school. I was in premed and . . ."

"I want to make this as easy as possible for you."

"I know. I mean, I'm sure you do. But it's no sweat. I'll collect the data, Xerox articles, send you copies of everything that's ever been written on the subject, as soon as you tell me . . ."

Rex Christian frowned, his face wrinkling like a deflating balloon. "I'm afraid that would involve too many legalities. Copyrights, fees, that sort of thing. Sources that might be traced."

"We could get permission, couldn't we? You wouldn't have to pay me. It would be an honor to . . ."

"I know." Rex Christian's miniature fingers flexed impatiently. "But that's the long way around, my friend."

"However you want to do it. Say the word and I'll get started, first thing in the morning. Monday morning. Tomorrow's Sunday and . . ."

"Monday's too late. It starts now. In fact it's already

started. You didn't know that, did you?'' Rex's face flushed eagerly, his cheeks red as a newborn infant's. ''I want to know *your* feelings on the subject. All of them.'' He pumped his legs and crept forward on the cushion. ''Open yourself up. It won't hurt. I promise.''

Victor's eyes stung and his throat ached. *It starts here,* he thought, awe-struck. The last thirty-three years were the introduction to my life. Now it really starts.

''You wouldn't want to know my feelings,'' he said. ''They . . . I've been pretty mixed up. For a long time.''

''I don't care about what you felt before. I want to know what you feel tonight. It's only *you,* Vic. You're perfect. I can't get that in any library. Do you know how valuable you are to me?''

''But why? Your characters, they're so much more real, more alive. . . .''

Rex waved his words aside. ''An illusion. Art isn't life, you know. If it were, the world would go up in flames. It's artifice. By definition.'' He slid closer, his toes finally dropping below the coffee table. ''Though naturally I try to make it echo real life as closely as I can. That's what turns my readers on. That's part of my mission. Don't you understand?''

Victor's eyes filled with tears.

Other people, the people he saw and heard on the screen, on TV, in books and magazines, voices on the telephone, all had lives which were so much more vital than his own wretched existence. The closest he had ever come to peak experiences, the moments he found himself returning to again and again in his memory, added up to nothing more significant than chance meetings on the road, like the time he hitchhiked to San Francisco in the summer of '67, a party in college where no one knew his name, the face of a girl in the window of a passing bus that he had never been able to forget.

And now?

He lowered his head to his knees and wept.

And in a blinding flash, as if the scales had been lifted from his eyes, he knew that nothing would ever be the same for him again. The time to hesitate was over. The time had come at last to make it real.

He thought: I am entitled to a place on the planet, after all.

He lifted his eyes to the light.

The dwarf's face was inches away. The diminutive features, the taut lips, the narrow brow, the close, lidded eyes, wise and all-forgiving. The sweet scent of an unknown after-shave lotion wafted from his skin.

"The past doesn't matter," said the dwarf. He placed the short fingers of one hand on Victor's head. "To hell with it all."

"Yes," said Victor. For so long he had thought just the opposite. But now he saw a way out. "Oh, yes."

"Tell me what you feel from this moment on," said the dwarf. "I need to know."

"I don't know how," said Victor.

"Try."

Victor stared into the dark, polished eyes, shiny as a doll's eyes.

"I want to. I . . . I don't know if I can."

"Of course you can. We're alone now. You didn't tell anyone I was coming, did you, Vic?"

Victor shook his head.

"How thoughtful," said the dwarf. "How perfect. Like this house. A great setting. I could tell by your letter you were exactly what I need. Your kind always are. Those who live in out-of-the-way places, the quiet ones with no ties. That's the way it has to be. Otherwise I couldn't use you."

"Why do you care what I feel?" asked Victor.

"I told you—research. It gives my work that extra edge. Won't you tell me what's happening inside you right now, Vic?"

"I want to. I do."

"Then you can. You can if you really want it. Aren't we all free to do whatever we want?"

"I almost believed that, once," said Victor.

"Anything," said the dwarf firmly. "You can have

anything including what you want most. Especially that. And what is it you want, Vic?"

"I . . . I want to write, I guess."

The dwarf's face crinkled with amusement.

"But I don't know what to write about," said Victor.

"Then why do you want to do it?"

"Because I have no one to talk to. No one who could understand."

"And what would you talk to them about, if you could?"

"I don't know."

"Yes, you do."

"I'm afraid."

"Tell me, Vic. I'll understand. I'll put it down exactly the way you say it. You want me to relieve your fear? Well, in another minute I'm going to do that little thing. You will have nothing more to fear, ever again."

This is it, Victor thought, your chance. Don't blow it. It's happening just the way you had it planned. Don't lose your nerve. Ask the question—now. *Do it.*

"But where does it come from?" asked Victor. "The things you write about. How do you know what to say? Where do you get it? I try, but the things I know aren't . . ."

"*You want to know,*" said the dwarf, his face splitting in an uproarious grin, "*where I get my ideas?* Is that your question?"

"Well, as a matter of fact . . ."

"From you, Vic! I get my material from people like you! I get them from this cesspool you call life itself. And you know what? I'll never run out of material, not as long as I go directly to the source, because I'll never, ever finish paying you all back!"

Victor saw then the large pores of the dwarf's face, the crooked bend to the nose, the sharpness of the teeth in the feral mouth, the steely glint deep within the black eyes. The hairs prickled on the back of his neck and he pulled away. Tried to pull away. But the dwarf's hand stayed on his head.

"Take my new novel, for instance. It's about an epidemic that's going to sweep the nation, leaving a bloody trail from one end of this country to the other, to wash away all of your sins. At first the police may call it murder. But the experts will recognize it as suicide, a form of *hara-kiri,* to be precise, which is what it is. I know, because I've made a careful study of the methods. Perfect!"

The underdeveloped features, the cretinous grin filled Victor with sudden loathing, and a terrible fear he could not name touched his scalp. He sat back, pulling farther away from the little man.

But the dwarf followed him back, stepping onto the table, one hand still pressing Victor in a grotesque benediction. The lamp glared behind his oversized head, his eyes sparkling maniacally. He rose up and up, unbending his legs, knocking over the bottles, standing taller until he blocked out everything else.

Victor braced against the table and kicked away, but the dwarf leaped onto his shoulders and rode him down. Victor reached out, found the bottle opener and swung it wildly.

"No," he screamed, "my God, no! You're wrong! It's a lie! You're . . . !"

He felt the point of the churchkey hook into something thick and cold and begin to rip.

But too late. A malformed hand dug into his hair and forced his head back, exposing his throat and chest.

"How does *this* feel, Vic? I have to know! Tell my readers!" The other claw darted into the briefcase and dragged forth a blade as long as a bayonet, its edge crusted and sticky but still razor-sharp. "How about this?" cried the dwarf. "And this?"

As Victor raised his hands to cover his throat, he felt the first thrust directly below the ribcage, an almost painless impact as though he had been struck by a fist in the chest, followed by the long, sawing cut through his vital organs and then the warm pumping of his life's blood down the short sword between them. His fingers tingled and went numb as his hands were wrapped into position around the handle. The ceiling grew bright and the world spun, hurling him free.

"Tell me!" demanded the dwarf.

A great whispering chorus was released within Victor at last, rushing out and rising like a tide to flood the earth, crimson as the rays of a hellishly blazing sun.

But his mouth was choked with his own blood and he could not speak, not a word of it. The vestiges of a final smile moved his glistening lips.

"Tell me!" shrieked the dwarf, digging deeper, while the room turned red. "I must find the perfect method! *Tell me!*"

WET SEASON

Madden watched the black crowd on the other side of the moving gelatin wall, as rainwater poured down in translucent sheets over the windshield. He did not listen to the patternless tattoo. Instead he followed with his eyes the group of black shadows floating past the car.

"I . . . I shouldn't have made you come, Lorie," he said at last to the black figure next to him.

She turned from the window, her lidded eyes not disapproving. "That's enough, Jim. I wouldn't have felt right, otherwise."

Madden pressed his chin to his chest, squeezing his eyelids shut. He cleared his throat and rubbed his eyes, and his fingers came away moist.

Again his wife spoke, very quietly. "You . . . were very close to her, I suppose. James, I only wish there were something. . . . Forgive me if I'm crude. But I only wish I could have gotten to know her better. That she might have become, in time, my little girl as well."

He pressed her cool hand.

"It was—just—all the *mud* around her—" He bit his lips and started the engine and roared up the cemetery road, spinning out and spattering mud as he went.

* * *

The Ford geared to a slippery halt under the wet sycamores.

Bart stood at the end of the cracked driveway, behind the main house, propping open the sagging screen door to his apartment.

Through mist Madden saw the controlled, mildly pleasant line shaping his mouth, leaving the face somber in a new and ill-fitting mask.

"Forget about the rug," said Bart. "It's filthy anyway."

"We're so sorry to do this to you, Bart." Madden's wife brushed water from her clothing. "But we thought the twins were really too young to, well, exactly have their faces rubbed in it."

Bart smoothed a hand over his protruding, black-T-shirted belly. "The kids are in the bedroom. Rain must have got 'em drowsy. Left them staring out the window, counting drops or something," he added gently to Madden, testing a smile.

"Let me see to them." Madden's wife started across the room.

The men waited until she was gone.

Bart faced him. "Come over here and have a drink."

"No."

"Really, boy, really now. You know how I mean it. Come on."

At once Madden felt his joints chilled and tired. "No, Bart. I . . . I don't need it." He lowered himself to the sofa that was bulging and splitting like a fat man's incisions.

Bart watched the misty screen door and compared it to the pale Scotch and water in his hand. Twice he shaped his lips to stillborn beginnings. He shook his head and said nothing.

"You look at the hole, and the mud," Madden began finally in a low voice, "and you think of . . . that human being there in a box, being lowered into the ground, and you wonder how it can be that—that a part of your body, a piece that has come *from* you like an arm or leg, can be cut off, killed and buried away, and you never being able to feel with it again.

"But you know, I worked with a man once who had lost an arm in the Korean War; and he said he could close his eyes anytime and suddenly it was *there* again, the nerves were restored and he could feel down into his fingertips. But when he opened his eyes to see why he hadn't touched what he was reaching for, his eyes told him there was nothing there anymore."

Rain began to tap erratically on a metal vent somewhere in the roof.

"And you know, I can still see the world through my little girl's eyes, feel it as she felt it, even . . . even though she's been cut off me, like one of my sense organs. I still *feel* her, feel *through* her, and my nerves, my ganglia just won't listen to the goddam facts."

Outside, water continued to fall and fall illogically, relentlessly, in what seemed to be the result of a vast macrocosmic defrosting.

Giggling, the twins came out of the bedroom.

Madden saw them and smiled wanly from the sofa. The two little boys acknowledged him peripherally and grinned, grasping their mother's hands more securely.

"How did it go, boys?" inquired Madden, generating concern, and immediately hated his own detachment. *You are my sons, now,* he thought, *my only sons, and I should hold you tight against me—*

"We had fun, Da-da. We had samiches."

"An' we tooka nap an' went out an' played an'—"

Why, noted Madden wearily, *they're actually speaking directly to me. . . . She almost never lets them do that. What is this, some kind of show for Bart?*

"Out? But it didn't let up today, did it, Bart?" he said.

"Well, uh," the dark man gestured firmly to Madden, "they—" and he dropped his voice, ready to spell out words before the children, "they begged to go out. You brought them in their raincoats and, you know, it was one of those things. For a few minutes is all. Made 'em real happy. God knows I have no practice in child-rearing. Jesus, Jim, I hope they didn't catch anything."

"Tad and Ray never catch colds," stated Madden's

wife, smiling her wide, smooth, peculiar kind of smile. "You did fine, Bart."

Madden watched his wife. Svelte in the gray light, she snaked an arm around each of her children's shoulders.

"We'd better go," she said. "It's Sunday and I have a Women's Guild meeting tonight."

"Thanks, Bart. I mean it more than I can say."

They walked together, heads down, to the door. A Sunday comics section for her hair and Lorelei and the giggly children clamored down the shiny, fragmented driveway.

Bart gripped his arm, looking deep into his eyes and nodding.

"You know I know. I can't say it. But I remember the Sunday we buried Mama." Hearing it said now, Madden felt no longer a memory of pain but a bond with manhood. "Just so's you know I know." And a slap caught Madden between the shoulder blades and sent him into the rain.

To a car where a somehow strange woman and children waited.

He switched off the ignition and sat very still, staring into the liquid pattern on the windshield.

"Ready, children?" asked Mrs. Madden, not looking to the back seat, taking her purse into her lap.

From the back seat came giggling.

Madden lay his head back to let his eyes trace the headliner of the car. Half a minute earlier, shutting off the wipers, he had caught himself hypnotized as the twin arcs of the wiper blades melted away. Now, motor silenced, he listened to the sound of endless beads beating their pattern into the top of the automobile.

In the back seat, there was whispering like the swishing of cars down an empty street.

"Let's go, children," prompted their mother. "There'll be plenty of time for secrets when we get in the house."

Abruptly Madden snapped to. He focused his eyes from the windshield to the woman next to him, attuned his ears from the drumming overhead to the whisper of cloth on plastic as the children slid across the back seat. He touched the handle of his wife's door; it was cold. Almost as cold as his hand.

Behind him, someone giggled.

Outside the picture window, premature dusk settled along the block like silent black wings.

"Won't . . . won't you eat something?" asked Mrs. Madden tenuously. She leaned into the living room, spoon in hand and spoke in silhouette from the yellow kitchen doorway.

He cleared his throat. "What?" Madden's five fingertips moved involuntarily to the pane. The glass was cold.

"Well," she intoned maternally, "you should have something. It's almost dark. Let me turn on the—"

"It's all right, Lorelei." *For God's sake,* he thought, *don't patronize me. Not now.*

Chilled and fatigued to the marrow, he sat in the newly rearranged and alien living room and tried to release his senses from the pain of here-and-now. He shut his eyes and tried to let his thoughts blow with the storm on down the blurred panorama of empty street.

She puttered for a time in the kitchen and Madden, curiously detached in the dark and the overstuffed chair, noticed again her effortless, liquid movements. The way she had of gliding over a floor as though it were polished glass, her legs flowing out and back with each step in a charming suggestion of no gristle or bone. No deliberate, angular bend to Lorie's arm, no; in her, stirring and pouring out and rinsing away became a Siamese rubber-arm ballet.

"Your soup is in the oven, keeping warm. And the twins are tucked in, so don't—I mean, they shouldn't give you any trouble."

Mrs. Madden paused in silhouette, then glided behind the enormous sagging hand that enclosed her husband.

"Lorie," he swallowed. Away in the bright kitchen, an electric clock hummed.

She sat on the armrest.

"Lorelei, do you ever . . . think about the decision you made ten months ago?" He tried to stop his teeth from chattering. "I mean—"

Her arms reached a pale circle around his shoulders. "You are the finest father my boys could possibly have. And I . . ." And she smoothed his hair with her oddly flat hands and did not finish. "Do you need to talk, Jim? The Guild meeting—"

Yes, he thought, pressing his eyes tightly shut until shards of gray light fired inside his eyelids, *yes, I need something. I hear your words but they're only words, I need more than talk, I need you warm against me, I need to live—*

He drew her into his lap. And at once it struck him.

She was *not* warm. Her skin was cold, cold almost as—

He pushed her away.

"Jim, I'm sorry. Is there something I can do for you?"

"No." He stared ahead into the night-filled room. "They're waiting for you already. There isn't anything you can do for me."

Picking up coat, purse and overshoes, Mrs. Madden pulled back the front door to a sheet of rain. A reminder about the soup, and she entered the falling sea.

The telephone refused to warm in his hands.

A sputter and crackle of rain and whispers on the wires between and across town, a mile away, a phone purred to life.

And purred. And purred.

"Yeah?"

"Hello, Bart. What am I interrupting?"

"Jimmy? That you, boy?"

"I hope I'm not interrupting anything."

"No, no. Listen. Lorie gone to her meeting?"

"That's right."

"Then you're alone." Pause. "Everything all right over there?"

"Yes. Aw, look, I shouldn't have called."

"You wanna talk, Jim?"

"I guess. No. . . . Bart, is someone coming over tonight? You going out?"

"In this weather? Look, is everything all right?"

Pause. "Uh, Bart, I wonder . . . I just wondered if . . . aw, never mind, I shouldn't have bothered you."

"Look. You wanna come over here? We could talk, if you want."

"Can't leave the kids."

"They're asleep, then, and you're alone over there. You want me to come over? Talk or something until Lorie gets back?"

Pause. "I have no business bothering you."

"Crap. Look, I'll come over, okay? We can talk, you know, like we used to."

"I'm pretty bad company tonight, I'm afraid. And the weather. Sure you want to?"

"My idea, isn't it? And look, how can you turn down a lonely ol' bachelor like me? See you in ten minutes."

"Thanks very much, Bart," but he had hung up.

Madden waited on the back porch, listening.

Far down in the darkness, the throaty thrumming of the frogs met with the rushing of running water.

All about his thin figure, dirty streams dripped from the roof to mingle with puddles at his cold feet, to slip on down over the slanting yard, to join larger tributaries that splashed their way through the thorny shrubbery of the ravine to feed at last with violent churning into the shrouded riverbed far below.

From in front, Madden heard wet brakes grip to a splashing stop. Shivering, he turned inside.

The two men sat across from one another in the living room, two men who knew each other best of all in the world. There was only a pale-moth glow from the kitchen. They spoke, and they did not speak, and from time to time Bart laughed and sipped from the brandy snifter in his lap.

". . . But then they threw the next game to the motherin' Angels," Bart was saying.

"Yes," said Madden.

Bart rose and ambled to the black picture window.

Abruptly Madden was aware that his brother had stopped talking.

Madden stared with him. He saw his brother frown. *Do you feel it too?* he thought. Vaguely illumined beneath the street lamp was Bart's car, leaning against the curb, weathering the storm. Idly, Madden had a vision of the rain pouring off the metal top, streaming over the rolled-up windows and down into the innards of the door, where the handle and lock mechanism were.

"Jimbo. God damn it."

Madden watched him. "What's wrong?"

Bart drained his glass. "I don't wanna say it. I don't even know I'm right. Or if I oughta say it."

"It's all right—I can talk about Darla. Probably it would do me good." He massaged his face, trying to relax. "I know I have to face—"

"No. That's not what I'm talking about." Bart pivoted from the window and the rain. "Listen to me, kid. *Do you feel it?*"

"Feel what?"

"Something, about this house, this town. I don't know how to say it. But can't you feel it?" Bart glared into the empty brandy glass.

"Something like what?" Madden lounged back into the cushion, ready to listen. *Now,* thought Madden, *this is the way. It won't prove a thing unless he says it first.*

"Damn," breathed Bart. He turned back to the night and lit a cigarette. "Maybe I'm going off the deep end. Look. Can I ask you a question?"

"Shoot."

"Something about this house. I don't know. The way it smells now, the way the chairs creak when I sit down, the color of the *light,* for God's sake, like the room is underwater or something. And all since she moved in." The cigarette reflection burned in the window. "Naw. Man, you're the one needs to talk at a time like this. I'm supposed to cheer *you.*"

"So you're cheerin'. Shoot."

"Look, it's just that—haven't you noticed anything, well, different about the place since Lorie and her kids moved in? That it isn't really yours anymore? I mean, it's like every person has a rhythm, a pattern to his everyday life. You go into a man's bedroom, it *smells* like him, the bed bends a certain way when you sit on it, because it's been shaped to fit every angle and bulge just right over the years. And you go into the kitchen, the way the dishes are piled up in the sink tells you more about the guy than a look at his diary, if you know what I mean. It's like the house soaks up what you are, the way you feel about life, and everything in the house gets to feeling the same way, too. And not only the place, but the woman he marries: she seems to fit right in, fit him, and the house . . . and that's part of it, too, Jimbo. She's—and I know I'm steppin' way over the bounds on this, but dammit, man, she's *not you,* you know? Let me ask: don't you notice anything unusual about Lorie?"

Madden shut his eyes impatiently. "She's an unusually attractive woman, if that's what you mean."

"No. But then I promised myself not to bring up any of this with you, at least not for a long time. . . .

"But it isn't just this house. Hell, we both grew up in Greenworth, I knew every turn in the river like the lines on my hand years before the government moved in. And it's changed now, somehow. First, it was just the way the trees started growing crooked along the banks, but lately the whole town seems, I don't know, *funny*. The way the air smells, the paint on the houses . . . I don't know. I just don't know. But I'll tell you this: if I were blindfolded and left here, I'd never in a year guess this was the same town we grew up in."

Outside, the moon slipped for a moment through a pocket of clouds, washing Bart's face fishlike-pale by the window.

"Bart. What is it?"

"I wish I could be sure, kid. Maybe you should forget it. I pray to God I could. Jim, do you know how many storms like this we've had in Greenworth in the last twenty-five years?"

Madden stirred.

"I'll tell you: three, before two years ago. And not one raised the river more than a few inches. But in two years, five big ones. Here." Bart spilled his coat pocket onto the coffee table. "What the hell—I spent yesterday in the library looking things up, I don't know what for. Something made me do it. But God, I've gotta show you."

Madden reached to the lamp.

Little white slips of paper fluttered in Bart's hands. For the first time in his life Madden saw his brother trembling.

"God!" he laughed nervously. "Help me, will you, Jim? Here are the pieces to a crazy jigsaw, it doesn't make any sense, but something in the back of my head keeps me from getting any sleep lately. Here, look, read it all and then tell me I'm nuts and send me home, but *do something!*"

" 'Deaths by drowning, County Beach: this year and last, total 31. Previous two years' total, 9.' What's this for?"

"Don't stop now." Bart fumbled at the liquor cabinet.

" 'Total rainfall in inches, adjacent counties last year, up 300%.' "

"See! It's spreading."

Another slip of paper. " 'New residents in Greenworth, past 24 months: Broadbent, Mr. and Mrs. C. L.; Marber, G.; Nottingham, Mr. and Mrs. Frank R. . . .' " Madden leaned forward intently.

"There's two dozen more."

He scrutinized his brother's now twisted face. "So?"

"So? So you're right, they're nothing separately, but put them all together—Let me ask you: Lorie never told you where she moved from when she came here, did she?"

"Now that you bring it up, no. But what—?"

"Listen to this. Last night I got out the phone book and dialed these new listings. Twenty-one are married couples. And every woman—" Bart emptied his glass. "Every woman is in the Women's Guild."

Ice water poured into Madden's stomach. "So?"

Bart jerked forth a folded clipping. "This was in the Gazette when one finally moved in twenty months ago."

Madden fingered the newspaper photo of 'Mr. and Mrs. Peter Hallendorf, newly-established real estate broker and his lovely bride.'

"Use this." A pocket magnifier hit the coffee table.

She *was* lovely. There in the enlarged dots was a face that was— "I don't see—"

Bart's shaking finger jabbed at the indistinct eyes, the mouth.

At first he didn't see it. Just that her eyes were softly, lethargically lidded.

Bart snatched a framed photograph from the bookcase and tossed it to his lap.

And there.

There were two sets of lidded eyes, two wide, smooth, peculiar smiles, side by side. They might have been sisters.

Madden groped. At the bottom of his consciousness, the pressure was rising now and he felt his finger giving way in the dike.

"Jim," grunted Bart. "I called the Community Center this evening. They never heard of it. *There is no Women's Guild!*

"And now. Just one more question. I hate to remind you, boy, but you've got to have all the pieces in front of you." Bart leaned over him, breath coming fast and pungent. "Tell me again how it was your little girl died."

Madden bit his knuckle. "Man, I don't know what you're driving at. Please—"

"Just say it!"

"She . . . she, you know. She drowned—in the—bottom of the tub." He fought up out of the chair.

Both men faced each other, white-faced.

"Goddam," breathed Bart, turning back to the darkness. "Goddam me for saying it."

Walking in the wet, Madden knew at last that he could leave the house behind and give himself up to the storm.

Slimy, tangled brush grabbed at his sopping clothes, but he did not think of it and slid down the ravine to the churning riverbed. In the glistening night he saw the swelling rush muddying over collapsing banks, and he remembered the first and worst storm, two seasons ago: how the ravine filled steadily to the brim, spilling up over the back yard; and then, weeks later, how the yard blossomed alive with all manner of new, unnamed wild plants and shoots and bloomed-faced flowers. And how he suddenly awoke one night to discover the moldering ravine an amphitheater of swollen hordes of singing insect life, a thundering of bullfrogs, a sweltering din of mosquitoes, a screeching chorus of crickets. Latent with life, pollen and cyst and egg had been carried by the water and given birth at long last.

Madden stretched through the wet growth to the river's edge. Facts and meanings swirled and eddied within him.

He saw the fresh water flowing on past, headed for the sea.

A paper boat or a leaf could float the five miles to the turbines, and beyond to the sea. But only something living could do the opposite.

Suddenly, as if by a signal, frog and insect ceased their noise.

In the new silence, above the rain, Madden heard a car door slam.

He began tearing savagely at the shrubbery. His hair and chin dripped and his clothes were torn and caked with mud below the waist, but he did not think of these things as he climbed his way to the porch.

He smeared a wet trail across the kitchen.

Lorelei came through the unlighted living room.

"Why James, I thought you'd be in bed. And your clothes, why—"

"Wh-where have you been?" He shivered.

She reached to touch his clothes. He jumped back.

He saw that her clothing, too, was dripping. Much more than from a run from the car.

"Why, James—"

"Get away! Who are you?"

The sound of giggling.

He ran to the bathroom door. He kicked it in.

Grinning in the stark white porcelain bathtub were the twins, Tad and Ray. They splashed and curled eel-like appendages up over the edge.

"What is this?" muttered Madden, blinded by the light. "What are you boys bathing for at . . . ?" Then he saw their smooth, shining skins glistening in the water in a strange new way.

So this is the way Darla came upon them that day, he thought. *So that was why, that was why. So now I have no choice. . . .*

He fell upon them, pushing their small heads under the water until bubbles floated up.

They came up grinning.

"So you know," she said.

He turned.

The bright, white tiles around him.

Lorelei, dripping, came toward him, holding out her arms as if to embrace him. An alien scaliness glittered anew along her neck, her boneless arms.

Behind him, the little ones giggled.

Madden stepped back before she could touch him. His legs met the tub and he tumbled backwards, seeing in a flash the bright walls and ceiling.

There was a resounding splash and then violent churning. And giggling.

And the sound of the rain outside.

I CAN HEAR THE DARK

There was a blackness and a struggling somewhere in the house; Willum could feel it. The others were busy again trying to be something they weren't, and he tried not to listen, but sometimes he couldn't help it. He had that feeling you begin to get when something is wrong but you don't quite know it yet. Still, wherever it was, he knew that he ought to find it, whether he was supposed to or not.

"How do you feel?" said the actress.

"Mother," he said slowly, "where do we go when we die?"

"Why don't you just let him outside so he can play with himself or something?" said the tall actor from the living room. "You know, you're going to turn him into a goddam vegetable, Leona, keeping him under wraps like this all the time."

"Into an agent," said one of the other actors, laughing.

"Don't be absurd," she answered, too softly for it to carry, tipping her head down close to the boy's eyes. "Willum's doing just fine today" She smoothed the hair from his eyes, and a tender, practiced pout appeared in a line below her mouth. "Aren't you, my baby?"

He nodded uncertainly.

"So. Why don't you run down the week for me?" said

another actor, the one with his hair over his collar. "I guess I've lost track, since that Dr. Whosit character put Jan into the hospital. You know." Fingers snapping. "The one they brought out from New York."

"Crispin, I think he was called," said the tall actor.

"Listen, there's some fresh fruit in the dining room," said the actress in her throaty voice, the one she used when she talked on the telephone at night, when the tall actor or Daddy, whichever one it was, was asleep. "And some of those good croissants, and your orange marmalade." She studied Willum absently. "I could ask Monica to make up another omelet with cream cheese. Would that please you, darling?"

"Leona, for God's sake," said the tall actor.

"All right!" She pretended to spit the words, making her eyelids flutter the way they did on *The Late Show*. "My G-o-d." She rose, still stooped, and kissed him dryly on his lips. "Take care, baby," she said. "Mother's just going to be a while longer. You can play downstairs, if you like, or—"

"Well," said the tall actor, "let's see. They finally got me divorced Friday. Just a minute. Leona!"

". . . So the way it went was this," said the third actor matter-of-factly. "Mm, what-was-her-name?"

"Jan."

"Right. Jan miscarried right after the rape. For a while it looked like they'd have her go back East to stay with her mother. But someone decided they should send this Crispin out from New York. And then it worked out that Jordan met up with his old flame again and filed for divorce. Naturally. These things never make sense. You're right, she used to be married to his brother-in-law, but you know how those things go. Sometimes it takes years. What do you expect? Just like a soap opera, right?"

"What I don't understand," said the younger actress, "was that part about the drug dealer, what did they call him?"

"Shorty something. Bernstein, I think."

"How was she supposed to carry on during all that, with this Bernstein trying to involve her in the trial, not to mention the custody fight? It was all so unbelievable. . . ."

". . . Of course you could handle it," the actor with hair over his collar was saying on the other side of the room. "Self-assurance is something a person is born with—and you certainly have it, Leona. How many pictures was it you made over there?"

"Twenty-two," supplied the tall actor, before she could answer.

"You see?"

"But," she said, "I've always had a role to hide behind, don't *you* see? Every word—"

"We have scripts, too," said the tall actor. "Don't we, Kurt?" He had to laugh. "Such as they are."

"There," she said. "That's just it. You've told me yourself that you hardly have time for anything more than the most rudimentary blocking and run-through." Her chair creaked, straining. "So you must fall back on what you *are*. Don't you see? In other words, you're not provided with an adequate mask." Pause. "I'd be petrified if I had to work your soap. How do you do it?"

"With your self-assur—"

"Of course, self-assurance, my God! But what about confidence? That's something one must learn. And I've never had to *do* that kind of acting before. Why, over there—"

"Then you simply play the surface," said the other actor, as though explaining to a child. "The line."

"Don't you think I know about playing the line?" she said. "My God, how do you think I survived all those *shitty* films?"

"A lot of actors play the line."

"What do you think episodic television is all about?" said the tall actor.

"I *know*," said the actress. "You could even say that Larry Olivier falls back on pure technique when he's not given enough to work with. But when one is concerned about playing the *meaning*—''

''Sure. The spine. Zohra, for example, plays the meaning. Did you catch her on that Kojak rerun the other night? But when her material is thin, that's *all* she plays, the meaning. At the expense of the line.''

''But,'' said the actress, ''what if one strives to play the meaning *and* the line simultaneously? My God. Do you know that I worked on one with Corman years ago that he shot in *four days?* Some funny little man was busy in the trailer typing out the next scene directly on stencils!''

''. . . I suppose that was why she had to do it,'' continued the third actor, across the room. ''Morton wouldn't accept the separation. And then when he broke in—''

''I watched the whole thing,'' said the younger actress. ''It was unreal. Like they had some third-rate writer.''

''Then you know. That was all she wrote. . . .''

I can hear the dark, thought Willum, on the floor in the hall.

If I listen hard . . .

''I tell you, I've never felt that way before,'' said the tall actor, walking in from the patio.

''Oh, you were just high on shock,'' said the other actor, following. ''You know. Hey listen, though, I'm glad we can talk—that's why I came by.''

''If I could only relax, if it would just let up. Some time to myself. You have no idea. The schedule—''

''So why don't we just kick back now, while everybody's outside? And you can tell me all about real life.''

The tall actor measured another Scotch. ''The daily routine? What makes you think it's worth the telling?''

''Might do you good.''

''You could run it down as well as I could, you know. All right, all right, what do you want me to say? First breakfast. Then an argument. Then somebody or other comes over for a visit. Or we go over there. Then work. And the crazy, irrational phone calls. Is someone up there writing this tripe, do you think? And the meetings. And the drinking. And the dinners, always at Tallboy's or the, whadayou call it? the Copper Kettle. Hey, Kurt, can you tell me why? Can you tell me how everything got to be so God damned repetitious? Monday, Tuesday, Wednesday. . . . Sometimes I wake up in the middle of the night wondering how I ever got caught in this stupid imitation of a life."

"Come on, man."

"That's all it seems to me anymore. Just like we're all trapped in some broken, cheesy videotape loop." He added abruptly, "Sometimes I think I could walk. You know? No matter what's about to come down."

The other actor said ironically, "Do you have a contract?"

"Yeah, you old son of a bitch," answered the tall actor mildly. "And you know as well as I do that there are some things we don't exactly sign a contract for. They're the things that are the most binding."

Hiding in the garden . . .

Willum padded to the end of the hall. He gazed around him in the half-light. Doors. To the bedroom, to the kitchen, to the bathroom, to the dining room. The stairway. To his room, where the tutor met with him five afternoons a week. The tutor would keep coming, his mother said, until he got better and could start school, even though he felt well enough to start right now. He had always felt better. And he knew Daddy would understand, and help him to start. Soon. Daddy always helped, when he was here.

He noticed the telephone. Maybe it would tell him something. It helped his mother lots of times. He touched his face to the cool, black receiver. If it didn't talk back to him with words he couldn't understand, the way it had when he tried before. And if it didn't make him cry, the way it made her cry sometimes.

From the living room came the voice of his mother, magnified by the walls of the corridor.

"I just wish Willum could be free of all this, oh, free to wander naked through the gardens of the universe!"

If wishes were camels, he thought, *eyes would have needles. . . .*

"Precisely," said the younger actress. "You have a career, and now you must use that to provide—"

"An access," said the actress, "is not an avenue."

"But it is a living, isn't it, Leona?"

"What you get is a living," said the actress. "If you're lucky. What you give is a life."

The tall actor sat her on the couch and tried to speak so that no one else would hear, though the others were waiting outside on the patio.

"It's going to be all right," he told her.

In the hall, Willum began trying doors. He was sure that someone had taken from him something irreplaceably valuable; but he couldn't remember who had done it, or even what it was. And no one would admit it.

"But they all know!" said the actress.

"That's right, and they're our friends—your friends, honey. They'll stand beside you. As I will. You know that."

The doors were locked, or did not lead to anything that didn't show. He could see that. The empty kitchen. The sweet-smelling bedroom with mirrors, her bedroom. The dining room, with the big table legs. And the stairway to his own room. (He knew where each of his toys was hidden, even if she did not.) He looked around again. There were the pictures of her lining the hallway, scary old posters showing the way she was on *The Late Show* or *Chiller:*

TERROR FILLS THE NIGHT AS
SHE STALKS HER PREY!

"I had to do it," she said. "What else could I do? He was going to take Willum away, in defiance of the court order. And do God knows what to me, if I got in the way."

"Self-defense," the tall actor said. "If you were going to be indicted and tried for it, which you aren't. Look, Morton broke in, trying to find him. The others were just arriving for dinner. Monica was out with the boy, of course—that part is true. You attempted to stop him. When he got to Willum's room he grabbed you, pushed you down. I came to your rescue, you ran for the gun, he took it from you, struggled with me, it went off. There. They'll all say they saw that, even the ones who didn't see anything—they'll claim they were already here, right? They stayed and talked to you, tried to calm you. You took a sedative. I called the police. Do you want to go over it again?"

"But why didn't we call a doctor? They'll think—"

"Kurt *is* a doctor, will you remember that? He'd practically finished his internship when he got his first part."

She sighed and made a small, strangled weeping in her throat. There was the sound of her pill box snapping open.

"Do you suppose he still loves me?"

Willum hesitated at the foot of the stairs, staring up into the blackness.

"Who?"

"Oh, Jordan, have I done such a terrible thing to my boy? Have I?"

The tall actor opened another bottle. "Jesus. You know something? I hate that damned show, but—"

"Then let's leave. Everything. Now. I'll get Willum and—"

"—But right now I wish to God life could be as simple as that stupid serial. A nine-to-fiver, with breakfasts, arguments, visits, phone calls, dinners, hassles, but little hassles, ones I could handle with my eyes closed. You know, God help me, I can't help thinking you'd be better off if you'd never come back from Rome with Morton, if we hadn't started up again, maybe if Jan—if we'd just—"

She made another, more desperate sound.

"I don't know why I said that. I didn't mean it. Forgive me, Leona. Shh, now. Shh."

Willum put his fingers on the railing and started up.

He felt it in the house, something missing, something gone away forever and never coming back, ever since he had come back from the park with Monica. And now he felt it inside himself. He paused at the first landing, peering back at the dimly-lighted hall and the last of the posters below.

THE HIGH PRIESTESS OF EVIL

He shivered and, for reasons he could not yet understand, a shudder passed along his spine. He thought: *A possum just ran over my grave*. That was what Daddy always said. But this time he would be brave.

He tried humming to himself under his breath, closing his eyes tight as he climbed the rest of the way.

"Where's Willum?" said the tall actor suddenly.

"He-he's fine. He's playing. He likes to play by himself. He's such a good, good little boy. Isn't he? Don't you think he is?"

"But where—?"

"Don't worry," said the actress. "He can't go upstairs alone. He's afraid of the dark. He always has been. I used to be, too, when I was his age."

"I'd better call the police now," said the tall actor.

"Yes," said the actress.

"And I'll tell Jack to be ready. In case we need a lawyer. You haven't touched the body since, have you? He's still up there, where he fell?"

She began to cry.

Willum came to the top. Soon he would be safe in his own room. Eyes still squeezed tight, he thought of the things he must do. He would go through his toys one by one, to be sure they were there. Then he would open the closet and feel around inside. And the bed, he would have to look under the bed. And maybe he would find it. And then. Everything. Would be. All right.

He went on singing his little song. Now he put the words to it again, or he heard them in his mind, he didn't know which, words from a movie on *Chiller* late one night:

I can hear the dark
If I listen hard
Hiding in the garden

Climbing up the stairs . . .

He got ready. He would open his eyes. Soon.

Then, with a curious, almost expectant smile on his lips, he reached out and felt the cold doorknob. And made it turn in his hand, turn and begin to open.

THE GRAVEYARD BLUES

He sat amid tall grass, shivering in the sun, waiting for a dream to come. But it was no use. He stretched onto one side and squinted through the comber of chickweed, running his fingers over the nearest blade; it was rough when you rubbed it one way, smooth the other. Patches of grass bent to the ground where he had trampled it coming, and all of it was davened slightly by a wind that had come and gone silently before him. The tops of the markers paved a solid granite band in the air above the grass line, and as he followed the slate-gray row with his eyes then he saw them, the dark, misshapen figures hunched one against the other, making their way down the hillock at the far side of the cemetery.

There were two of them and they were wrapped around in bolts of a stiff cloth that cast sawtoothed shadows over the untended ground. They came to the stones and the larger one felt a way for the other, the ratchet edge of her skirt jerking ahead unsteadily around heavy, unseen shoes.

He stood above the warp of the grass, staring blankly at their progress as the wind came up again and a bird, conspicuous by its absence, quieted somewhere in the papery trees.

He could not take his eyes from them as they felt around

the graves, tapping spasmodically, feeling, feeling. He heard the rough swishing sound of their garments; once he thought they had found it—they spread their hands in a crooked circle in the air over a headstone, only to break the circle as soon as their bodies closed to the plot—but it was not the one and they pressed restlessly on.

When they found the site they fell upon it, but slowly, twisted leaves settling to earth. He saw knotted hands buckle and extend like unnatural insects on the face of the granite. He saw the hands become smooth and sleek as praying mantises then, sentient hands, quick, delicate tendrils, antennae, to measure inscriptions with caliper precision, scanning with eye stalk fingers, gesturing faster, seeking to tap wrists, tug clothing, bend together in sightless discovery.

And, suddenly, the memory of another Saturday: six years old and wakened by a smell, the Cream of Wheat he never liked, filtering under the door to his room and a dream fresh as a new bruise inside his head. No one asked, of course, not yet, not Mama or Daddy and not Vin when he crooned *Could Mars-ton come out to play today?* at the back screen. But he asked himself about it, over and over during breakfast and the tentative beginnings of play by the black walnut trees in the lot, answers that were indistinguishable from questions fading in and fading out on the dim backdrop of his inexperience like the unreadable words of advice that floated up on the underside of his Magic 8-Ball when he shook it and waited for the cloudy ink to clear. The dream: he had stolen a Radio Flyer wagon from Vin's double garage, had compounded the sin by hiding it under twiggy mulch at the edge of the graveyard where he was forbidden to play. Noon came and Vin was called home for lunch, untold. Then, scuffling over unearthed roots, a stripped bamboo stick for a sword in his jeans loop, about to be called in for soup and sandwich himself, Marston felt a need to run after Vin, tell him, apologize for the transgression. But how stupid Vin would think him, and Vin's mother and sister Nancy; they would courteously ignore him as always, reaching over his head to stack dishes or retrieve the wash from the service porch sink. How were you supposed to apologize for a dream? Mama talked with Uncle Ralph and Uncle Harold after supper sometimes about something like that, he knew, and he heard them in the driveway, through the kitchen window, and Daddy had had to meet over the dining room table with a man he was sure Daddy had never seen before about something like that, and silly Aunt Frances still brooded with Mama in the hall about Eddie Who Had Been In The War and when was he going to come over and make up for the way he had cursed her at Dentoni's? and Mama had told her *Hush, it was only a dream,* and Aunt Frances had said *What do you mean, only a dream? You know what's right and wrong, Mabel,* and Mama had said *You know better than that, Fran,* in that righteous way of hers, *You know it doesn't work both ways, it never has* and Marston had known that that had something to do with it, too. So that when Mama finally called for him out the back door, and he did not answer because he couldn't yet, because he had not told Vin, which he couldn't do, he ran—not to the back door and not across the street to Vin's but away from both, lighting out across town in what turned out to be the direction of the Plunge; and then the rest of it. And he felt something close to that now, here at the edge of the graveyard: he wanted to leave, to go back, something was not right and what he saw upset him, and yet he could not go, not yet, fascinated as he was by the sight of the two mysterious figures hugging a tombstone, something he had not seen or ever even dreamed of before.

And so he ran away from both choices, not toward home and not across the cemetery. He headed off across town in a direction he did not want to have to think about.

"Ol' Marston's got the graveyard blues again," said Joseph when they came into the kitchen.

"Marston," said Mama.

She did not glance up from the fryers on the drainboard but continued to lay out the cut-up pieces, gazing at them as if they were somehow objects of pity. The smell of burnt pinfeathers lingered.

"Here, now, you gave your . . . ." *mama such a scare,* Grandma almost said, but he was no longer a child, though she still spoke of his 'going out to play' when he left the house to go into the arbor or to tend the bantams, to sit next to the coops. "You are hungry?" asked Grandma.

"What a question, Karen," said Joseph.

"I . . . hope you're not planning to go out tonight," said Mama, not turning.

"Your mama wants to talk to you," said Grandma. "Here, a piece of French twist with butter. Go and sit now."

"Oh, Mama," said his mother.

"Mabel, Mabel," said Joseph in his loud voice, which always seemed out of place in the breakfast nook, "don't hover over the boy, will you? For God's sake. Right, Marty?"

"I'm not going anyplace," offered Marston.

Later, after supper, dishes more or less done and drying on the white tiles and Marston tipped back against the wall in his chair, his ear next to the radio on the telephone stand, Mama hung up her apron and left the kitchen. That surprised him. He leaned forward to the table and listened to her footsteps leaving the kitchen linoleum, onto the carpet in the hall, the floor heater grille screaking when she walked on it, the voices from the dining room louder, then muffled again as the door swung shut after her, pulling a thin cloud of cigar smoke in around him.

He did not hear her coming back down the hall, only the sudden flurry of low conversation as the door swung open again.

Mama, wielding a heavy, oversized book, squeezed into a chair on the other side of the table. She positioned the book on the tablecloth. It looked to be an old heirloom. She smoothed her hands, reddened from the sink, over the padded cover, at the same time studying her son's face until he could no longer avoid looking back.

"How much longer is it till your birthday? Marston, can you tell me?"

"Oh, you know, Mama."

"I want you to tell me," she said.

He could not read her expression. At least she was not angry in that way that made him ashamed. "I'm gonna be sixteen day after tomorrow. Monday," he said, a little proudly, and felt a little embarrassed about it. To change the subject he tried, "Is that Grandma's Bible?"

Her eyes focused through him. "Something like that," she answered. "And I'm not being sacrilegious." She considered opening the book. "Sixteen years old. Already," she said softly; and he realized the subject had not changed after all.

He sat straight, feeling tall, and tried to talk to her in a matter-of-fact way. "What book is it?" he said, pushing grains of salt into the white tablecloth. "Mama?" he added, and then realized that his voice had cracked and that it was no use.

He folded his hands and waited.

She was ready to say something, he knew, but was trying to put it off, at the same time trying not to back away from it. She propped her elbow on the table edge and held her chin in her hand with controlled casualness, lifting the heavy cover with her other hand.

"It's such a shame you never knew your grandfather." Then she said, "He would have been able to talk to you."

The book fell open. Marston caught a glimpse of pressed letters written in broad, faded fountain pen script.

"This was his Book, the first one. He carried it with him all through the War. The others, the family Books, we started after he came home."

Marston tilted his head sideways to show interest.

"He was in the infantry. He and Mama came over from the old country in nineteen, oh, nineteen-eleven, yes, see here? And he joined the service, of course, when war broke out. He was a very striking man . . . my dad."

When she said 'my dad' her lip began to move, but she

held it tight with her hand. Marston fidgeted, reached out tenuously and raised other pages. "May I see?"

The pages he lifted were filled with handwriting; and now he felt an unease because it was not what he thought; it was not a Bible and it was not a scrapbook.

To speak, to say something to get her past tears, because he would not be able to do or say anything once she started but would have to sit quietly, eyes averted, he said, "Is it your—is it Grandfather's diary?"

"It was his Book," she said in a forced sing-song, "his Dream Book. But I suppose you know about the Dream Books, don't you?" and it sounded almost like a gentle accusation. At last he made the connection. He had seen the others, quickly, once, at their bedroom door: Daddy had been putting the large black volume in on top of the stack in the cedar chest, had turned his head, said *Yes, Marty? Can I help you?* with a false calmness, something he never said at home, and then he turned back to twist the key in the Yale padlock, missing it the first time.

"Your grandfather was . . . a very *special* man. You've heard me talk about him before, but I only wish you had known him."

Shifting to another level, her voice picked up. Marston had the feeling she was not talking to him, not quite.

"He . . ." and here she shut her eyes so, as if seeing a scene she had rehearsed many times over the years thrust now suddenly before her, no putting it off this time, ". . . he recorded every dream he had, starting over there, and then, back home, here, and for a while Mama shared it with him, but then he gave her her own Book. . . . And Ralph, Uncle Ralph and Uncle Harold, and I had one, too, we all did, with my name on it. When Aunt Frances and Aunt Marcella joined our family, and Bill—Daddy—then they were given . . ."

She was getting at something—why wouldn't she say it? He blinked faster, then kept his eyes closed a second, two seconds; her outline, the hair, the reading glasses flashed in relief on his eyelids. He knew she wanted something from him and he had been trying to give it, he always did for her when she asked and when she didn't, if he could guess, but now he was not sure. He smelled night-blooming jasmine through the window screen, masking the wind from the slough, and cigar smoke.

"What about the dreams, Mama?" He felt a burning in his eyes, and he said, "What do you want me to do? I mean," and here he made a jump, hoping he was not going too far, "I know you want me to tell about what I dream at night—but what for? Mama, what for?" Then, retreating slightly, seeing her eyes again, the glasses coming off, the fingers rubbing, "Is it a game I have to learn, is that it?" Foolish, that was a foolish thing to say.

"It's no game, Marty."

Joseph, standing there how long? The cigar smoke. Marston looked up. Joseph was not smoking, he was not allowed to smoke in the kitchen, but it was in his clothes, in his breath.

Her eyes held on Marston. "We're having a talk, Joseph."

"I say you ought to out and tell him, if you're going to. One way or the other, Mabel. You've got the boy so he doesn't know whether he's coming or going."

"We," and she backed off a bit, he could hear it, "we were having a talk, Marston and I. About . . . about the way he's been spending his afternoons."

Joseph tucked his shirt in over his belly. His fly was unzipped a third of the way, as always.

"What's she trying to tell you, son? That it's picture albums and good old stories? That's not what it's about. You read it careful. Trenches and blood. That's right. And your grandfather Stolberg watching a man die that didn't have to, his best buddy it was, now get that. You see? It didn't have to happen, wouldn't've if he'd been able to understand the dreams back then."

Mama cleared her throat.

Joseph's big hand clasped him firmly at the back of the neck, as though to hold him from running.

I'm not trying to run away, he thought. Was he? He kept looking to his mother. No, it wasn't true; he only went there to get away, to think, to know what to say, to come up with something Mama, something all of them would want to hear.

"Now, Joseph," she said.

"You like being part of this family, don't you, Marty?" asked Joseph.

Marston, his face burning, lowered his head.

"Well everybody pulls his load here," Joseph began lecturing. "Your daddy—"

"Uncle, I'm trying . . ."

"—And your granddaddy, they pulled their fair share—more. Nils, he taught us all. So there'd never be any more hurt. And there hasn't been, let me—"

"Uncle!"

Her voice struck the close walls, the tiles. Out on the other side of the sill a cricket stopped in midchirp; even the talk in the dining room seemed to pause.

She pushed up out of her chair. Then, her hands locked at her waist, she said, "Whatever I'm trying to explain to Marston . . . what*ever* . . . I'll do it in my own time, and in my own way. What is best for my boy. If you please!"

Joseph stopped himself, mumbled, shook his head, ran a glass of water, touched it to his mouth, poured it down the drain and walked loudly back to the other room.

She sat down.

The sounds of the evening returned slowly, and after time passed she said gently, "Why don't you . . . you can go to your room now, honey. Or you can look at television. I don't think anyone else is in the living room yet." She had one hand curved over her eyes. "But what am I saying? You're not a baby anymore."

She glanced up, her eyes red. He wanted to stop playing with the salt shaker and touch her arm or her hand but could not.

He said, "I guess I'd like to hear about—about Granddad."

She studied him tiredly.

"There's nothing for you to worry about, Marston. I've never fibbed to you, have I?" She tried to smile. "I want you to stop worrying about it."

"Yes, Mama."

She took a breath and her eyelids fluttered. "I don't want you to worry about anything. Honey, all you have to do for now is this . . . . I want you to start keeping a Dream Book of your own. Use your school notebook if you like until I can get you a good one. That's all. It's just something everyone in this house does. I was waiting for your father to speak to you but he's, well, Daddy's not very good at talking to you, you know that. It was really always my duty, though, because it started with my dad."

She waited, watching him. "Look, I know. You can use the tape recorder I promised you for your birthday, if you like, for the time being. You may as well have it now. If it makes it easier."

"But," he began uncertainly, "but when you told me to start remembering my dreams, remember? I asked you if—if the others would have to hear, too. And you didn't answer. You didn't. Why not? Will they?"

"Well, we don't all sit around and talk about each other's dreams. It's not like that. You see, honey, I wanted you to tell just me at first, so you could get used to it. You have to get the hang, and it takes patience, I know. You have to learn how to wake up gradually, so you keep a thread of it to hold onto, and then you follow the thread back in, this is the way I like to think of it, back in, so you don't lose the whole thing. You have to keep the gist of it, that's what counts."

Marston turned in his chair.

"But I didn't answer your question, did I? You know what else? I think it would be all right if, well, if you just let me listen to your tape recorder in the mornings, after you're through, and then I could, I could explain to the others, tell them what it was about. That way they wouldn't have to listen, or even read it, if you didn't want them to. At least not at first. I'll ask Grandma, but I think it will be all right. How does that sound?

"Because, don't you see, they all, we all have to know something about it. And then, oh, we can talk it over, have a kind of meeting. You know those times when everyone goes into the other room after breakfast, while you're out to pl—outside? Well, that's when we have our meetings. That's the way it's always been. We single out any messages that we think we ought to act on as a family, and then your Uncle Ralph or Uncle Harold, whoever's sitting at the head that week, they decide what would be the right thing to do. This week it's your Uncle Harold."

The after-dinner talk in the dining room grew louder again. He could imagine them talking about his dreams, what they would say if they really knew: how they would laugh, the way the men guffawed and the women made their shocked sound when Joseph told one of his stories about the time he was a salesman. He knew, and imagining made him feel knotted inside, the way he felt on the last Sunday night of summer vacation when he knew he would have to start school again in the morning.

"Marston."

When she said his name like that he knew there was something more, and that it was something he would as soon not have to hear.

"I really did want to talk to you about that other, too."

"About what?" he asked warily.

"It *is* a point I think we ought to clear up, don't you? You know, it really isn't very nice the way Uncle Joseph has to go out looking for you in his car like that after school."

"I do all my chores in the morning."

"I know, honey, but why do you want to go out to that place? It is consecrated ground, after all, and private property. . . ."

"There's no sign."

"Yes, but I'm sure they don't want strangers just wandering around in there. It isn't something that decent people do."

"I don't go there very much."

"Marston . . ."

"Well, not every day. Nobody says I go there every day."

"But why go at all? You have such a good mind, and there are so many interesting things you could be doing, instead of . . ."

"I just go there sometimes to be alone."

"But you can be alone right here. You have your own room."

A soreness started in his throat.

"Do you go there to meet someone, is that it? Some friends you don't want to bring home? You know, if they're decent young people . . ."

"I never see anybody. Except for—"

Just then chairs creaked and the men stood up on the thin rug in the dining room. Loud voices and then the men came out, thumping the swinging door, and followed each other through the kitchen to the service porch and out the screen door to the backyard.

Marston didn't look up.

"Who are they, Marston?" she said after the men passed through.

"That's just Daddy," he tried lamely, wishing it hadn't come up, "and Uncle—"

"You know what I'm talking about, young man."

He gave up. "I don't know!" he said too loudly. "I don't know who they are. Just some people. I didn't talk to them—I don't talk to anybody. They are just two people, they were wearing all black and they walked funny. Like they couldn't see, or something."

She let out a breath that sounded like it would never end.

"So you have seen them. I was afraid of that. Grandma was right. She said you would, sooner or later."

"Well, so what? Who are they?"

"You must have seen Rosie," said Mama, her lip beginning to tremble violently as she stared into a spot both on the table and beyond it, "and Cousin Erna. I knew they'd be going again. That's why I didn't want you going over there. There was no reason for you to know about them yet. Our dad is buried there. Your grandfather Stolberg."

She began to cry openly.

"My sister Rosie, and Erna. They left the family . . . the family ways a long, long time ago, before you were born. I tried to warn Rosie, but she wouldn't listen. She just wouldn't listen. And look what happened to them! I didn't want you to know yet. I didn't want you to be frightened, but now you know, now you've seen for yourself that it isn't a game . . ."

She went on, and there was nothing for him to do but wait, and he couldn't bear that. So, as quickly as he could, he maneuvered out of the chair, took a step, and bolted.

Slipping out the screen door, letting it drift shut without a sound, he forced himself to move slowly, hearing the sounds and stories from the arbor, from the grapevines and the milky fig trees, and he crossed the driveway cracked with crabgrass, followed the driveway out into the blue street, past the black walnuts to the house where Vin had lived before he moved away; he let himself out the gate at the back of Vin's lot and began walking fast, then running over other lots, heading across town. Moving in the twilight, he remembered that first time he had run off: not home and not to Vin's but somewhere, anywhere, to be alone, to think. And the way Mama had wept and clutched him to her cold cheek late that night when finally he had been found. It was the only moment he still remembered about that night, but it was enough. He wished—he wished—

Now, of course, he was too old. But he couldn't help wanting—he didn't know what he wanted. There was only one thing he could hold to now: to get away, far away, to some place like the old overgrown grove by the churchgrounds, the place where he had gone so many times lately to think up a dream that would sound right, that would be what they wanted, that would not be laughed at. He would lie there in the copse, among the creepers and broom and moss, waiting, waiting perhaps without even knowing it for those strange blind women to return. And there, while he waited, he could think hard about who they were and why they had left and what secrets they might know about living apart, and the price, about how steep, how terribly steep it truly was.

ON THE PIKE

His name was Geoff and he had been seeing her for seven weeks, ever since; almost exactly, in fact. Her name was Sherron. She was nineteen-and-a-half and a Fine Arts major, and he had met her at the semiannual Students Arts & Crafts Sale in the sculpture patio among the kilns and unfinished steel and bronze weldings, the finished ones as well all jagged, angular jumbles resembling knives, halberds and rusty sheets in the sun and concrete shadows.

A crowd of women in floral print dresses cooed over her bowls and ceramic teapots; her dishes were going like hotcakes. He had short-cut through the Arts wing on his way back to the House, and now circled in the unexpected activity, arriving at her table by natural course.

Tracing with his finger a caricatured Uncle Sam glazed blue-and-russet on a centerpiece plate she had tagged *not for sale,* he thickened his lower lip and nodded in a knowing wrap-up and turned to leave.

"Wait!" She waved through her customers, edging to the end of the table.

"You talking to me?"

"Um. Do you have a match?"

She was pretty, cute, close enough to it, at least. He nodded and fished in his windbreaker.

"Thanks." She ignored the pottery hounds—they were picking over the last few pieces, anyway—and watched his eyes. "Do you have a cigarette?"

He watched back, came up with two.

She cradled her elbow in her other hand and flexed the cigarette in her fingers. He lit hers and then his, waiting ceremoniously for the sulfur to burn off first. She cupped her hands, small and gray with dried clay, around his and inhaled.

"Do you have a car?" she asked, without blinking.

He had to laugh. "What's your—" Only then did he recognize her as the girl his roommate had pointed out in the cafeteria. That one'll help you forget, man, Greg had smirked. She'll go out with an-y-one. For one night. "Your name's Sherron, isn't it?"

"Mm-hm. I have to get to the USC Dental Clinic by three o'clock. I have an appointment."

She stared him down.

He glanced at his watch. "Three o'clock, huh?"

"I thought afterwards we could go to my place. I could make you some Ovaltine, or something."

When he looked up she was smiling. Really smiling.

"You're not putting me on, are you." He said it like he already knew the answer.

"No," she said. And she wasn't, either.

So it had gone: from icepacking a wisdom tooth socket all the first night, to breakfast *and* lunch *and* dinner, to the friendly, slippery morning showers, till it was too damn much trouble driving back to the House for periodic supplies of books, money, underwear and socks. He had moved out, and moved in. One night they passed in and out of each other's eyes for hours, each leaning forward as if to enter a mirror held by the other, and out again, and then again. So they would get married—no shit. She acted as if she didn't care about that part at first, though she warmed to it after introducing him to her sisters in West Covina. Some nights he dreamed he had stuck his neck out an open skyscraper window, but made himself leave it there on the sill, daring the window to come crashing down and behead him. He had broken through to the other side, and he was going to stay there, no matter what.

So that now, after a basketball game at the Long Beach Sports Arena, they found themselves mousing their way back in a determinedly unhurried stumble-pace to the car. A few colored lights remained on along the Nu-Pike, an old boardwalk fronting the parking lot, and the bulbs reflected in the easy tide lapping the sandy bar, breaking up like winking Christmas lights in the gently strafed waters.

"Hey," she said, "I wanna ride the roller coaster!"

"Naw," he said, tightening his arm on her neck, steering, "come on, they tore it down, remember?"

"No, then, well, so what?" insisted Sherron. "We can still have fun!"

"You want to get mugged? There's nothing over there but winos and sailors."

"Come *on*. You can buy me a cotton candy, or something."

A country-and-western bar was letting out in the amusement park. The couples sashayed away, all sequin shirts and wide dresses, their dishwater children, he imagined, left under blue TV screens in paper-thin rooms somewhere; he couldn't hold back a bitter thought of Jeannie and the hick veteran she had run to the altar with—was it only seven weeks ago? Some kind of square. He had seen him once. Probably has tattoos, thought Geoff.

Sherron led him past boarded-up concession stands, a fortune-telling parlor with frayed tassel drapes and a palmistry chart the size of a hyperthyroid octopus. The pavement glistened with stains of indeterminate origin, shiny smears like the ones found on garden leaves and walkways the morning after a rain. A huge plastic model of a hot-dog-on-a-stick thrust out from a stand in an obscene beckoning. In the dim glass, beyond her reflection, he saw dark and cooling game machines and wilted stuffed animals. He stood staring, trying hard to think of something, when she began pulling excitedly at his sleeve.

She pointed to a spot a hundred feet down the pike, where stragglers had drifted to form a crowd in front of a small wooden platform.

"It looks like a show! Oh, can we go?"

A man with a neck microphone was gesturing at the canvas behind him, and now Geoff heard a tired voice reverberating between the rows of empty rides and abandoned booths.

He caught up with her just as the pitchman introduced a girl in a turquoise harem costume. The pitchman promised a mystifying, stupefying and mesmerizing demonstration, "one which you will remember the longest day you live.

"But first," he pressed on, his moustache brushing the microphone like the sound of a riffled stack of bills, "allow me to call your attention to what I hold here in my left hand. . . ."

He held up a blue roll. All day long, he said, he had been selling admissions at one dollar per. He made a rhetorical bet that some "within the sound of my voice now" had paid that full price time and again to see the very same show that was about to go on again inside the tent.

"But this is our last performance of the night and, tell you what, I'm going to put these away." He held up a pink roll. "That's right, fifty *cents*, the regular child's price—this time and this time only!" To a faceless man in the booth: "Herb, don't sell any more of these adult tickets tonight. . . ."

"I bet he says that every time," whispered Geoff.

"Shh!"

Then the barker called everyone—there were only twelve or fifteen—in close to the platform, so they would not miss the mind-boggling demonstration he had promised.

He tied her wrists to a splintered, cross-like T-square (to force truth from her before the trick was over?). Geoff watched her writhe in the soft ropes, her bejeweled navel rising and falling above a low gilt belt. Now the latecomers, almost all men, pressed intently to the platform, their eyes rolling over her like ball bearings on a washboard.

"She's wearing a wig," Sherron interjected. "And there's a rip in her armpit. *Poor thing.*"

The barker pitched and persuaded and promised and enticed and the audience, grown restless, flicked eyes from the word pictures flying like spittle-moths from his mouth to the painted poster renderings strung up against the tarp:

Pin Head, an androgynous mystery.

Mister Frozo.

Petrified Man.

The Human Pin Cushion.

A sword swallower with the neck of a giraffe.

A fire eater.

And a geek, curiously unexplained.

He started a portable phonograph, promising admittance for those in line before the music stopped—"Limited standing room!"—and then, don't blink, the girl whipped her freezing hands out of the ties, hiding them in her veil as she ducked inside.

They got in.

Geoff smelled sawdust and something he didn't want to name as they inched from the closed flap. His eyes strained to open to the dim light. Sherron hung on his sleeve, her breast pushing into his arm, and he liked that, and then remembered why: Jeannie, walking home from school in their sophomore year, before he had gotten his car. He hadn't known what it had meant, that memory, until now, and he fought it, everything about Jeannie, Geoff and Jeannie, Jeannie and Geoff. Well, the hell with her. He had something different now, and better, he told himself, and he wasn't going to give it up. It didn't, it didn't matter what his friends said, that he was "on the rebound" . . . .

He put his arm around his fiancee.

The sword swallower slid an assortment of smooth chromed blades into his gullet, starting each one carefully and then allowing the weighted handle to glide it down all the way. He wiped them before with a rag reeking of antiseptic, drawing them swiftly up and out and wrapping them neatly away at the end.

"That's easy," confided Sherron, "see, he just tips his head so far back his whole throat opens."

"Yeah, sure, but how does he keep from throwing up?"

"Aw," said Sherron, "I wanna see something good!"

The magic show was slow and tacky; it was the sword swallower again, doing double duty. He struggled through a levitation with the girl in the harem costume. He got her up on the board, then kicked out the chairs, *then* put the sheet over her—he had forgotten; and every time she started to tip one way or the other he had to yell back at the shabby curtain for someone to tighten the wires.

It was the last show of the night, all right. Geoff felt embarrassed for the man, he couldn't help it. But Sherron laughed. She was getting restless, he could tell.

Pin Head was asleep, they were told.

Mister Frozo was down for the last time, too, laid out on a bed of nails surrounded by twenty-five-pound blocks of ice like the ones that come down the chutes of vending sheds in small towns. You didn't want to stand too close to the table, with the dirt and straw melting to mush underneath. Mister Frozo, a beefy pink man without expression, appeared at first, too, to be asleep, and perhaps he had been for hours; the outline of his body had sunk deep into the icy supports; when he got up, if he would when the show was over, he would leave behind a mantle of Goudi architecture, clear shivering crystals like the pointed slopes of translucent icebergs.

But just then Mister Frozo, prodded, did sit up, lifting slowly at the waist like a rigor mortised cadaver, so that all could see the deep hole-like indentations quilted into his back.

"Sit on him!" someone suggested, and a girl laughed.

Shuddering, Geoff stepped ahead to the next stall. The cold was beginning to get to him. He rubbed his hands, breathed into them.

Next in line was the Petrified Man.

Geoff stood reading the signboard while Jeannie, no, it was Sherron, moved over with him, and then the others led by the sword swallower. The sign was crudely lettered and spelled, as if by a child. This is what it said:

THE MAN 14,000 YRS. YOUNG!

This perfect Specimen of a MUMMY unearthed in North Amer. Continent by Archeologists in the Place: Puebla, Mex. in the year: 1939 A.D. The Prehistoric Man was a member of the Clovis Culture (12,000-10,000 B.C.) and made his own Lanceolated Spear Points using the Flint or Chip Method of design. He is therefore assumed to be a Hunter, several of his Tribesmen were found nearby & were also known to be Hunter's also. He made his home a rude Wickiup made of sticks or branches and the skins of Animals he Tracked & Killed. He is preserved so timelessly by the High Altitude & Dry Climate, so that he was preserved whereas his Tribesmen were not. Look carefully and you will see authenticated Hair, Finger-nails. You have just witnessed the Most Perfect Speciman of Man of his Era on Earth!!

Truly An Unforgettable Sight

The sword swallower recited the same words out loud. And that was that, except that those who wanted a closer look were given time to file past Petrified Man in his plastic-capped pine box, a very realistic mock-up, brown and taut and convoluted as a chestnut. Uneasily Geoff noticed the teeth.

Sherron no longer clung to his arm. He turned and snared her wrist out of the stragglers shuffling to the far end of the tent.

"You don't want to see any more, do you?"

"Well, what do you think?"

"I think it's a stone drag," he answered soberly.

"Oh, come *on*," she said, "we never have any fun," and that brought him up short.

A drunk, a pair of sailors similar as bookends, a girl from the country-and-western bar, an overweight, rumpled, lonely man with perpetual five o'clock shadow, a young crewcut with his sleeves rolled, picking his nose slowly after a hard day and night at the pinballs, Geoff and his girl and three or four—who could be sure?—other furtive presences on the fringe. They found themselves clumped together before the last platform.

The sword swallower went into a low-key spiel about fire-eating.

Someone yawned loudly and left the tent.

Hearing that, the sword swallower gave up. He dropped to the edge of the platform and tried an informal huddle.

First he dipped a black-tipped wire—it was something like a coat hanger with a charred marshmallow at the end—in fluid and ignited it with a whoosh.

He spat out a medicinal lozenge and showed the inside of his mouth. He lifted his tongue. "No," he answered candidly, "my mouth's not coated with anything. You don't *need* anything to do this," and Geoff believed him. In fact, this casual revelation was the first thing he had believed tonight.

Fixing his eyes on the ceiling, the sword swallower popped the fireball in and closed quickly to extinguish it. "It's the fumes," he said. "The fumes are what's burning, not the wad. You cut off the air, that's it." He picked a second wire from the jar and lit it with his Zippo. Black smoke wisped upward.

"See, I can put my fingers right through it." He cupped his hand through the glowing aurora around the fireball. "See, it's the vapors burning," he said, flashing his smudged palm. "That's what you call the fumes."

"Don't you ever burn your mouth?" someone asked.

"You get numb to it. I been doing this for years." He plucked two more torches, holding them between his knuckles like xylophone sticks, and ignited them. "The trick is to hold your breath, or you suck fire."

"Yeah, but did you ever get burned?"

He twirled the first torch toward his lips in a graceful, surprisingly feminine gesture, dousing it quickly, and then the pair of torches together. He inserted them rapidly, aiming cleanly into the center of his open mouth. A second longer and the flames would lick his nose and chin, would sweep up the rod to his fingers.

"Sure, I been burned. Wouldn't you?"

He hunkered closer. He stretched back his thin lip with his thumb to reveal a beaded chain of small blisters lining the inner membrane. Someone drew a breath.

"I been burned more times than I can remember. *Every part that can burn has been.*"

Geoff took a close look at him. The face was one of those the age of which, once past puberty, is incomputable, rawboned and alert, every trace of self-indulgence long gone from it. The eyes were a startling eggshell blue, transparent as water, the nose pointed, nostrils pinched, the bridge pitted with blackheads as his cheeks were pitted with scars. The short, coarse hair shone from working in the sun, and the skin reflected a bright oil sheen. The expression on the sword swallower's face was a kind of detached mercilessness, toward itself as well as the world. It was a face seen at shooting gallery machines in Greyhound bus depots the country over, and it was a law unto itself.

"You all probably want to see this," he said.

He felt behind him, came up with a forty-five rpm record. Geoff tried to read the label. The sword swallower held it as if displaying a product, and a certain indefatigable pride showed through now in spite of the late hour.

He bit the record about an inch into the grooves, grimacing, his teeth dry and white and bone-like. The vinyl cracked and crumbled. He showed the disk, a rough half-moon missing from the edge. He began to chew. His eyes clenched, his jaws vibrated. The plastic broke and ground to powder. He chewed till nothing but black grounds remained in his mouth. He balled the powder into a clod and wiped it into a handkerchief.

A girl's voice tried to interrupt.

He held up a hand and went on cleaning his teeth and gums with his fingers. Then, "Hey," he called behind the curtain. He waited, hand out. "You know what I want." The curtain wobbled. A deep, unseen voice grumbled. "Don't give me any of that," he snapped.

He dropped his eyes to the bottom of the curtain, reached over and picked up a light bulb.

He turned it in his fingertips. Then he cracked it on the stage like an egg, took a curved, opaque wafer and positioned it in his mouth. He began to chew in a rolling motion, grinding it to dust. He extended his tongue to show the pile of shining particles, then picked off the ground glass cautiously, daubing with the handkerchief.

"Why don't you swallow it?" asked a girl.

"Who said that?" he asked coolly, but the spectators were hidden in the shadows. "I can swallow it. You want to see me swallow it?"

"Don't it hurt your innards?" asked a man's voice. It was one of the sailors, in front, and he sounded genuinely interested.

"Sure it does. What do you think? Let me ask you something. Wouldn't it hurt you?"

No answer.

"What did you say?"

Finally, "Then—" The sailor did not finish.

"It's something I do," answered the sword swallower.

He took a bent pack of Kools from his pants pocket, straightened one with careful strokes. He lit it, inhaling deeply. Seconds passed. A board fell outside, and heavy shoes somewhere.

"Let's see you put that cigarette in your mouth," said a girl.

He looked into the darkness, his face hard as rock. Then he laid the cigarette on his tongue, the glowing tip protruding from his mouth, and simply flicked it inside like a chameleon. Smoke blew out his nose. Then he opened his mouth, flicking the cigarette back out and down.

"Satisfied?" he said to the darkness. He wasn't smiling.

"Let's see you put it out."

The sword swallower held a deep breath, let it out slowly and with great control. He cocked an eye knowingly. "Let's hear the rest of it," he said.

A giggle.

"No. Come on. You want to say something, say it."

"Let's see you put that cigarette *out* in your mouth, I said."

No, thought Geoff. Don't let her make you.

The sword swallower sat forward, elbows braced on knees. He stared at the cigarette. His expression was unreadable. He took a hard drag and tapped the ash, rolling the cigarette between his fingers. He made a short, bitter sound that might have been a laugh, straightened his back, crossed his left ankle on his right thigh, dragged again, tapped the ash again so that the bare coal was hot and bright in the air.

"I can do it, you know. I've done it before. It'll blister for four days, then it'll hurt like hell. But I can do it. What's the matter, you think I can't?"

Geoff cleared his throat. "Man," he offered, "you don't have to prove anything." Uncertainly he added, "The hell with her, see?"

The sword swallower looked at Geoff, or as near as he could come to him in the shadows. The eyes, sharp and steely, would not give him away. Strange eyes, Geoff thought. The eyes were looking at him.

The sword swallower put his feet down and flexed his legs, half-standing. He opened his mouth, showed his tongue. Then, you know what he did. You know what he did then.

He put out the cigarette on his tongue.

"Didn't it . . ." A throat caught. "Didn't it hurt?"

"Sure it hurt." The sword swallower stepped up to the curtain. "Sure I feel it. *Wouldn't you?"*

Geoff pivoted, somewhat unsteadily. The show must be over, he thought.

Now where was she?

The others stretched and bumped together like wind-up dolls suddenly activated on the dirt floor.

"Exit to your left. This show is—"

"Hey, you're the Pin Head, right? I seen this show before."

Geoff craned his neck. The fat, rumpled man was speaking. To a new man on the platform, come out from behind the curtain.

And there was Sherron, edging over.

"Psst," whispered Geoff, "over here! You're blind as a bat, aren't you? I was looking for—"

"Is that the Pin Head?" She gave him her hands but not her attention.

Geoff sighed. "That's all, honey," he said, "there ain't no more."

"I am the Human Pin Cushion," said the man on the stage.

"I wanna see some more," said Sherron.

The man heard her. "Very well," he said, since the sailors had stopped by the tent flap, blocking the others from leaving.

Her fingers were cold. Geoff wanted to pull away, but made himself hold on.

The man, the Human Pin Cushion, was old, old. Bushy brows. A tight, unexpected cupid's-bow mouth between his hanging jowls.

Sherron laughed.

"Don't—" say any more, thought Geoff. There was something about her voice he did not like.

The old man checked his watch resignedly, slid back his sleeve as he took out a pair of spectacles. He had an old leather eyeglass case clipped over his pocket. Without enthusiasm, he produced a long, gleaming hatpin from an envelope. He waved the people closer and prepared himself, pinching up the loose rice-paper skin on his wrist. It pulled into a familiar fold.

"Hey," said a girl, "that picture outside, it shows you sticking pins all over your body."

"That is correct." The old man hesitated, needle poised. "I have passed steel through all areas of my body. I have performed for *The Johnny Car—*" He stopped himself, drew off his glasses, gazing out. "What is it you would have me do?"

"Stick it through your . . . your . . ." Giggle. The girl's voice. "Oh, through your tongue."

Geoff forced himself to look.

It was Sherron. It had been her voice all along.

"My God, Sher . . ." He tried to say her name. "My God."

The old man was looking at her, and so was everyone else. She had come up close to the stage. "No, not that. I've already seen that. Stick it through . . ."

"Yes, young lady?"

". . . Through, oh, your ear," she said impatiently. "Stick it in your ear!"

The old man checked his watch again. The show was folding. He studied her. He pushed back his hair, badly in need of a cut, folded his long ear forward. Salt-and-pepper hairs encrusted the opening above the pendulous lobe. Light from a single miniature spotlight turned the flesh a warm peach color.

He raised the long needle. He held his ear with one hand, placed the point behind the lobe, and pushed it through.

"Not there," said Sherron, "anybody can do that!"

The old man stared her down. He folded his upper ear and pressed with a slow, trembling force, driving the tip through the cartilage in a tiny stirring motion.

He stepped to the edge, the needle penetrating his ear in two places. He looked down past his chins at the girl. At Sherron.

"You are satisfied now?" he asked.

"How come you don't bleed?" she said defiantly.

The old man stepped back. He grasped the ball on the end of the needle. "This show," he said, "is over." And then, to Sherron alone, he said:

"What do you think I am? Don't you think we are human?

"Of course we bleed."

He pulled the needle as if lowering a sword from salute.

A stream of blood coursed immediately from his ear. It gushed down his neck and spattered to the boards.

Then he left the stage.

Geoff forced a path out. He put a hand to his forehead

and hurried away from the pike. He was aware of the tarpaulined machinery of thrill rides, canvased shapes and empty attractions. A mist of dew was already forming on the glass of the fortune shop but he did not see it as he passed. He zipped his windbreaker and continued to his car, refusing to break stride, and as the girl named Sherron strove to keep pace, laughing at him, cajoling, finally silent and unintentionally merciful as the fog rolled in, he felt, no, he knew at last that he was alone now, after all, quite alone.

KEEPER OF THE LIGHT

It is a small thing, really, very slight, but it happens like this:

Drowsy in the seat, your legs folded by the thick pane, you hear her pattering up the spiral steps. You stand. Your foot is asleep and for a moment you sway before the glass, reeling atop the white masonry tower that is mercifully cushioned from the breaking sea by soft folds of outside fog. Then she comes up behind you, touches your neck with her hand so like a cool fish brushing near in the luminous dark; you turn and take her up in your arms and turn again into the night.

"How's everybody tonight?" she asks.

Your eyes follow hers up ladders to the sky. To her friends.

"They're happy, aren't they? See? They've got all their lights on." She dabs a spot of frost on the glass. "Look at the Seven Travelers. They're not blinking. Calm. Don't you think?"

The cluster of lights she has named waits above you, wheeling peacefully over the low mist.

"Well, I don't know. Look at Old Three Eyes," indicating a line of bright, flickering points in another part of the sky. "And what about the porpoise?" A string of white motes spilled across with the familiar milky roadway. Once, years ago, they had resembled a ladle to you, but that was before you met Luanne.

"Oh, they're flying easy, too," she assures. "See how clear . . . how they're watching us. 'Content,' I guess, is the word."

Kiss her by her ear, in the soft place between cartilage and short, wispy strands of hair. "Don't you ever get tired of being here," you ask suddenly, "just us, for so long? Tell the truth. I mean, six months—"

"—Is beautiful!" she answers. "*They* are so beautiful, and they seem to want to make a place for us, to remind us what peace is really like. You know. So we won't forget, back in the city." Her eyes sparkle, her lips shine under the billion members of her personal family. In a sense, she has created them, for herself and for you. It makes her happy. You would not have it otherwise.

It is hard to believe that so many ships have run ashore and wrecked on this coast. So soft, it appears, this fogged haven on the north California shore. Thinking of it, you imagine that you hear the twisting of rusted iron, the buckling of hulls and the cries of the lost washed onto the rocks, but you shake your head to throw it off. Only it doesn't go away.

"Listen!" she says, incredulous, hearing it, too. Far below on the beach there is the sound again, as of grinding motors and bent propellers thrashing the sand. You look at each other and then head down the stairwell.

He is squat, rumpled and fatigued, and as he sips coffee in the cottage your eyes are drawn to his pallid hands, smooth and flounder-white.

"Salesman," he sighs, baring his teeth. "I was on my way to a meet in Marin County this afternoon, figured I'd shave a few hours if I cut down on the cliff road. Jesus, Joseph and Mary, I haven't seen a gas station for two hours!"

"Listen," you decide, "no way you can get a tow out here tonight. Rest your bones till morning and I'll have a look at her in the daylight. I used to be a half-assed mechanic myself. My wife can make up the couch here, and—''

''I'll get you a fresh cup,'' Luanne chimes in. Her eyes crinkle up, smiling, actually pleased to play hostess.

The man stretches, expands, not at all embarrassed. ''Say, what do you folks do out here? Godforsaken place, eh? That is a lighthouse I saw out there, isn't it?''

''Lu and I stay here every year, spring through fall. Ryman Scientific owns the facility, actually. Bought it all from the Coast Guard when the automatic beacons went up, six-seven years ago. We watch the bottom measuring devices for them, drop the lines, chart wind and rain and, oh, you know, read dials and gauges. We get room and board and a small stipend. Very small.'' You rise. ''You know, it's quite a break from city life. My wife doesn't seem to mind. . . .''

''I love it!''

''There you are. Come on. I'll show you around.''

Cursing the terrain, he stumbles out and over the grounds and into the lower levels with you, muttering *hmm* and *yeah* and *well then there now,* disturbed that the whitewash comes off on his hands, bumping his head on the old acetylene-cluster burners on the way up to the light. You fire it up for him, showing off a little, perhaps. 400,000 candles beam out, tipping the water with phosphor. You are proud, somehow.

''And you? You're in sales?'' you ask, crunching back across the field between the vegetable garden and the poppies and daisies, past the mums and roses and giant sunflower plot, touched and ordered by the delicate, ever-widening network of her personality. She has transfigured us all, you think, and the cold leaves you for a minute.

''Toys,'' he says, warming to his subject. ''Yeah, I sell the little monsters—their mothers, really—one kind of diddlyshit after another. Heh. It's a living. Say, you folks have kids?''

''We're trying.'' You wink at Luanne.

He veers to his car, racked up blind in a ditch. ''My

compliments, here. You'll use 'em someday. The least I can do, if you won't take my money."

"Oh, let's see!" says Luanne excitedly.

"If you'll just give me a hand, then, with these samples . . ." and he loads you with boxes from the back seat of the station wagon.

His favorite is a tabletop planetarium. The living room is small but the walls and ceiling make perfect projection surfaces. You switch off the light and as he thumbs the rheostat on the plastic toy, a semblance of stars limns the room, faint, then bright, then unbearably brilliant, unnaturally coruscating aureoles, cold and riveting.

Luanne gasps.

The salesman wields his electric pointer and begins to entertain with an impersonal lecture, rehearsed for his sales conference, no doubt. He traces lines between the points until he has interconnected them all.

"This one is Ursa Major, of course," he rattles off, "the Big Bear."

"It's really a porpoise," says Luanne in the dark.

"No, no," he corrects with cool finality. "And here's Orion, his belt, right?" He raises his bright arrow.

"Old Three Eyes," she objects.

"And over here," he explains, rather pompously, "the Seven Sisters, got it? And . . ."

And so on and on. He names every constellation in the heavens, rotating the black pinholed shell, whirling you through season after season. The effect is disorienting. Every pet name, every reassuring personification she has created is laid to rest, stripped from the sky, replaced by the neutral abstractions you thought you had forgotten and which Lu had never known, had never wanted to know. Some he calls again and again, until their names become unfamiliar, abstracted beyond meaning, dissociated utterly from your lives. It must seem that way to her. To be honest, you feel something of it yourself. He directs you to Sirius, to Alpha Centauri and to Mars, god of war and dissension, 40,000,000 miles from Earth, far, you think, far, far away. In place of signposts he leaves nomenclature, in place of beacons he leaves disinterested classification, in place of recognition he leaves a universe too distant to know in any meaningful way. In any way at all.

Luanne breathes moistly across the room. It has gotten to her, all right. Such a small thing, really. You wish you could find her, touch her, warm her, be with her. The salesman breathes heavily, tiring, as his strange, surrogate stars continue to blaze down with an icy certainty, laid out like dots separated forever on a graph of alien geometry.

In the morning she is awake too early, moving aimlessly around the small house, busying herself without purpose. By noon you have given up on the wagon and phone for the tow truck, and he departs as he had arrived, in a grating moan of machinery.

She waits between the cottage and the lighthouse. Her eyes are wide, implacable. You walk up to her and she lets you take her arms in your grimy hands. In her eyes is neither resistance nor consent.

"What is the Pleiades?" She says it oddly, as if she does not expect an answer. You don't know what to say. You shake your head, a pale gesture of resignation.

She slips away. "Hey, wait . . . !" You try to hold her while you think of something to say, but she eludes you.

From the top of the tower you can see her puttering around the house in no particular pattern. You try to make sense of it, but it is a random ballet of Brownian motion.

All day you sit in the tower.

Then, as night comes in, all the way into the crow's nest, you realize that the beacon is still burning. You shut it off. You sit that way for hours; once you stand to stretch, searching for something like a man looking for an answer in the back of a book and finding the page torn out, and you gaze down at the jagged boulders on which the station is built. The water laps all around. It tears at the rocks in perpetual erosion. Without malice, without design, without end and you remember that one day the rock and all that has been erected upon it will fall into the swirling black-crested waves, and the thought sobers you, and you blow on your greasy hands, still trying to warm them.

It is something you can live with painlessly enough. You have seen far worse things.

You want to explain that to her. But you wouldn't know how. Besides, it is a small thing, really, very slight.

Yet many days in the weeks that follow you find yourself sitting like that, alone in the tower. From there you can see her easily as she comes out from time to time, looking for something to do in the garden. But the plants go untended more and more as the season drags on, and when she moves her gait grows more deliberate each day; once you even see her weeping as she walks softly around the grounds. You stay on to the end, of course, and when you leave she says that she doesn't care if she comes back next year or not. As simply as that. She mouths something about the weather. And so you go back to the city, to pass the years ahead together, and to forget that night soon enough, both of you.

Still, there are nights when you find yourself trying to call up from within her something she seems no longer to have to give, and that seems strange to you; and on some of those nights you go to the window, to sit by the window remembering from an old dream the way the tule fog used to settle in like a blanket over the coast, masking the stars until they were but microscopic pinholes staring blindly out of an indifferent sky, and that seems to you the strangest of all. It is a small thing, really, a very slight thing in the course of a life for a man to remember at all.

BLACK SUN

I live on a hill. Tonight the dark came too soon. I was down cutting the grass for the landlady and I came up for a drink of cold water about seven o'clock. The wind started blowing over from the east side of town then. I had to stop by the back door. All of a sudden my face and neck were cool. The wind was from the cemetery. I closed my eyes. It smelled sweet and damp and full of roses.

Inside the house was filling up with blue shadows. Shyla never liked that time of day.

The living room.

Sitting in the rattan rocking chair.

How to tell you? Begin anywhere:

"I think I'll kill myself tonight," she sighs. "There's nothing *else* to do."

I stop long enough to manage a wan smile. "There's always Scrabble. But in a little while. I almost have Series II licked."

"What do they want to know now?"

" 'State the nature of your belief,' " I read from the 150 Form, " '. . . and state whether or not your belief involves duties which are to you superior to those arising from any human relation.' "

"Nosy."

" 'Explain how, when and from whom or from what source you received the training and acquired the belief . . .' "

"I wonder," asks Shyla, "why they don't just ask you to define the universe and give two examples? In twenty-five words or less."

"Don't exaggerate. They give me two whole blank lines here."

I watch her as she shifts her hip and lays her long legs up on the madras coverlet. She has to be moving every other second now; it is the macrobiotics, part of the natural high.

"That's Section III, I believe," I tell her, cracking my cramped knuckles. "You've been through this yourself, haven't you. Don't lie." I lift the typewriter off my knees and stretch my back. "Jeezus. This is worse than that last term paper."

I look over at her. The round rice-paper lantern moving slowly behind her head. She is absorbed. She is filing her nails with a long emery board very carefully, as if playing a rare violin.

"You do remember that weekend," I remind her.

"How could I forget? You, your typewriter, the kitchen table. Thank God you've learned how to type since then. I had to sleep in a chair, at your beck and call."

The bamboo wind chimes are tinkling outside the window.

I pluck off my glasses, rub my eyes and make a truce with myself again for a time.

Trying to get a fix on her through the blur.

"When do you . . . What's his name?"

"Dr. Soeul."

"Ha. With a name like that, he must get more word-of-mouth business than he can handle." I raise my hand. "Don't. I know he comes recommended. I was the one who turned you on to the whole thing, remember? But when do you see him next?"

Her glance has grown needle-sharp now since the diet. "Tomorrow night, seven."

I feel myself moving closer to her.

Her hands fold together like slender, pale fish. "I'm sorry, David. I love you." I see her slip up to her outer level, a silent *click*. "I think we both do," she tries.

My eyes clasp hers and my hands her warm cheeks, and then I bend to kiss her mounding stomach through the cloth. I am aware of my hair again. "What are you worrying about?" she asks as she touches it.

"Nothing."

"The ba—"

"No. Of course not."

She waits a beat. "The C.O. thing." I start to answer again, but her fingers tighten on my head. "I know it's getting to you." Her tone: strangely serene, as if separate from the words.

"It's nothing."

"Nothing," she says then, "is something inside out."

I have to look up. The dark eyes slip back to that other place. I can't help trying to press deeper into them. . . .

This is one night.

The horror lies in that there is no horror.

I sank back into the dry, distended hand of the chair, the chair crackling, accommodating me. Out somewhere the crickets began to chirp, a sound like the clicking of poker chips.

Rocking. Trying to rock. I held my breath. I couldn't smell then. Or see. I tried not to feel. Only the motion. And the story.

I remembered our first week. My II-S had expired that quarter. The first days of our relationship were like the first bites of a watermelon before you hit a seed. It started at Santa Monica. She was walking out of the sea and the sunlight was firing blinding bolts around her silhouette and I stood transfixed and just watched her come up to meet me. The next day my eyes peeled burned skin. She said she had run away from a place where they wrapped her in wet sheets. When she found out I lived in Silverlake, too, she asked me if I had a car. I told her I didn't and she moved into a new apartment ten miles away just to test me.

I was the one who gave her the book, along with *Albion Moonlight* and *From Bindu to Ojas* and some others. Of course you will blame me, as you should. Naturally. It started with a visit to his office in Little Tokyo; you know the type: Monday night Zen classes served up with brown rice; the following night another course. The regimens. Something. I didn't go. The vigil at the Friends House, a WRL meeting, maybe a counseling session somewhere or hours alone just going over and over my duplicate file. I don't remember.

When she came home I had turned down the bed. Afterward she shook herself like a puppy coming out of sweet grass and smiled around the house and left her hair down the rest of the night. In the morning she woke me to announce that she had dropped something. We searched the floor for her last pill, more valuable than a contact lens—it couldn't be insured. She wished it had been an IUD. Later she tried to drink a bottle of Jergens Lotion while I was out mailing a letter to the Board. "It smelled so good," she said. "Just like burnt almonds!"

After the Form was filed I had to beg the usual collection of "imminent piety" reference letters. Then the reclassification: I-A. No surprise. It did not take long; the Justice Department is no longer involved. Then the appeal. Then the request for a personal appearance. Then the letter requesting an appointment with the government Appeals Agent, a Compozed Larry Blyden impersonator who knew nothing. A formality. I can no longer remember when her thinness first became frightening. Then the personal appearance and the two counselors along as witnesses: refused admittance, of course: one more detail duly noted in case of a court test. The refusal to reopen the classification. Then the appeal to the County Board, where it is said the rubber stamp falls like a blade every eleven seconds. Then the filing of Form 151 with the Local Board, followed by their refusal to reclassify and rewind the appeal procedure for another replay. Then the preinduction physical, follow the colored stripes up and down the stairs and get in line for short-arm inspection. Later the fellow next to me bit his lip and spat blood into the beaker and it almost worked. Then the appeal to State Headquarters. Their reply. Then the letter to the National Director. She spidered her fingers around cups of mu tea, talked rapidly of tests in darkened rooms and small bottles and extractions. Then the first set of induction papers. Then the change of address through a front in San Francisco. Then the flight up to the Local Board there for a transfer of induction — $11.43 each way on PSA. Then the National Director's refusal to intervene. Then the new induction date in Oakland. Then the transfer back down here. Then the letter from the Friends counselor pleading for a new hearing. Then the letter requesting another appointment with the Appeals Agent, adjusting his glasses with sweaty fingers, handshake clammy. Then the new induction date. Then a final transfer back up to the Oakland Induction Center. . . .

Shyla. Shyla. It grew more and more difficult for her. I don't know how it happened. I don't even know what happened to her. Her condition was not enough for a III-S under the new law. For a time I thought of her like the place where I had met her: storms rend the sea but never change its hardness. If anything she seemed to be growing softer, more sensitive. That was good. I thought that.

One night coming home from there like so many other nights.

Looking up and seeing her halfway through the bead curtain.

Her body like one of those starving African children, bloated belly and pencil-thin wrists.

I stand and take her hands. "Hey, your gloves are cold," I tell her.

"I'm not wearing any."

I breathe on her fingers. We sit. After a while I say, "How is . . . ?" The way she looks, I don't want to press it.

"H-he's pleased with my progress. He said so. The examination—"

She creates a little pull at the corners of her pallid mouth but her eyes lid over. Her finger makes a fine tracing around my jawline.

"David," she pronounces. That is enough, I think. Then her lashes fly together and I can feel the strain growing as it draws together in her. It feels something like desperation. "David, let's get out of here." Her eyes open. She is unbelievably sanpaku, I notice, and for some reason, though I know better, I get a cold rush in my chest. "Now. Tonight. We could start fresh—in Mendocino. Anywhere. Oh shit."

"Hey, hey."

I see she is struggling to stay ahead of herself. "I can't have it this way. I want to get out of here, out of L.A. We have to, don't you see? This place is some kind of—of necropolis for—for the waiting dead." She shudders, unbelievably.

I have no idea what to say to that.

Then her eyes, flicking between mine, lose some of their depth and withdraw in the manner of a camera iris stopping down, *click*. And I know she has remembered my case and the way its weight has me anchored here.

I take her head in my lap and stroke it. Now there is neither resistance nor consent. . . .

She casts the yarrow stalks. She sits cross-legged, staring as into scattered entrails. She is still for a long time. Then she takes the book down from the shelf and unwraps it and the three coins and throws them, too. I ask her for the reading.

" 'If the bridge is weak at both ends,' " she recites in a dull, emotionless voice," " 'it does not matter what happens in the middle.' "

The hours unravel and I cannot think of a thing but her.

In bed she tosses just outside my arms. Once she sits up.

"*What is that?*" she whispers out of what sounds like terror.

"That?" I try to follow the trajectory of her stare. "That?" I get out of bed, pad to the corner, find a thing, pick it out of the dust. "Well, what do you know?" I turn it over and over. "It's nothing. It's an old pretzel! Ha."

"Oh." She sinks back.

I start to toss it over to her but I am afraid she might scream.

Just before I drop off, I study her face, the flawless line of her nose, her soft lip, her shoulders. I can no longer be sure when she is asleep, awake.

There are marks in the muscle of her upper arm.

I bend closer. Everything is a grainy blue-gray in the near dark. But there they are: tiny specks also dot her face around the eye sockets, her forehead, her temples, her cheekbones. With a shaky finger I tip her head to one side on the pillow. Marks along the tendons of her neck. I wonder how many marks there are.

Dr. Soeul, I realize, has been practicing—what?

What do they call it?

A fist tightens in my stomach.

She has promised that she is seeing an obstetrician as well. I believed her. I was busy.

She is weak. It is more than that. It can be stated simply. Something in Shyla is missing. It has not always been this way.

In the middle of the long night I wake at the sound of her voice close by me.

". . . All cold and clammy and brassy like a mummy's fingers . . . !" Her voice is racing, lost.

"Shyla?"

No answer.

I try to sleep some more. But I keep listening to her dreams. It is as if I need to hear them.

I wonder what happens when the dreaming stops—or goes mad.

Morning and I come out of it to find her on her back staring into the mottled pattern the sun makes on the ceiling.

I kiss her. No response. I feel like a man who has awakened to find himself bound in cement.

I blow the spider web of hair off her forehead. "Sleep okay?"

"For a while I couldn't," she replies. "The moon on the bottom of the bed wouldn't let me."

I blink, resume breathing.

But "I thought I heard a voice calling me," she goes on. "Then in the dark I heard a voice answer, 'yes?' "

I can't even shudder.

Finally I come up with, "Well, I hope you feel better than you did last night. You know—"

"Last night," she says, still staring at the ceiling, the walls, "I felt my brain shaking like jelly. And the water seeping into the ground."

I just look at her.

"It's all right, David," she says. "You understand what's happening, don't you? I'm only coming closer and closer."

"To what?"

"To the far away."

I laugh, tight-lipped. I try to think that it is beautiful to have a woman who knows things she will never tell me. I try. She must know. I have to believe in her. I have to return the belief.

She grew thinner and thinner. I continued to fight my case. The time came. Almost came.

Mostly I remember the shadows of the leaves on the trees covering the walls of the living room in a moving black wash through the glass. Shyla on the couch. This one day she chose the darkening living room. I don't know why.

She wouldn't leave the city without me and I had to be with the lawyers at the CCCO. And she wouldn't change doctors. I must have tried and tried. You would think so.

She had been reading a lot of Patchen that day. Lastly she was studying the cold black flaming on the wall. Sun through leaves. Black centers deeper than the light.

"I need the dark," she says suddenly, settling the squirming shape behind her almost translucent belly. Her voice is like a rustling now, her body dotted all over. I haven't left this room for three days. The file. "Do you know? It gives all . . . and it takes nothing back!"

Turn from the pane. Start to speak. But see. There is no longer any Word possible between her and the dark now.

Something quietly leaves the room.

The sun nails black to the wall . . . .

I sat in the chair. There. After cutting the grass. The sun outside gone away. I don't think I even noticed when it happened. They say it will rain tomorrow. I don't worry about the weather. I haven't for a long time. The sky has lost control.

This afternoon I burned my draft card. I thought about it a long time. I read it over and over. Then I knew you can never decide from the words. Consider the spaces. She taught me that. I think she did. I squirted it with lighter fluid and touched a match to it and threw it on the air. It flared to something black and fell apart. After that I took my file and scattered it down the hillside.

A little while ago I sat in the chair. Then I got up.

I went down the hill. The place called me. I used to go there a lot evenings when I was a kid and it was warm and I was thirsty after helping with the lawn or something.

I wasn't thinking anything. Down the hill. The leaves at the corner crackled at my heels. I turned round half-expecting to see myself. Fosselman's was cool neon at the end of the long block. I thought it looked good.

Went in the store. Too many flavors to pick.

Got in line. There was a girl in front of me with a snowy streak put in her hair. She turned around and looked at me and the second time she smiled. But I just turned away. Her dress enclosed her like a self-addressed envelope. She swept out with a cone and didn't look back. I noticed her ice cream: it was almost colorless, sort of a brain-gray.

The counter was stainless steel and plastic frosted over

on the underside. Leaned my palms on it and looked down.

"Double or single?"

"What?"

Mr. Fosselman gave me a look.

"You wanna buy something, or you come here to sprout roots?"

He didn't recognize me. The hair, the way I don't care anymore. Maybe he did, maybe he did.

Right then a chill touched my face.

And I knew that I didn't want anything there. I turned and clipped over the waxed linoleum squares, past the wrought-iron chairs, the peppermint shaft and the cardboard boy licking it so patiently.

It was cold outside, but a cold that numbs, without a chill.

I rolled up my sleeves and then threw away my jacket and started east across town, stripping off my shirt, everything as I went, through all the yellow and red lights, stepping on every crack, all the way.

Tomorrow I will find him in among his sharp gold needles and small bottles; I will take them all back from him and I will kill him and read his bloodstains like a Rorschach test and find an answer.

Then I will come back here. They will never find me when they come looking, if they do. I have left everything behind. Maybe I will live here, in the trees and bushes, the lawn and the shadows of the shrubbery, and the headstones. Maybe I will.

WHITE MOON RISING

It went like this: in her room at the top of the stairs in the empty sorority house she lay warm and rumpled in her bed, trying hard to sleep some more. It was now near noon and the light streaming through the open curtains had forced her awake again. She did not seem to care if she ever got up; she had no classes, not for a week. Still she could not make herself relax. The late morning flashed a granular red through her eyelids. Then she heard the front door down below open and close, the click echoing through the abandoned house like a garbage can dropped in an alley at dawn. Probably it was one of the few remaining girls returning from an overnight date or to pick up books before leaving for vacation. Lissa hoped so. Now she could hear footsteps treading up the stairs. She tried to imagine who it was. The footsteps reached the top of the stairs and stopped. Firmly, deliberately the footfalls turned and came down the hall, toward her room. Maybe it was Sharon. She wanted it to be Sharon. She kept her eyes tightly closed. The shoes thumped deep into the rug; the loose board in the middle of the hall creaked. Finally whoever it was reached her room—there, just on the other side of the door. Lissa felt ice crystals forming in her blood. She waited for the knock, for the clearing of a familiar throat, for the sound of her own name to come muffled through the door. But there was no sound. Still she waited. She held a breath. The blood pulsed coldly in her ears like a drum beaten underwater. She wanted to speak out. Then the sound of a hand on the loose doorknob. And the almost imperceptible wingbeat of the door gliding open. I know, she thought, I'll lie perfectly still, I won't let anything move in my body and I'll be safe, whoever it is won't see me and will go away. Yes, she thought, that's what I will have to do. Now she clearly felt a presence next to her bed. She was sure that someone was standing there in the doorway to her right, a hand probably still on the knob. She had not heard it rattle a second time. Time passed. She counted her heartbeats. At last she knew she could hold her breath no longer. She would have to do something very brave. With a rush that screamed adrenaline into her body she sat bolt upright, at the same instant snapping her head to the right and unsticking her eyes with a pop. There was no one there. The door was still closed and locked. The room was empty. Suddenly she realized that her kidneys were throbbing in dull pain. She knew what that was. It was fear.

The sunlight washed in through the window.

"Oh Joe," said his wife, "it makes me sick, just physically ill. And I know it gets to you, too."

Joe Mallory cleaned up the steak and eggs on his plate with a last swipe, then hesitated and let his fork mark a slow pattern through the smear of yolk that remained.

"No." He cleared his throat. "No, honey. Just a job." Gently he removed the newspaper from her side, poked it in half and tried to find something else to read.

"Joey," she said. She reached across the tablecloth suddenly and covered his hand. "I know you. And I know I shouldn't have let you take this job, not this one."

He looked up and was surprised and strangely moved to see her clear brown eyes glistening. As he forced his shoulders to shrug and his mouth to smile, she placed her other hand as well over his. From the open kitchen window sprang the sounds of bright chains of children on their way to the elementary school. He could almost see their black bowl haircuts and dirty feet. He wished he could help them, but it was already too late. He blinked, trying to concentrate.

"Babe," he said calmly, resurrecting a pet name they had abandoned before he went overseas. "One more semester and I'm finished with night classes. Look. You know the size of the government checks, and you know they aren't going to get any bigger. We both know Ray can't take me on without a degree—"

"You know he would, Joey, if you ask him again. What's a brother for?" Instantly she darkened, regretting the last. She held to his hand, hoping that he would let it pass.

"Now let me finish," he said slowly. "I can't handle a position like that yet, not without leaning on someone half the time. I have to do it right. This damned uniform is just a job until I'm ready. Till then, well, what else do I know? Really, now?" He flipped her hands over and warmed them with his. "I have to make things right before I go ahead, to feel like I'm my own man. I thought you understood that."

"Oh, I know all that. I'm sorry. I know. It was just all the details, the whole horrible thing, these last few weeks. It sounds so awful."

She rested her forehead on her arm and cried for a few seconds. Then she pressed her nose and stood up, stacking the dishes. "Come on, you big jock. You'll be late."

He pushed away from the table and crossed the kitchen in three steps. He took his wife in his arms and held her close for a long minute, while the electric clock hummed high and white on the wall.

She rocked back and forth with his body. Finally she began to laugh.

"Get out of here," she said, trying hard.

"Meet me at work," he said. "I'll take you to Fernando's for dinner."

The tears settled diamond-bright in her eyes. She kissed him noisily and pushed him out the door.

She watched him through the window.

He came back in.

"Forgot something," he said. He walked briskly to the breakfast nook, picking up the morning paper, and dropped it in the waste can. "Give my love to the ice cream man," he said before he shut the door again.

"Hey, I don't even know the . . ."

He was gone and she stopped laughing. She went to the can and picked out the paper. She spread it on the table and stared down at it.

"Shit," she said very seriously. "Oh shit, Joe. . . ."

The latest headline read:

Security Doubled
ANOTHER BRUTAL COED SLAYING

Lissa, now in tank top and embroidered Levi's, toed into her sandals and slipped down the stairs, her thin fingers playing lightly over the handrail.

"Sharon?" On the wall at the foot of the stairs she noticed the poster Sharon had brought with her from New York. It was one of those old *You Don't Have To Be Jewish To Love Levy's* advertisements, showing an Indian biting into a slice of rye bread; Sharon had replaced the Indian with the horribly burned face of an Asian child, and now she saw that someone had written across the face with a red marking pen the words *You Don't Have To Be A Unicorn To Enjoy The Tapestry* in an unmistakably feminine hand. She wondered what *that* meant. "Has anybody seen Sharon?" she called, tapping her nails on the railing. Then, "Is anybody here?"

She thought she heard voices and stepped off the stairs. But she saw only the bright, still day outside the open front door, and the two familiar Security guards at the edge of the dry lawn. They stood with their hands behind their backs and, Lissa thought, peculiar smiles on their faces; as they rocked on their heels their billy clubs swung tautly from wide, black belts.

Something about them gave her the creeps.

Her eyes listlessly scanned the living room, finding nothing to settle on.

She stepped away from the open front door. Sharon must have left it open. On the way out, probably to see Eliot.

She could call Eliot and find out, couldn't she?

She took two steps toward the phone. She stopped. The thought of the newly-installed tap put her off again. Damn it, she thought. It irks me, just the idea of it. It really does.

She sighed. She stood in the middle of the rug, her left hand resting on the back of the sofa and her right hand fingering her left elbow. She took a breath, held it, let it out. Then she went over to the big front door and nudged it shut. With her back. She didn't particularly want to look outside.

Officer William W. Williams was doing push-ups on the grass.

"How many I got, John?"

"Uh, forty-seven by my count, Bill."

"You lyin'!"

"You're not going to break no record today, Williams," said Officer Hall around a lumpy chili dog from the food service machines.

"You shut up, Hal." Williams spat to one side and pumped three more times. The muscles on his shining arms inflated with each stroke.

"Fifty," said Joe matter-of-factly, "and still counting."

Williams quivered high on his corded arms for a beat, then dipped again.

"Mother," he breathed.

The sun, setting some kind of record for April, beat down in shimmering waves, now mercifully on the tin roof of the pergola so that the officers were able to remove their spongy hats, at least for half an hour. Joe felt not quite a breeze but at least a shift in the hovering air layers here in the shade; the sweat in his short black hair was beginning to evaporate, cooling and contracting his scalp. It was, he thought without knowing why, a day for ice cream. Williams, however, chose to remain under the sun, bridging again and again over the blanched grass.

"What did the Chief have to say this morning?" asked Joe. "Sorry I missed the briefing."

The men did not answer.

As far as Joe could see the campus was deserted, the gray buildings flat and silent, the sparsely-sown trees moving not at all in the noonday heat. Though he knew better, Joe wondered idly if anyone other than Security was on the grounds today.

Old John, white-haired and better suited to a Santa Claus costume than a black uniform, folded his hands unsteadily.

"It was another one of his pep talks, Joe. You know Withers." Joe didn't very well, but it didn't matter. "I guess you didn't miss anything."

Hall resumed chewing.

Joe realized that Williams had suspended over the lawn. Finally he moved. *Down.*

"Well, I hope we get him," offered Joe, "and soon. A guy like that has got to be sick, and needs help."

Up. Williams stopped.

Hall stopped eating.

Joe felt odd. He repeated to himself what he had said, trying to figure why they were uptight. Something about Withers, maybe. Except for Old John, they didn't seem to like the Chief. That must be it.

"Hell," said Hall, "this is the easiest job in the world. We don't have to do anything. A person commits a violation, he does himself in." He spoke carefully, as if laying out a scientific fact. "Because if he's human, he's ashamed of the act. That's all the lever we need." Barely changing his tone he said, "Look at that one, will you?"

They looked. A young girl, slender and poised, was crossing the parking lot in old Levi's, very tight, and a form-fitting top.

Down. "Hoo. That one is sweet and tough," said Williams. *Up.*

"You take girls like that," Hall went on. "They don't *have* any sense of shame. Man, somebody's got to teach her a lesson."

"I'm not sure I follow you," said Joe.

Down. Williams rolled over onto his back. "Gimme some of that Dr. Pepper."

Hall cackled and took the bottle over to Williams. He knelt and whispered something. Williams nodded, then drained the bottle and lay back, gazing dreamily through the low trees by the pergola. "Somebody gimme my shirt an' gun." He sang a few notes to himself. "You know what we need around here?" he asked. "Bows an' arrows. That's what we had in 'Nam. Pick a sentry out of a tree at a hundred yards. *Whoosh.* Simple as that. Don't make no noise."

The girl was disappearing from sight.

"What time's it getting to be?" asked Joe. He reached for his walkie-talkie. "We'd better check in with the command post."

"No reason to hurry," said Hall.

Williams rolled over onto his belly. *Up.* He started counting again. *Down.*

Up.

Down.

"Hey, you can knock it off," Hall said to him. "She's gone."

They all had a good laugh over that.

Lissa walking across the grass: What were they laughing about?

Beyond the glimmering parking lot she glanced over her shoulder at the pergola, blurry without her glasses, bouncing behind her with each step. She shrugged and went on.

She looked down. She slipped her shoes off and felt the warm grass, following her feet past the Library and the new Student Union, staying on the shade. At the far side of the campus she climbed the cool steps to the lab.

"Knock-knock?"

She slid around the open door.

The stink from the tiered cages was overpowering; she knew at once that it would be too much for her.

She heard someone clear his throat. She held her breath, tucked in her top, and walked forward between the skittering enclosures.

"Oh!"

An elecric buzz rattled the cages.

The rats scrambled over one another, hundreds and hundreds of rats. She almost screamed. The buzzing stopped. The rats subsided.

A hand, cold and clammy as sweating brass, touched her neck. She stiffened. It seemed to be trying to press her straight down into the floor.

"Ah, but you're not Sherrie, are you." It was a statement. "Apologies."

She was released. She turned. She saw a moist left hand recently relieved of its rubber glove; as she faced it, an acrid fume sliced up her nostrils. Formaldehyde.

She stumbled back. "W'll, hi, Eliot. I was looking for Sharon." She rubbed at her watering eyes. "I was on my way to your apartment, but I thought I'd stop by here first." She looked up into his pallid, implacable face. And shuddered. "You haven't seen her?"

"Afraid not, Lissa."

He simply observed her, waiting.

She wanted out, but she said, "Well, what are you up to in here, anyway? I never saw all these—these *mice* the last time I was here."

He snapped off his right glove and moved to the sink, applied talc. He pocketed his pale hands in his white coat and leaned against a supply cabinet.

"A low voltage is discharged through the bottom of each cage," said Eliot, "every two minutes, twenty-four hours a day. At various stages I remove typical specimens and dissect the adrenal cortex, the thymus, the spleen, the lymph nodes and so forth, and of course the stomach. There is a definite syndrome, you know."

Are you for real? she wondered, drifting to the window. Below, a fat, greasy-looking mama's boy with horn-rimmed glasses gazed up at the window. She had seen him hanging around a number of times lately. Too many times. She stepped away from the window.

"The adrenal cortex," continued Eliot conversationally, "is always enlarged. All the lymphatic structures are shrunken. And there are deep ulcers, usually in the stomach and upper gut."

He's not kidding, she thought. She looked outside again. The young man was gone. She felt relieved. "What do you call it?" she said, almost reflexly.

"A stress rig," said Eliot. Cheerfully, she thought. Then, "Sherrie's probably back at the House by now. Be careful going home, will you? I know I don't need to remind you." When she did not say anything, "About what happened to the others. It was a combination, a choke hold from behind, forearm across the throat, under the chin, one arm in a hammerlock. Fractures of the larynx, internal hemorrhaging. And this vertebra, this one right here, at the base of the neck. That's what finished them. He had to lift them off their feet. Here." He reached out to show her.

Suddenly, jarringly, the cages buzzed.

Let me out of here! She felt sick.

"Well, I'll see you later, Eliot." She did not wait for an answer.

Outside and down the stairs, a breeze was coming in with the dusk. It's really summer, she thought. She wanted desperately to be at the beach. She could almost smell the Sea & Ski basting her skin. A bird sang high on a telephone wire. O let there always be summers, she thought. A hundred, a thousand of them. That was what she wanted. She wanted there to be a thousand summers.

Joe trod blankly along University Drive. Off duty at last, he was on his way back to the campus, where his wife would be waiting.

"How long has this been happening?" he asked, a little dazed.

"Ed Withers's been paying off Hall to keep him quiet

ever since, Lord, seven-eight months,'' said Old John, strolling with his hands behind his back, his voice low as a moribund bulldog's. ''Anyway, Joey''—he had never called him that before—''I figured you ought to know. What I mean to get across is, try to keep to yourself as much as you can while you're here. They're a kind of—oh, they're a bunch of what you would call motivated young officers. Highly motivated.''

''What I can't understand,'' Joe persisted, ''is why everyone is keeping his mouth shut.''

Old John averted his eyes and took an unexpected number of steps to answer. He fingered his handcuffs nervously; they glinted in the day's dying rays of sunlight. ''Job's a job, you know what I mean,'' muttered Old John.

Joe turned those words over and over as they came to Portola Place.

What in the world did that have to do with it? He stopped at the curb. ''What does that have to do with it?'' he asked.

But Old John was trekking on down Portola Place. He continued to keep an eye on Joe, however. Joe saw him put a hand behind his ear.

''Nothing,'' Joe shouted. Nothing at all. ''See you Friday.''

He shook his head. Even here, he thought. He took a too-deep breath of the lukewarm air, squinting as the setting sun peeped its staring red eye from between the buildings. He started walking again. He lowered his head and watched his feet move, crossing the street at a fast clip.

So Hall's wife was getting pumped by the Chief of Security. And Chief Withers was being—was there a less melodramatic word for it?—blackmailed by Hall. With a promotion thrown in. Joe throttled a bitter laugh. He wondered whether Hall's wife knew that end of it. And whether she was smugly enjoying the benefits with her husband. What the hell, what the hell, what the hell, Joe thought aimlessly. And heard a rustling in the bushes.

* * *

"Where's the cook?"

"She's not coming in again till after vacation."

"Well, where's the House Mother?" said Kathy. "I know, I know, there's no House Mother here. Ooh, I wish I was still at PT!"

"Better not let Madam President hear you bitching," said Sharon. "She'll kick you out on your lily-white ass."

Kathy groaned and went upstairs.

Lissa laughed. She had seen the House Mother for the Pi Taus; her face had more lines in it than *War and Peace,* which she had been reading for English 260. Trying to read. Part I had been on the *Six O'Clock Movie* Monday. Dutifully she had watched it, but for some reason she had had to miss Part II. Part III had been on for a few minutes now.

"Henry Fonda's the only one who acts like he read the book," said Sharon, giving up on the color controls and laying her legs over the arms of the couch again. The set, which rendered everything the color of bile, did look, as Sharon had once remarked, "like somebody took a whiz on it." Lissa tried to follow the plot, but by now it made no sense at all to her.

"Who's been leeching my Marlboros, anyway?" said Sharon, digging under the cushions.

Lissa flipped over to Channel 11. "Hey, *Chiller's* on."

"Right arm," said Sharon.

"Is that *Frankenstein*?"

"Fuck yes," said Sharon. "I've seen this flick so many—"

"You know, I've never seen it all the way through," said Lissa. "My folks would never let me."

"Ha!"

"No, really."

"Well, go ahead, knock yourself out."

Fascinated, Lissa watched the scene in which little Maria so innocently shared her flowers with the Monster on the riverbank. One by delicate one they cast daisies on the water. Then, very slowly, the Monster's expression began to change, as the child ran out of flowers, as the scene began to fade out.

"That's the part they always cut," said Sharon. "You should see his face right after this, before they find her with her neck broken. You know what I think? I don't believe he ever meant to kill her at all. I think he just sort of, you know, crushed her to him. You know what I mean? I don't think there was anything evil about it. They were both innocents. Neither one of them knew anything about it."

A bald-headed used-car salesman appeared on the screen, his face a sneer of chartreuse.

Joe stood stock-still and waited for the next sound.

It did not come.

He stepped onto the blue-shadowed lawn. His hand steadied on his flashlight.

He heard footfalls on the other side of the hedge, close to a house.

He let himself into the foliage, deciding to follow it up. Leaves, small and shiny, tracked past him on either side, hard branches skidding off his head, almost knocking his hat to the ground.

Close to the other side, he saw a man's back moving quickly away from him along the side of the house, toward the front sidewalk. The house was dark, probably empty; he hoped so. He felt disoriented for a fraction of a second, almost as if he were not really here but somewhere else entirely. Then he saw the figure stand straight and slow to a normal gait, crossing under the street lamp. Then the figure returned to a crouch and headed into the trees on the other side. Peeping Tom? Or the one he had been hired to catch? Well, if this is the one, he must be one poor scared son of a bitch right now, even if he doesn't know he's being watched. In fact, Joe realized, his own heart hammering at the back of his badge, that part wouldn't really have anything to do with the feeling, not anything at all.

Joe pulled free of the hedge and backed up. He moved down behind the next four houses in line and then continued forward to the street and crossed at the end of the block. He cut into the alley just past the houses.

He stayed close to the wooden fence, navigating around trash barrels—empty, they would drum an alarm down the whole of Sorority Row.

He heard tennis shoes grinding into the gravel.

A young man crossed the alley not fifty feet in front of him.

They heard Kathy put a record on the turntable upstairs.

The TV screen receded into the deepening shadows of the living room. A cricket started up, sounding so close that Lissa glanced nervously about to see if it was in the house with them. Outside, an elderly officer paced past the hedge, hands behind his back.

"Look at that old codger." Sharon's ash flared and hissed before her face, then arced down. "I'll bet they still don't give them real bullets to use. Yeah, I saw his gun one time. The barrel was plugged up with wood or bubble gum or something. I wonder if they're going to do any good now that we need them? Somebody needs them. The only thing they've been good for so far is to *remind* us all. D'you see what I mean?" She sat forward. "God, I've got to get away from here for a while. I'm starting to vegetate. When's Eliot coming over?"

"He didn't say."

"He always takes his time. I don't know what he does on his way over here, wandering around jacking his brain off with some new pet theory."

"Sharon!"

"Well, it's the truth."

They sat with the sound turned down. The cricket synched with the record for a few bars, then continued on its own again.

"Can I have one of those, please?"

"I didn't know you were smoking now, Lees."

"I'm not. Not really."

The young man crossed the alley.

Joe froze.

Then he followed.

Passing between two houses, he stopped again and dropped to one knee.

He saw ahead to the next street. The young man had already crossed over and was now hesitating by one of the huts on the other side. Houses, he told himself. Now Joe looked between the trees and houses as down a tunnel: as the street lamp flicked on, the pavement mottled under the new light, his eyes focused through to a square of still-bright sky visible now above the long campus parking lot.

He waited.

Another figure, nearly a silhouette, appeared against the sky.

It was a woman.

He snapped to, aware that he had lost track of his prey. The young man was gone. He had slipped through, probably to the lot. But—*had* he gone through, or was he still somewhere on the block between, sidestepping from house to house?

He had blown it.

He started to move anyway.

Then it hit him. The woman. The woman waiting in the lot.

It had to be his wife.

"Eliot," said Sharon, "is very into it. And therefore out of it. If you know what I mean. There are moments with us. Not many, but there are. You were right, though. Sometimes I do wonder if it's worth it. God, I've been staring into this box too long. Now it's beginning to stare back." She clicked off the TV with her toes. "I don't need to turn on the tube to see rape, murder, and perversion. I can get all that right here at school."

Lissa heard a record droning upstairs. It sounded like Dylan.

turn, turn, turn again

"Tell her to turn it over, will you?" said Sharon. "That song's bumming me out."

Lissa felt her way to the top of the first landing.

"Lis-sa? Bring down something to scarf, will you? Um, Screaming Yellow Zonkers. Whatever she's got hidden up there. An-y-thing!"

Lissa smiled.

turn, turn to the rain and the wind

She walked on down the hall.

Joe had squatted so long that his gaze was fixed, almost as if the rectangle of light sky had somehow been looking back down into him instead. His eyes stung.

Fatigue. He hoped. Four days a week had seemed fine at first. Enough time to do some good, maybe, but not enough to—but it was late now, much later than he had thought, judging from the color of the sky. Marlene, he realized, blinking alert, had been waiting—how long? How long had he crouched here? And how long before, at the other village? Block, he reminded himself, block.

He crossed the street, his breath jangling in his ears like dog tags.

He shot a glance at the patch of sky and the dark figure of his wife.

His pace quickened.

As he headed over a lawn, a young man bolted out of the shrubs, a pair of horn-rimmed glasses clattering from his face.

With Ritz crackers and a five-pack of Hydrox cookies in one hand, she drew the knob toward her, cutting the sliver of light from Kathy's room, and made for the stairs.

There was a knock on the front door.

The stairway was an unknown in the dark. She waited.

Finally, "Sharon? Can you get that?"

The knock again.

She descended, pressing against the wall.

"Just a—" She felt a catch in her throat. Why?

The door swung open.

The kid was squirming on the lawn, his face jumping.

"Whatsa matter? I'm on my way home from a study date! Whatsa *matter?*"

Joe closed the cuffs, pressed the key into the notch and set the lock.

Something in the young man's face, swarming in a film of sweat, refused to let Joe relax. He shoved the glasses at him and pulled him to his feet. He glanced ahead. The sky was dark, too dark to see her.

He whipped up the antenna on his walkie-talkie. It shook in his hands, waving back and forth in the night air.

She saw a woman, backlighted in the open doorway.

"I'm sorry," said the woman. "But I wonder if you've seen my husband. He was supposed to meet—"

"No, I—" stammered Lissa. "Do you mean he was outside?" Where was Sharon? *Where?* She left the doorway. "Just a minute, okay?"

She felt around the room. "Share?" she called. I know, she thought. She said she was hungry. I'll check the kitchen. If I can only find the light!

"Sha-ron!" she called, and wondered why her voice was breaking.

"We don't want to hurt you," Joe said. "Believe that."

He drew his prisoner through the shrubs, crushing twigs and unseen garden creatures in his path.

He turned up the gain and depressed the call button. He needed back-up. His throat was dry and the back of his tongue hurt.

A shrill electronic sound whined close by. Instantly he recognized it. It was feedback—his own signal being picked up on another receiver.

"I guess you wouldn't know who I mean," the woman said from the doorway. "But he's one of the Security . . ."

It's so dark, thought Lissa at the door to the kitchen. She forced herself across the chill linoleum, her arms outstretched like antennae.

She heard a sound—a low voice. It was singing:

some folks like t' talk about it

some don't

A wind from nowhere blew through her chest.

He pushed the kid ahead of him, following the sound. Louder. Joe was relieved. Reinforcements were near. Then he noticed his prisoner's stare.

At the rear of the last house by the parking lot, dark shapes were moving.

She seemed to swim through darkness past the smooth pulsating refrigerator where there were always tooth marks in the cheese, to the drawer from which the tools had been quietly disappearing for weeks, clamoring for something, anything with which to protect herself. It was silly, she knew, but—there. A butcher knife.

Joe released his own wrist and locked the kid to the branch of what might have been a rubber tree.

"We'll be back for you, Charlie," he said.

She felt herself drawn down the short stone steps from the kitchen to the storage porch, to the low singing and other voices and what sounded like a scratching close to the screen door that opened into the back yard.

The officer plunges through the shrubbery. At that someone slams out the back door, sees dark forms and the girl held to the dirt and reflexly cocks back an arm, white moons rising on the nails that clench the knife. The officer sees the downed girl, uniforms, another figure lunging into it. There is no time to question, not now while there is still time to stop it before it happens again. He remembers them sitting there dumbly in their baggy pajamas, their wooden bowls empty of the ice cream a few minutes before it happened, and how he had gone away and done nothing, not even when he heard the laughter and the grunting and the automatic fire. And the screams. But not this time. He dodges and grabs the empty hand, wrenching it into a hammerlock as he encircles the waist with his left arm, releasing the wrist with his right and setting his forearm under the chin. The back arches and the legs kick madly, but the hand refuses to let go the knife. Faces turn up. One of the officers stays atop their victim. It is Williams who closes in from the front, spreading his milky palm across the distorted mouth, covering it. "Nice going Joe." He grins. "Now you one of us, too." Joe does not yet understand. Now he feels a slip in the neck and the body swings like the clapper of a bell in his arms. Now he hears new footsteps behind him and a sudden skull-splitting screech. It is the scream of a woman. He thinks he recognizes it but it is too late, now it really is too late as the girl in his arms swings one last anguished time, as her knife slices at the dark with a flash and he sees a face reflected in the blade for an instant before it drops into the leaves. But he must know what he has seen. He has seen the face of a killer. It is the same face he has always seen.

The moonlight washes down on them all.

THE CHILL

The thing that shocked him was that he wasn't shocked.

Morgan came out of the health food store, cut over the grass at the corner and was about to dig into his jeans for the keys when he clipped it with his foot. It was soft and rubbery.

Then he was stumbling into some kind of pothole, flailing one arm for balance—only there was no hole. At least there was not supposed to be.

It was then that he saw the people gathered around.

He laughed at himself and shook his head. But he wondered why they, all fifteen or twenty of them, continued to watch. He touched his fly, glanced down.

And saw that he was standing in a small hole in the sidewalk. The cement was cracked down in a concave circle, like a shallow crater.

"Now wait a minute," he muttered. He shifted his armload of groceries uneasily.

It was screwy. *I walked this way twenty minutes ago,* he thought. *Same side of the street, too. And there was no hole—there wasn't.*

"Move along, son."

"What?"

A cop supported Morgan's elbow, helping him out of the chuckhole.

"Keep the area clear," said the cop, to the others as well. He was big and flat-chested; Morgan got a close-up glimpse of his gun, the polished rosewood grip. As he led Morgan he kept his head down, as if afraid he might step on something.

Morgan looked down with him. And did a double-take.

The cop was high-stepping over a pair of white tennis shoes, set out on the pavement at a nice, neat angle. The laces were still tied.

"Wait a minute," he said again.

He stopped. The cop kept walking. His fingers left Morgan's elbow.

"What's going on?"

Some of the people turned away. A man in a shiny suit escorted a woman through the glass doors of a building. She glanced nervously back at Morgan. At Morgan's *feet*.

Morgan looked down again, and to the side and behind him, and saw finally what he had nearly stepped on the first time.

A hand. A man's hand, gray like the cement. The hand was attached to an arm that led under a mound of dull army-green canvas. The bulk of the tarpaulin lay in the street, between the wheels of a parked car.

Morgan stumbled backwards, staring at the formless shape. He stumbled again at the curb, regained his balance and crossed the street quickly to the parking lot.

He sloughed the groceries into the car and stood there by the open door. He started to step in onto the floorboard, then paused, balancing from foot to foot on the blacktop, watching over the roof of the car.

He thought about the body under the tarp. It must have hit at terrific speed—and, unbelievably, bounced, judging by the dented sedan at the curb.

Well, the building was tall enough, he guessed. He craned his neck. Ten, twelve . . . twenty-six stories. Offices or apartments, he couldn't tell which. Gray and black and hazy silver, layered between floors with a thin, dirty metallic icing: mid-twentieth century Crackerbox Imposing. It reminded Morgan of a stack of folded aluminum deck chairs. The filtered glare of the sun, down now behind the crow's feet TV antennae atop the laundromat, glazed the rows of smokey windows, the reflected light wavy on the glass panes that were lidded by unmoving metal awnings. At the very top, on the roof between a pair of blocklike structures, stood two figures, their trouser legs blowing like flags.

Morgan considered. The vitamins would keep, certainly, but the half-gallon of raw milk, the natural cheddar, the pound of frozen DES-free ground beef . . .

He couldn't take long.

He locked the car and, dragging his feet, went back to the street.

He stood at a decent distance, his hands in his back pockets.

"That was the car, was it?" A man in walking shorts and black socks sidled up to him. The man inclined his head conspiratorially. "You saw him get hit, did you?"

Morgan made a noncommittal gesture. He needed answers himself. But he knew the police would not bother with his questions now; they were preoccupied with notebooks, with squad car radios, with each other, talking their own kind of reassuring shop in low voices that seemed not to move their lips. An ununiformed man with crewcut handled a walkie-talkie officiously, aiming it like a pointer at the figures on the roof.

A woman in a sleeveless blouse came up and took possession of the man in walking shorts. Morgan heard a clucking begin in her throat.

"Excuse me," he said, and crossed the street.

At the curb one of his feet caught, nearly causing him to fall.

He felt a chill coming on as he hurried to the building. At the doors a security guard waved him back.

"I live here," he tried. The guard hesitated. Morgan ducked inside, not looking back, and slipped through the milling crowd in the lobby.

The desk phones were all in use, hunched over by nervous, quick-eyed men who cupped their hands around the mouthpieces as they spoke. At the elevator he finally looked back at the glass doors. He saw a station wagon stenciled with the call letters of a local TV channel parking across the street. He punched the button and waited.

He waited while the other elevator opened and closed once, twice, three times; each time a full load of passengers squeezed out, followed by two officers who blocked the door with their shoulders as a third man checked names off a list; then the officers reboarded and took the elevator up again. He watched the light on the wall move up and down and up without a stop.

The light over his elevator never wavered from the top floor. After a few minutes it went off, and the words NOT IN SERVICE blinked on.

He pivoted slowly, casually—only to find himself reaching out for balance again. He groped, found an ashtray, steadied himself, hoping no one would notice.

He scanned the busy faces. No one had.

What happened?

His foot, no, his whole lower leg was asleep.

From standing, waiting so long? That was it.

He pretended to adjust the ashtray, a sand-filled canister into which countless cigarettes had plunged and extinguished. *Shake a leg,* he thought, *shake a leg.*

He made his way down the hall.

Morgan found a service elevator at the first turn, at the end of a row of offices, flanked by a maintenance closet and a restroom for EMP. ONLY.

He thumbed the button and tried to focus through the safety glass, waiting for the compartment to lower into view.

The double doors parted; it was already there.

He leaned his head back into the padded interior. He shut his eyes.

He squinted down through slitted lids at his legs. The right leg still felt cold. The foot, through some oddity of perspective, appeared very far away. He tried to thrum his toes but felt nothing, though the round, scuffed rubber end of the sneaker flexed like a mound of earth beneath which some unseen creature moved.

In fact the sensation, or lack of it, had now crept up to his knee; he rocked forward, took a step, but felt nothing. No blood coursing, no pins-and-needles. Only a coldness.

The floor locked into place, and the doors slid back.

Well, he could still walk.

He hobbled into the hall.

2642 . . . 2644 . . . twenty-sixth floor.

The elevator thumped closed behind him.

He had come up here for something. *What? So I'm just as morbid as the rest of them,* he thought. *Maybe worse.* No, he decided, not worse; they'd all be up here now, too, if they could, just to see where it happened, to savor the thought of it, turning it over and over before their minds' eyes like the secret behind the door at the end of the hall in the middle of the night in a house they thought they'd forgotten.

But he was already as high as the machinery would take him. He'd have to take the stairs the rest of the way, to the roof.

All but dragging one leg, Morgan tried to make it to the end of the long hall.

He passed door after door, yet he had the impression that they were moving past him while he remained in place, as if struggling on a treadmill. Each door was closed tight, sealed. Only if the doors were suddenly to swing wide could the lives they hid impinge upon him, or he upon them. And what then? Would their eyes recoil at the unexpected contact, would they slam soundproofed doors at his passing? Or would they stand frozen, fascinated?

Probably neither, he decided. They would most likely pretend that he was not there, that he did not exist.

He wondered in passing how many of the guests, insulated within these structures in which their lives played out—how many of them knew what was down there in the street right now? Would they *want* to know? What *about* the one who had chosen to leave his hermetic safety, to climb out under an alien sky, to scream down, straining to burn like a shooting star in the steely dusk?

He stopped, breathing heavily.

He leaned against a wall, and felt something cold touch his skin.

He turned: a fire extinguisher.

In the glass, behind the words BREAK IN CASE OF EMERGENCY, the reflection of his face.

The dim image reminded him: twenty-five, thirty extra pounds, so that the lines of his features were now soft, the face puffed, the skull beneath almost hidden by granola, wheat germ, yogurt, honey, unpasteurized milk, acidophilus culture, dessicated liver, torula yeast, turbinado sugar, dried fruits and cashew butter and whole wheat spaghetti and Brockmeyer's ice cream and date nut bread and carrot cake, and brown rice . . . it was *good* food. But now he looked at himself, unable for the moment to walk, and the fear returned, the fear that sapped and took the place of his will, and he forced himself to see and be reassured. But he could not look back, not for long. *That's right,* nodding sadly, turning away, *you can serve it up, can't you? But when it's on the plate, you can't see it.* Can *you?*

"Shit," he said aloud. The first thing he had thought when he saw him in the street was, *I'm glad it wasn't me!*

The left side of his body was cold, and growing colder.

But still he wanted to be there, to be up there, to be where *he* had been, to know what it was like.

He had to swing one leg around, using the other as the axis, and reach down with his good right hand and hold the knee from folding. In that way he managed to go on. To the fire door.

The stairs were a problem.

* * *

From here Morgan could see the Pacific Ocean beyond the shadow palm trees at the end of Wilshire Boulevard. The shoreline was broken by the ragged teeth of silhouetted buildings and, above it all, the clouds seemed to be bleeding dull colors that were illuminated from behind, masked by drifts of suspended particles.

He approached the edge of the roof.

He felt currents of air rising to meet him. He stopped between the two blocklike structures, which he now recognized as ventilation outlets. Droplets of moisture fell on his face and neck. They were like warm pinpricks.

The left side of his body, from toes to fingertips, was icy cold, numb.

He moved closer to the edge.

When he looked down, there was no sense of dizziness. At this distance the body on the street would be just another dark spot on the sidewalk.

He could not see it.

There were only a few raptorial stragglers left around the entrance, a single police car, the sedan with the dent and the TV station wagon. The man under the tarp had been cleared away. It had all started when he touched the hand, the empty hand curled heavenward; the cold hand. He wondered about the body. He pictured a collapsed sac, crushed bones, the pools of blood inside.

He heard a door slam. The door to the roof. But he had closed it. The wind? He stretched his neck but could not see around the air outlets.

Then he heard voices.

Police, probably. Or in-house security, checking, rehandling the details like beads until they satisfied themselves that it was a simple suicide.

And what would they think, finding him here?

But they could not see him. They would not, as long as they stayed away from the edge.

He turned back, swaying slightly.

Now several new dots angled on the sidewalk, and others moved jerkily across the street to gather at the front of the building. With a peculiar calmness, he realized that they were clustering together to watch him.

How long had he been standing here? Long enough for the police to notice, to send someone up? Did they think—

He waited, taking more and more of his weight onto his right side as the left side of his body grew heavy, a dead weight, unresponsive; and still he waited. He no longer had voluntary control over the stiffening joints, the leaden shoe. He watched with detachment as it began to move in the rising wind. The foot lost contact with the graveled roof, rose an inch, two inches into the air and swung, slowly at first, then in an increasing arc, nearer and nearer the edge. Now in space, now over the roof, now in space, now over the roof.

He waited, watching with growing concentration and concern, and presently he began to wonder which way it would fall.

Heads cocked and eyes fixed, his own and many others.

THE SMELL OF DEATH

The little girl bundled in the back seat of the Falcon wagon was covered with pink blotches, and as the man from the diner leaned over her she released fast, shallow breaths almost directly in his face, breaths that smelled of bread hot from the oven. He drew back and stood shakily, a shudder passing down between his shoulder blades.

"I can't say what we'll do," whined the woman, "if we can't find that doctor. He's the only one for miles and miles. He's supposed to be fishin' all weekend, that's what that lazy nurse of his told us, but . . ." Her voice ebbed and she sank again into the shadow of the headrest.

"I *tol'* you," whispered her husband hoarsely, a big, uneducated man with cracked hands, "t' stop it. Now we just got t' bear it. It's no one's trouble but our own."

The man from the diner turned away, dredging up a sigh from so low it shook his dry, thin chest, and kept his face from them. He walked back inside, made three ham sandwiches and two coffees in styrofoam cups and snapped on the lids and brought it all out to them in a tight brown paper bag.

"Scarlet fever, is that so bad?" asked the wife hopefully, peering around her husband's shoulders from inside the car.

"That's not what it is," he told them. He handed the bag in and took the three wrinkled dollar bills, one for the gas, two for the food. He unfolded them, pocketed two, handed one back impulsively. "Two'll do it."

"It ain't the fever, then?" said the husband, still suspicious, grasping for an alternative as he took back the bill unquestioningly. In the light through the windshield his face took on a sallow look.

"Scarlatina," he said shortly. Before they could react to that, he waved a dark hand and directed them. "Go straight down the highway to the first turnoff, veer right, and in about 30 miles you'll hit Alamagosa. There's a kind of clinic there. It's run for the Indians, but they'll see you. Ask at the Phillips station."

"Well, come on, then," said the husband, slamming the worn transmission into reverse and hunching his head around over his big shoulder.

"No need to hurry," the man from the diner said. The car hesitated, the back end dipping on worn-out shocks as the transmission strained mightily to hold to the underside of the car.

He decided not to say anything more.

He walked around to the back and looked inside as the woman said, "I just can't thank you enough." She seemed ready to release a stream of words that had been locked up tightly for years, like a five-year diary waiting to spill open at the first touch. "You seem to know so much," she added, leaving the sentence up in the air in a kind of polite awe.

He emptied his lungs and bent a last time over the girl child, whose cheeks were the color of the inner surface of shells found on a beach at sunset, and took a heavy, very heavy breath. What he had been hoping not to find was there. It was there and so there was nothing else left for him to do. He stretched inside to his waist and put his sunburned hands on the girl's face as if feeling for a fever.

The child was already delirious. He lowered his ear to her lips. She was muttering like lightning, most of it incoherent, but he caught a few words:

". . . green stars going up to the sky . . . ride my bike. . . ."

He cupped his hands around the sides of her neck, meeting his fingers at the back in the sweat-steamed twists of blanket. He gazed down, hoping to see her eyes, but they were lidded over by almost translucent membranes streaked with veins swollen full of blood. He saw the jerky movements of her eyes fighting from side to side in their sockets. He held his breath, forcing the infection from his nostrils, and made an adjustment in her neck. He felt a nerve slip out of place. The girl's brow knitted quizzically for a passing moment, and then she died.

He stood up.

"You're a kind man," said the woman, extending her hand from the front window. He went around but did not let her touch him. "I want to thank you. When Rose Ann's well," she rushed on, trying to get it all out before the car bounded away, "we're going to stop back by here and—and buy the biggest dinner you ever served up!" She beamed. "That'll be all right, won't it, Mister . . . ?"

"Raven," he said, his mouth dry as dust, and turned on his worn heel and walked quickly back to his diner, head down, eyes hidden, not looking back and trying not to think of them again as the station wagon pummeled the rocky dirt and ground away down the highway, heading east.

He hoped it would be a long time before they checked the back seat.

The screen door slammed like an old overshoe against the door jamb. He shut his eyes as the air inside hit him. Doughnuts. Bologna and sharp brown mustard. Horseradish. Coffee, fresh and old grounds. Open packages of bread. Cheese, American and Swiss. And the acrid bus tray blue with silver cleaner where the dirty forks and spoons were soaking. And apples and oranges and bananas, and the warm stickiness of runny chocolate.

And the sawdust.

Nostrils flaring, he stormed behind the counter and began rewrapping everything, twisting the end of the bread, hurling the cheese into the groaning refrigerator, screwing the cap back on the mustard, burying the can of chocolate syrup deep in the cupboard.

He turned to face the empty diner. The chairs dry sticks of kindling. The flowing window glass frozen in still heat mirages, the sills below burial pyres for the mummified flies.

He swayed over the sawdust.

It was a knife at his nostrils. And even as he shook his head the fume of the oranges crept again from behind the door to the back room, the chocolate beginning to pour down invisibly from the crack in the cupboard, the old smells of slowly decomposing food filling the empty desert air like a crowd closing in on him from all sides.

He cursed, the pungent air barely moving in front of his shiny, creased lips.

He brought his hand down suddenly on the counter top with a force that stung his fingers and rattled the napkin holders. He brought his hand down again and again, slamming wrist and forearm as well, firing needles of pain that blocked out everything else again and again and again.

In his rage he did not see the figure approaching until the screen door screaked, bouncing lightly.

"Hey, you're open, aren't you? You gotta be."

It was a man, late twenties, coat slung over his shoulder, wide tie loosened at the bulging, moist collar.

"Menu's on the table," mumbled Raven. He turned to the water glasses.

"Uh, you run the station, too?" The young man hooked a thumb toward the pump outside and the garage.

Raven glanced back at him. He hadn't heard him drive up. He squinted, trying to see through the gaping rents in the weathered screen door.

The young man dragged his dusty feet to the counter and closed a shaky hand around the plastic tumbler. He drained it noisily in one pull. Raven flinched at the grease and gasoline permeating the man's skin, the almost rancid rilling in the hair curling behind the ears, and something else, an expensively androgynous floral cologne mingling with the perspiration, the mixture of smells strongest in the darkened armpits of the wilted sport coat over his shoulder.

"I said, would you mind?" the young man was saying.

Raven refilled the water glass.

Halfway through it the young man slowed down.

"See, ah, my car quit on me back there" (no direction that Raven could judge, just back, way back) "oh, five miles, maybe." The young man snickered at himself. "I haven't had this much exercise since I quit the rowing team!"

He meant it.

Raven nodded. He reached behind for the strings to his apron. "Get in the pickup," he said. Cost you five dollars, he started to add. But the thought of leaving the diner, all of it for a while, however briefly, seemed to lift something from his shoulders.

The keys almost burned his hand. He led the way outside, and the young man hauled himself up and in as if mounting a horse for the first time. They bounced onto the road and drove west, canvas water bags thumping against the bumper.

Raven breathed deeply, grateful for the clean chickweed and mesquite and the old blacktop baking in the sun. "Where you headed?" he heard himself ask.

The young man seemed relieved to talk. "Driving straight through to L.A.," he said, pulling his hair off the side of his face. "I thought I might find what I'm looking for out here, but there doesn't seem to be much but sand and lizards. Talking to the natives hasn't gotten me much but thirsty."

"You're looking for something?" asked the driver, keeping his eyes on the road, unnecessarily since the first curve was not for two miles.

"Well, I guess I should explain. I'm a reporter, sort of. With *Sandler's Monthly*. Was. Supposed to be on assignment, but I'm afraid my leave is about up. I wasn't able to get the story, so I guess they'll write the whole thing off somehow. They'd better."

The reporter blotted his forehead with his sleeve and put

on his dark glasses, continuing to watch the flatlands for something, anything.

"It's crazy. A guy nobody's seen for fifteen years. Named McCabe, used to work for NASA. No family, his friends swear they haven't seen him since, not even the Internal Revenue's heard a word. And I'm supposed to find him. Ha! 'How I Spent My Summer Vacation.' Don't ask."

"This way's shorter," said the driver, downshifting and spinning out as the truck left the road. A tumbleweed lodged in the passenger's side of the truck, which had no doors; the reporter kicked it away and picked nettles from his dusty cuffless trouser leg.

"Some country," he said. "A guy gets lost out here, he may as well find a rock and start scratching out a headstone."

"Takes some getting used to," admitted the driver.

"Yeah, you could really lose yourself. I guess I'm a born city boy, though. I'm not ready for a place to escape to, at least not yet. Though I may need one, when I get back to New York empty-handed."

"It's not so much an escape," said the driver, his eyes on the distant hills, "as a haven." He added, "The air is relatively clean out here."

They drove on, passing the bleached skull of an animal of some kind half-buried next to a cactus. The sandy ground, nearly white as salt, was fairly firm and smooth-packed, so that the driver had no trouble controlling the truck.

"Tell me about your friend, the one you're looking for."

"Aw, it all happened a long time ago. It's a pretty depressing story, I'm afraid."

"I wouldn't ask if I weren't interested. Besides," the driver added flatly, "a man can get too used to being alone. Builds up a need for talk."

"Well then there now."

Breathing heavily, sweating like a pig, the reporter went ahead.

"See, this McCabe was part of a four-man team they were training in Houston for the first manned satellite program. You remember how long ago *that* was. They put them through this 188-day milk run in a lab mock-up. Self-contained air purification, moisture retrieval, you know, the whole bit.

"Anyway, if you really want to hear it . . ." The driver said nothing so he kept talking. "What happened was this: at one point in the test they were supposed to be cut off completely from 'ground control'; it was planned that way, to simulate a power failure in the model space station's communications systems. For thirty-six hours. During that time audio-visual contact was suspended completely. And that's when it happened.

"In spite of the really unbelievably thorough immunization against any kind of infection or disease—permanent, lifetime inoculations, by the way, some in the experimental stage then and hush-hush now, reserved for Presidents and like that—despite every precaution, *something* went wrong. The X-factor, Jesus factor, whatever you want to call it. Something happened, and the guys at NASA still aren't exactly sure what.

"At first they thought it was murder, but nobody had any idea why. They still haven't come up with a motive, but the label still sticks, I guess. I didn't buy it at the start of the investigation and I don't buy it now, though it looks like I'll have to since I haven't come up with anything better. Needless to say, all four men had been screened by probably the most complete battery of psychological tests and interviews in the history of the planet. But when contact was finally resumed only one man—McCabe—was alive. The other three, McReynolds, Armbruster and . . . I can't remember the other man's name, but—"

"It was Willard, wasn't it?"

"Ye-es, I think so. Yes. They were all dead. Just like that. Some vital nerve." The reporter reached around to touch a spot high between his shoulder blades, and had to squint as the sweat ran into his eyes. "Right here, at the base of the neck. Something to do with the medulla.

Actually that part isn't as weird as it sounds. Nerves, pressure points, all that stuff was part of the hand-to-hand training for the men who served in Special Forces in the war in Asia then, which includes McCabe, of course. He had seen duty in Danang and Phnom Penh."

"Let me ask you one thing," interjected the driver, bearing straight across the sands toward a point he had fixed on. "Why wasn't he charged?"

"Well, there wasn't time. Washington was red-faced, naturally. Kept him under wraps and shipped him off to San Diego, where he apparently put on an orderly's clothes one day and just walked out the front gate. And he hasn't been seen since. Vanished. That," sighed the reporter, "is about as far as I've been able to get with the story. Which is about exactly nowhere."

"They still think he murdered them, then," said the driver, his voice distant.

"What else? The big question still is: why? By the way," said the now curious passenger, "where the hell *are* we? If you don't mind my asking. Seems to me my car's over that way somewhere. Or there. . . ."

The truck crunched on over pale, porous rocks and sand, farther and farther away from anything remotely man-made. Downshifting, the driver took them in a short arc between clumps of white sage and salt brush and pulled up short. He lurched back on the hand brake and closed his tanned fingers over the key ring.

"Wo-ow," puffed the reporter. "Listen to that." He suctioned his hands over his ears, pulled them loose with a pop. Now, the engine stilled, there was only the water in the radiator bubbling and settling. Finally that, too, was stilled.

"What is it?"

"Nothing," said the reporter, surprised. "That's what's so groovy. And the air! Man, it's clean, empty. Except for the dust back there, when we hit the sand, there's *nothing*. My sinus cavities never had it so good."

"Yes, clean, but not really empty." The driver leaned back and flared his nostrils distastefully. "Take a deep breath, if you can stand it. Gypsum. Caliche. Limestone. Even the damned silica."

"You can tell all that?"

He looked at the reporter with one hawk eye, not turning his head. "What I'm really interested in is your friend."

"Yeah. Well, you know, I think I'd better get—"

"Murder is an absolute term. You have to be absolutely sure before you use it."

"Oh, I wasn't accusing—"

"Imagine for a minute," bristled the driver, "that he wasn't responsible for their deaths."

The reporter puzzled.

"Suppose they were gone already."

"What, then? I'm sure the autopsy—"

"They were looking for something to substantiate the obvious, nothing more—and that's giving them the benefit of the doubt; you remember the Kennedys; at least you've read about them."

"Man, you're blowing my head! You know that?"

The driver darkened. He hoisted his pack from the boot and riffled carefully through the contents: a Kelty backpack, a sleeping bag, a smaller, open pack with emergency supplies like nylon rope, canned water, halazone, vitamins, biscuits, pep pills, pemmican and salt, an eight-blade Army knife, a Mallory pocket flashlight, a light nylon-over-steel shovel. A compass. And a long Bowie knife. This he unsheathed, examined the fine burnished blade of Swedish steel, resheathed and snapped to his belt.

There was a tense pause as the reporter lay his head back and squeezed his eyes shut. "Let me have a little of that water, would you?"

The driver complied.

There was another silence, all but unbearable this time. There was no breeze in the air, seemed as if there never had been.

"Man," the reporter broke, "this is really too far out. In more ways than one." He got out and stood looking around with his soft white hands half-hidden in his back pockets. "Anyway." He squinted and adjusted his dark glasses, as though they magnified the sun beyond endurance. "What'd you expect me to find out here?"

The driver swung down and led him a few yards past a sagging, stickled juniper palm.

There, just beyond, sat a huge rock, six, eight feet across, pitted by a thousand patternless holes, like a mound of termite-ridden wood, or the surface of a burned out tubercular brain mercifully relieved of its skull case.

The reporter shuffled around it, leaving a snake pattern in the sand with his chukka boots.

"Whew. Looks like this baby got caught in a sandstorm for a million years, huh? Hey, dig this." He bent and slipped inside, found room to sit.

After a minute the man from the diner said, "I don't give a damn about the rock, you know."

The reporter said nothing.

"But I know what you came looking for."

The reporter, straining to hear, said, "What?"

The man stepped closer. "You don't fool me."

"Well, thanks," said the reporter, not hearing. "Think I'll drive over here and take some pictures after my car's fixed. How far are we?"

"Don't move."

"You think you can fix it? Just sort of went off the road. Lost control. Not my fault, though. Something—"

"I said don't move!"

"What?"

The man took the knife from his belt slowly. He held it pointing forward, its tip honed as sharp as a broken piece of razor. He stepped closer, moving only his feet.

The reporter tensed, his trousers stretched shiny over his locked knees.

"You don't have to," he said weakly. "I only wanted to talk to you. . . ."

The man laughed. He hit it, a small coral snake, swiftly and silently as it lay coiled in the dark by the reporter's foot. A quick spinning flicker of afterlife sent the young man from the opening in a paroxysm as intense as the dead snake's. He glanced down at his leg, at a flowing run of thick reptile blood, and instantly lost his balance The knife blade had nearly split the slender head from the triangulate, yellow-black-and-red-striped body but the tail continued to writhe, jerking s's through its own blood drying on the heat of the rock.

The man from the diner wiped the blade on the sole of his boot.

"Might have been a ground snake, harmless, but I couldn't be sure. Out here you learn not to take chances."

"Jeezus," whispered the reporter.

"He shouldn't have been out here. Worm around where you don't belong and you're playing loose with your life."

The reporter, grinning in a confused rictus, said simply, "Hey, you don't want to kill me!"

"I'm no murderer," spat the man from the diner. "Get that straight, you nosy son of a bitch."

"It was my job," gestured the reporter helplessly.

"Is it your job, too, to understand?"

"I think I could. You know?"

"Like it was *their* job to understand something they'd never come up against before. Sure. Maybe you would," he snapped suddenly. "But what about the rest? They have names for what I did, their own terms. Because they've never seen real suffering and had to pull together enough guts to help another human being through the misery of dying."

He stood. "I'm sorry, kid. Sorrier than you know. But that's a feeling I've had to live with for years and years."

He started to walk away. He stopped. He poked at the bloody remains of the still-quivering snake on the rock. He stirred it with his knife blade. A strong whiff drifted up to him, and he angled his face away from it.

"Is it dead?" asked the reporter, because he couldn't think of anything else to say but knew he ought to go on talking. Nervously he smoothed his hair back from his face and drew his hand back quickly, his hair so hot and shining it stung his hand.

"It's dead, all right," said Raven, his stomach churning. "I'd know that smell anywhere."

* * *

A half hour later Raven was back on the highway. He found the car on the shoulder of an ill-paved detour that would cut several miles through the roughest terrain before reaching Alamagosa. The reporter must have read the map incorrectly, as a few unlucky tourists did from time to time; the broken line seemed to intersect the highway at a point just before the rest stop but in fact bypassed it by more than a mile.

He pulled over and braked, relieved again by the absolute silence. In a few hours, as night enshrouded the desert, the silence would deepen till it reached all the way from the blaze of the Milky Way down to the lonely sentinel arms of the saguaros scattered on the horizon. Then the cold would cut through the crystal air like a guillotine.

Raven started to work.

He loosened the chain on the winch at the truck's tailgate. Then it occurred to him that the boy might be lying about the car, too. But he dismissed the notion, considering the heat and the location of the car. The young man had been lucky, all right. He must have had to walk the quarter mile back to the highway, another two miles on to the diner.

That was less than a fourth the distance he would try to walk today. Without a compass.

Raven got down on his back and sidled under the car, an old Rambler station wagon. The trouble was in the front end. The right tie-rod end had been snapped loose, probably by the impact of running off the road, or maybe by a bump that had sent the car off the road.

So he would have to tow it in.

He knew what he would say. That he found it abandoned on the roadside, that he went looking for the owner and had finally to give up. By that time—

That was just the part that made him sick. It was the first time that he had had to do this, to leave a man to die to insure his own safety. Not like that time years ago. Something had gone wrong with the air system; some kind of bacterial contamination in the diatom filters, that had been his guess. It got to Jack, to Rob and even to Willard, and for hours he sat next to them as they died by the most painful progressions, until he could bear it no longer. It was unmistakable. He had read an article something like that once, about a nurse in a terminal cancer ward who swore she could predict which ones would die the following day; she said there was an odor given off by the dying, which once smelled was never forgotten. He had shrugged at the article then, of course. Then came the test. *The filters*—why didn't it affect him? For hours he sat strapped in, hearing the agony of the dying around him, filling the capsule until it filled his head, driving him almost mad with waiting. But it never hit him. Antibodies, genetics, some damned advantage or other he happened to possess. Or maybe it was the others, perhaps they had had trouble with the inoculations, like smallpox vaccinations that don't always take the first time, though that seemed almost too ludicrously simple to believe. But the infection got them and when it did he had to give them the only peace it was in his power to give. Once he had known for sure. And he had known. It was unmistakable.

Tell them that part of it when you write your damned— But this was one story that would never get written. It was too late for him to face the accusations, the questions, the disbelief; too late to live steeped in the rankness of city life ever again.

He wrapped the rubber guard over the bumper, wound the chain through the frame and locked it, reached in the cab of the truck and threw the lever that activated the winch.

The car nosed up a foot, two feet. It stopped abruptly as the winch shivered, overloaded, and shut itself off.

He knelt and peered under. He saw nothing. He dropped to his back and hunched underneath again.

Crawling farther back, he twisted sideways on his shoulders. The A-frame was still good, near as he could see.

He crept on. There, the rear axle, straddling the edge of the ditch, the left wheel caught awkwardly on a chunk of granite. So. He'd have to lower the car, push it back with the truck and try again. Back out like a sidewinder, trying not to think of anything but—

Wait. The car creaked over his body. Hold it hold it—He saw the frame tipping. He had forgotten to set the hand brake on the car. But too late *too late*—He jerked his head to the side. The rear wheel broke free of the rock and the car slipped halfway down the ditch.

He screamed as the car crunched to a stop, crushing his left arm deep in the gravel. His cry was muffled and lost. His head lolled from side to side, his face knocking loose bits of dried mud cake and grease into the corners of his eyes.

Seconds passed. He felt his ruptured life seeping into the ground.

Then, very slowly, he turned his head a last time to look at the remains of the arm pinned beneath the chassis.

Slowly, very slowly he reached his right hand to his belt, found the sheath. Grasping the handle decisively he drew up the burnished blade. It trembled briefly, its sharp point scratching the oil pan. More fragments of dry underseal fell onto his body.

He smelled oil and gasoline. He smelled burned axle grease. He smelled the stuffed upholstery up inside the car. He smelled no other person near and knew he would not.

Pinned in shadow, it seemed as if night had already fallen here.

He knew he had nothing else left to do. He had done almost the same thing several times since. They had been passing through. They had been truckers, problem pregnancies, fevered children with the cold sweat already sealing their eyes. He had had no choice.

He left his head turned to the side. There was no mistaking it. The arm, cracked open to infection, its systems destroyed, cells and tissues already mortifying in the dirt, would go first. Then the chill and the ache would spread up, not far, to his heart.

Quivering again, then steadying his hand with a grip of

practiced resolution, he moved the sharp, curved blade toward his blood-soaked shoulder. *If thine eye offend thee,* he thought.

He knew what he had to do. He knew. For he had smelled it, that smell, and he knew what it was. He knew too well.

It was the smell of death.

DROP CITY

Bus let man off.

"Hey, uh, wait, I—" He squeezed frame of dark glasses in circle of midfinger and thumb; then patted down nondescript tie strung loosely around open collar, fastened top two buttons of coat, smoothed flaps of pockets. He cleared his throat. "Right." It *seemed* right. "Thanks."

"Take care, pal," said the bus driver.

The man looked around. Hill, narrow road curling up the side; not many trees, dust motes dappling the air. He was reluctant to leave the bus, and afraid to say so. He left his foot on the step-up.

"Up there, is it?"

"You got it."

"Uh."

"Yeah?" The driver clocked his hands around the big steering wheel.

"Why'd you let me off here?"

"Hey, now. You said the next town, right?"

"Right." He guessed so; he could hardly remember that, even. Something about a highway. Ditch. Crawling up through tumbleweeds. He saw his hands. Cut. Not long ago, either. "Only, it seems like we came close to a couple of other stops before this. Doesn't look like much here."

The driver hit the pneumatic lever. *Hiss.*

"Those weren't the one. I'm not even supposed to stop for them. *At* all." He said it like he would have said "Move 'em out." He fixed straight ahead as the door pumped, trying to close.

"Well, thanks anyway," said the man, retrieving his foot. "Wish me luck."

"You got it," said the driver. The door hissed again and sealed and the long mudspattered steel sides moved out.

The man started up the hill. Well, here goes, he said to himself.

Near the top, he stood and wiped his face with a handkerchief he found in his jacket pocket. He got a look at the fields opposite: rolling acres of an unknown rust-colored crop in endless unkempt rows. Like wheat covered with dried blood, he thought.

He turned. Something had moved nearby in the dry weeds. Then again, again. He raised his face and brimmed his eyes with his hand.

The dim lights of a truck swung around the top of the hill. He realized it was getting dark fast. More gravel careened over the edge and skittered through the grass near him. Listening hard, he heard or thought he heard the motor sputter and die and the ratchety pull of a hand brake. He folded the handkerchief away and started trudging the rest of the way to the top.

When he came up, it was blue twilight. He saw a funny old town on the plateau, lots of trees and tended fields backed up all the way to the shadows under the far hills.

He snorted at the dust in his nose, pulling his hair back behind his ears with his fingers and went to the building with the neon sign. THE MOONMILL, it said. The truck, an old Ford pickup, rested in front. It was the only one of the wooden buildings he could see that had a light on yet.

The door, hewn from heavy planks, thumped behind him. He peered. It was pitch dark. Music played from a scratchy phonograph record.

green, green, promenade in green

"Hi, hon." A woman's voice. He turned, turned again. "You just get in?" Close, by his shoulder. He felt her take his arm. He made an uncertain step with her, only to bump his knee on something. He made a sound. Reaching out, he felt a stool.

"Well, what have we got here?" said the woman. "Is it a man or a mole? Ha ha ha!" She touched his dark glasses and drew them off. "Well, well! Aren't you a sight! Hurt yourself, hon?"

He slid onto the stool. "I'm all right," he said. Reassuring himself, maybe. Reflexly he touched the knee. The fabric was torn, and he noticed other rips and frays on the suit. He left his hand over the knee.

"Harlan," she called. "A glass of dark for my friend here."

He saw her clearly now, twenty-thirty pounds overweight, not too bad though, bleached hair, cheeks that looked like they held an acorn in each for the winter. And the bar: old wood and black leather, a couple of working men covering beers in the corner, a fishtank, one of those long, slim ones with green crystal paint on the back and a purple light that made the fish shine.

"Here you are, sir."

He swiveled on the stool, almost knocking over the beer at his elbow.

"This here is Harlan," said the woman, "the best barkeep we ever had." At that she laughed again.

"Harlan Shiply," said the small, thin man as he dried a glass. His voice was thin, too, and precise, and one would more likely order a pair of eyeglasses from him, say, or a book on theosophy, than a drink. The thin man put down the glass and extended his hand.

It was the kind of handshake he expected. At the same time the woman placed one of her dimpled hands on his knee.

"My name's Eleanor. This here's my place, you could say. For the time being, anyway."

"Uh," he said, "my name's . . ." He couldn't think

what to say. Frantically he scanned the walls, trying to spot a word, a name. All he could see were beer advertisements. ''Miller,'' he said finally, without much conviction.

''Oh?'' inquired the bartender politely. ''What line of business are you in, Mr. Miller?''

The woman frowned at him. ''Harlan,'' she said sharply.

''S-sorry,'' said Shiply, ''I forgot.'' He returned sheepishly to his sparkling glasses.

''To tell you the truth,'' he blurted, ''I'm not in anything at the moment. I'm looking around for a new line, actually. I was in, uh, the retail market before.'' He caught a glimpse of a sign for Danish beer. ''Imported. Importing, I mean.''

''No, you weren't, hon,'' said Eleanor, moving her hand around in a circle on his knee, ''but that's all right. It'll worry you at first, but before long—Look at that.'' She looked at his knee.

''I don't know how it got torn,'' he said. He put his hand over hers, stopping it. ''Well, actually, I was trying to fix my car. Broke down back there on the highway, and—''

''See? It moves around like that, just like it wasn't even attached. That's why they call it a floating kneecap. Ha ha!''

''I guess I should clean up.'' He lifted his hand from hers but she drew it back, pressing it warmly. ''It's been quite a day. Matter of fact, I'm feeling a little disoriented.''

''Mm-hm.''

''Is there someplace, a motel? It's too late to do anything now. About my car.''

''Mm-hm. Boland's is right down a block. Don't you worry about a thing.''

''Thanks.'' He stood. He glanced between the two of them, smiled tautly, tipped his head. ''I appreciate—''

''Don't you go off just yet, hon.''

One of the men in khakis started the juke box again. The same record boomed out.

green, green, promenade in green

She pushed the wet glass against his knuckles. "Here, now, you need it."

Oh no, he thought. He reached for his back pocket, hoping. It was empty.

"You're not going to believe this," he began.

They were both looking at him.

"Cheers," said the woman.

He smiled and shrugged. He drank the glass halfway down. It was cold and thick and it tasted like gold.

They were both looking at him.

He reached inside his coat.

She held his hand against his chest. "Don't worry," she said.

"My pleasure, sir," said the man behind the bar.

He felt something firm, drew it out. It was a shiny black breast-pocket wallet. He turned it over. No initials. Inside were several crisp, unfolded bills, fives, tens and twenties. He drew out a five absently, searching for a driver's license, a credit card, anything. But there was nothing else. Just two words printed in gold in the leather. He looked closer. "Pinseal Goathide."

"You just put that away," she insisted. "You have that money for a purpose, now."

"Thanks," he said. "Thank you very much." He smiled at the bartender. "Mr.—what was it?"

"Shiply. You're quite welcome, Mr., I beg your pardon?"

He put the wallet away. "Forget it," he said. "I'm having a hell of a time remembering my own name right now. Tired, I guess. But what is it they say? 'Sufficient to the day is the, something, thereof?' "

"That's all right," said Eleanor. "You're just like everybody else."

He thought it was a joke, and forced a laugh, and finshed his beer.

He walked over to the hotel as the crickets came out. He reversed the ledger and signed "Mr. Jack Miller," though the desk man—the owner, judging by the size of the place—did not bother to ask. He made up an excuse about luggage, but that didn't seem to make any difference to Boland, if that was his name, one way or another.

"Is there a" (hospital, he started to say) "doctor in town?"

"Thought you'd be asking," said the hotel man.

He got directions, found the office in an unmarked storefront. Doctor Leveland put down the phone and leaned against the doorjamb, drawing on a cigar. He seemed to be expecting someone.

Inside, the office was surprisingly well-equipped with what appeared to be very new, miniaturized instruments, most of them so new, in fact, that Miller had never seen their like.

At least he thought he hadn't.

"Cigar, Jack?"

He accepted it and a wooden match and stood in the office, shifting his weight and hearing the sounds of what he took to be a television program on the other side of the wall. After a while he had to say something.

"This is a Marsh Wheeling, isn' it? Uh, Dr. Leveland?"

"Make it Roland. Indeed it is. Bite a wee bit more off the tip, why don't you. A real Pittsburgh Stogy is what that is, all right. They'll stop making them pretty soon, I hear. But I've got—" He puffed forward proudly and conspiratorially. "—Quite A Few Cases put away, in there with the refrigerated supplies."

He rocked on his heels.

Just then a series of gunshots cracked loudly. Miller jumped. It was no television set. A backfire? He gazed out the open door but there were no cars in sight. "Alcazar Theater," said the doctor. "The ass-end of it's flush with my wall, there. Showing another one this week about all those poor cops dying for our sins."

"Look," said Miller irritably. "Aren't you supposed to ask what's wrong with me?"

"What's wrong with you?" asked Dr. Leveland.

That stopped him. He held out his hands, feeling like a damn fool. "I was jacking up my car," he tried. "Do you have anything for a cut?"

The doctor threw back his head and roared. He slapped a hand around the back of Miller's head and led him into the other room. Miller realized that he hadn't been touched like that by a man since he had been a small boy. Wait a minute, he thought, that's something. He tried, but it was no use. He couldn't remember. He howled loudly with the doctor. By the time they got to the examination room his face had twisted up and he was no longer laughing.

The doctor sat him down.

"Listen, now. I know why you came to see me." He was aware of his coat coming off, his sleeves rolling up. "You think you're the only one, don't you." The doctor, if that was what he was, spoke in statements, authoritatively, not patronizingly, and the effect was oddly reassuring. He felt a coolness on his arm, then a needle slipping in. "You think, 'Why did this have to happen to me?' You think, 'What did happen to me?' You don't know yet, do you? Of course not. You feel like you want to cry, but you're man enough not to. It'll come to you, though, what to do, how to live, in time. It always does. You understand me? Always."

"Look. Doctor." He opened his eyes. "I'm tired, beat, and—"

"I know."

"And I'm a mess."

"That's right."

"And, God help me, I don't know what the hell's going on!"

"Of course not."

He felt his head tipping back. His eyes closing.

"And you don't remember how you got here, what your name is. They did a real job on you. That's right. They always do. Take it easy for a minute, now. It'll pass. It's just working its way through your bloodstream." He chuckled. "It's sleeping medicine. I'll help you back over to the hotel. They always need to sleep first off, and the longer the better, I say."

He felt a warmth spreading up through his legs to his groin, where it burned, a big, hot balloon, and on up his chest to his head. ". . . I must have been fixing my car. It fell on me. Or an accident. Or I was robbed. On the road. You know, hit on the head." If that was true, though, why was he still carrying money? But the ID, that was gone, all of it. "Was that it? You think that's why . . . ?" His head swelled up like an inflating dirigible and he tumbled backward through open sky, no land in sight. He started counting down his altitude in thousands. "Where am I now?" he asked.

Far away, the doctor chuckled. "Drop City, I call it. That's as good a name as any."

"Doctor," he said, sinking fast. "I . . . I feel more like I do now . . . than when I came in."

"That's all right. Tomorrow's a whole new ball game. Or the day after. You'll do just fine here. Glad to have you with us, Mr.—"

He tried to stay up long enough to hear his name.

"—Miller," said the doctor.

He slept for two days. He started out of bed lost; then enough—the town, the bar, the hotel, the doctor—came back to make him pound his forehead in anger, but the drug hangover brought him right back down, suspended in a limbo between righteousness and terror. Feeling like an inmate in a nudist camp of the soul, he took a shower, went downstairs for breakfast.

He bought a razor and a toothbrush.

Days passed. Whenever he found himself explaining his predicament, in the coffee shop, at the general store, he was eased away from the subject with understanding cluckings and almost cheerful misdirection. For some reason he did not understand, he did not return to the doctor's office; all he knew was that he did not *want* to. He stopped questioning.

At first he did not believe that there was no police department. "Leveland's takes care of everything," he was told more than once. But when he searched the streets, covering the entirety of the small, self-contained town to its perimeters several times, it was true, all right. Neither was there a bus station. He wondered about that, standing on the ridge overlooking the highway where he had been let out; there was not even a sign to suggest that a bus should stop there. Soon he gave that up, too. If no one else seemed to find anything remarkable about his condition, well, why should he? In a real sense he felt free. After all, how many men are granted a new lease?

The feeling deepened as easily as the taking of a breath, and the days passed just as easily one into another.

First he spent a lot of time in the park lying under trees marked on their trunks with strange eye-like knots. He would wink at them, first one eye, then the other, when the sun fell too low behind the branches, the leaves like burning black coins, their shadows washing over his hands and face. He moved out of Boland's Hotel, found a quiet rooming house on an unmarked lane. He walked and walked, nodding his head and learning to smile again, luxuriating in his new anonymity.

Soon he came to feel that things had always been this way.

One afternoon he found himself at the town's only gas station, drinking a soda and watching the pump ring a dollar's worth of regular into a '47 Studebaker. It was the old glass style pump, like a model of a lighthouse, with the gasoline visible through the sides. There were few cars in use on the streets and he didn't miss them. He felt at ease here, leaning against the soft drink cooler, smelling the sweet dangerous smell from the pump after each slow sale.

"Hi, Earl," he called to the station man. "How's it going?"

"Howyadoing, Jack? Come on out back. I'm workin' on a real crazy one today."

He followed past the tire tub and the collection of old brake linings to a Volkswagen, its dingy red paint long oxidized to the color of a mass of tubifex worms. It was a model from the early fifties, with the small round backseat windows and pinched, slant-eyed rear panes.

"Crazy looking, ain't they? I don't get many."

"You don't? How long you been here, Earl?"

"Long as I can remember. Losing power, he says."

Miller stooped under the bonnet. The plugs were laid out on a dirty cloth the same color as the automobile, and a caged lightbulb hung over the exposed carburetor. "What's the compression like?"

"Hell, number three valve's down to ninety-five. Looks like she's in for a ring job. Yeah," he mused tiredly, "I'm gonna have to pull the engine on this baby."

"Hmm," said Miller. "You got any diesel fuel around here?"

He took a two-pound coffee can full and poured it slowly through the carburetor with the motor running. Steaming gouts of white smoke billowed up around him. Halfway down the can, he cupped his hand over the intake, felt it suck hungrily for air and die.

"Cut the ignition," he told Earl.

They shared a leisurely break over two more bottles of soda, and then he started her up again, gunned her real good and emptied the can through the bowl.

After that, the compression was up to 120 in number three, and within ten pounds all around.

"Where'd you learn a trick like that?"

"I don't know, Earl. I really don't."

"Well, you must've been a mechanic, sometime or other. Jack, my boy? How would you like yourself a job?"

His money would run out soon, anyway. Besides, he felt at home in the station. The pay wasn't much, but it kept him in the rooming house, and kept his hands busy so that he didn't have time to think. Nights he ambled back through the quiet streets, smelling the roasts for dinner and the figs on the trees and dodging sprinklers that spilled over the cracked sidewalk. He wound up at Eleanor's more often than not. She kept at him, pushing up against his arm in that teasing way of hers, but he held back. There was something, something. Though he couldn't remember what. Though he didn't especially try.

And one night he bought a ticket to the Alcazar, because

he liked the slow, downcast smile on the girl in the glass booth and the way she looked in her uniform. The same the next weekend, and the next, and after a while he didn't think about what picture was showing, just stepped up and bought his ticket, then waited to talk with her in the lobby when the last show went on and she had to empty the butter machine and lock the candy counter anyway. After a time he guessed she was in love with him or thought she was, and then one particular Saturday, after seeing the show for two nights running, as they walked back to her house as usual, she held his hand very tightly until they got to her corner, when she suddenly drew into herself and tried to make believe she was watching the cracks in the cement.

"What's wrong?" he asked.

She wouldn't answer at first. Then, "Oh, Jack." It sounded like all the breath went out of her when she said his name this time. "Before I met you, I didn't know anything—and now I'm confused. Are you happy here?"

He stuffed his hands away and counted the cracks with her. "Why shouldn't I be?"

"I don't know. There's something about you."

He tried to sling his arm around her neck.

"No, really. I knew it the first moment I saw you. The way you used to dress, that suit."

"What about it?"

"It was handmade, for you. And your shoes, and the, I don't know, the way you carried yourself. You're part of something else, something that *can't* figure here. Oh, don't say anything, I can tell. And if that's true . . ." She tilted her head from side to side, reasoning. "Then, someday you're going to want to get back to some of the parts, at least, of that other kind of life. It's just too far removed. You can't forget everything. That kind of thing is in your bones."

He pulled her over by one of the eye trees. "That's not necessarily true," he said.

"It's not that I care what you were running away from before you came here. How could I? I don't even want to know about it. I promised myself never to try to find out. Of course I couldn't, nobody can, anyway, but that's not the point. . . ."

"What do you mean, nobody can?"

"You know. The way it is for all of us."

"No, as a matter of fact, I don't know."

"Dr. Leveland's supposed to explain it to you." She sounded suspicious. "Don't you even know that?"

"I'll ask him," he said, an unnerving feeling taking hold. "I will." Maybe there is something wrong with me, he thought, just going about my business here as if I really do belong, not wanting to know. Maybe I *am* running away.

They came to her house. They passed the tall hedge but, instead of sitting down in the lawn swing, she continued straight to the porch and took her key out of the pocket of her purple and gold uniform. She fumbled long enough for him to catch up with her.

He lifted her chin. "Come and sit with me, for God's sake."

She looked at him painfully. She was pretty, he thought, even like this, her straight, brown, pageboy hair. The light from the yellow porch bulb made her skin look like—

He kissed her. Her mouth was warm at first, then unyielding. When he pulled away her eyes were still open.

"Do you love me, Jackie?" she asked.

"Butter," he said. That was it.

"I always smell like butter," she said flatly. "It's my job. I'm sorry I asked."

He stepped off the porch. He touched her elbow gently and she followed in spite of herself, as he knew she would. They sat apart on the swing.

She was right. The sense behind her words reached him. He had lulled himself into ignoring a key question of his existence; he really didn't belong here, and sooner or later his life outside would impinge. He could not hide forever. He had no right to pretend, to allow this girl to go on building a fantasy future for the two of them, one which by all odds had no right to exist. A ringing began in his ears and he suddenly had the overwhelming idea that he had seen all this a dozen times at that movie theater of hers, or on the late show.

"Irene," he said. "How long have you lived here?"

"Why do you ask that?" Her eyes grew steely. "A few years, I guess. Ever since. What difference does it make?"

"Since what?"

"Look at you. Your face," she said dolefully. *"I'm beginning to lose you already, isn't that true?"*

"Wait."

"Well, isn't it? Oh, why can't you just be happy with what you've been given? Most do, you know, even after we know."

"Know what? You're not making any sense." Nothing was. He felt afraid, now, for the first time since that first night. "I want you to tell me something."

"I can't. Dr. Leveland . . ."

"The hell with Dr. Leveland! Listen. The others in this town." He had to find out. "How long have they been here? Listen! I know I'm not the only one. They don't remember anything either, do they? *Do* they?" It was all coming in a rush now. "They treat me like it's normal. Well, is it, for them, too? Is that it? Don't *you* remember, either?"

Her head collapsed in her hands.

"Listen to me! Where were you born? What date, what city? Where did you grow up? And your parents, what were they like? Tell me, tell me, damn it!"

"Stop it!" she shrieked. "Stop all your questions! I can't take it! I can't, I just can't!"

He reached out blindly for her, grabbed her to him, a terrible coldness frosting his insides. "Sh, now," he heard himself say as he stroked her hair, her neck, her forehead, her face. He kissed her deeply, putting his hand over her breast and keeping it there. "Shh, now, it's all right, I'm sorry, it'll work out, I promise, shh now, shh. . . ."

She threw her arms around him then and in the moonlight, as she cried and cried and would not be stopped, he saw the inside of her arm where the sleeve drew up: something that chilled him to the marrow.

He held to her very tightly, his eyes wide open to the lawn, the street, the town and the unseen and unseeable night.

So he resolved to see Leveland. It was time for answers, big ones to some big questions.

The alarm went off but he didn't need it. He set out, deciding on the way to detour by Earl's and let him know that he would be late. Earl had been decent to him, and he owed him some explanation. He could do that much, at least.

Half a block from the station—he heard a *ding* from the air tube—he noticed a long black limousine pulling slowly away from the pumps.

He crossed kitty-corner, the early morning sun sending its first tingling shock through his skin before it began to warm him.

"Hey, Jud?"

The sunlight blinded him. He lowered his head and bore on across the street.

"Judson! Hey, buddy! Hey, it's me!"

The limousine had drawn up to the curb. The driver was waving.

Judson. For a split-second the name seemed to mean something. Then it did not. Is he talking to me?

He approached the car.

"Jud, old boy! I was starting to think I'd never find you! R'lly!"

The driver extended his gloved hand. The grip was firm. A young man, middle twenties. Dry, sun-bleached hair curled surfer-fashion below the edge of the black cap.

"Do I know you?"

"Do you know me, he says! Bro-ther, what a greeting after all this time. Don't you know your old buddy Allen? After all the driving I've done for you?" His straight teeth beamed out of a tan years deep. "Mr. Bledsoe," he said enthusiastically, "hop in. You don't know how glad Mrs. Bledsoe's going to be when she sees you!"

"Just a minute." He wasn't sure. Something sounded within him, its resonance as yet subaudible. "I'm on my way to work."

As soon as he got in, the window rolled down and the door locked by remote control, and the big car, as distantly responsive as a boat, cruised out from the curb and through the streets which now appeared almost too narrow for such a luxury liner to pass. The huge, soft tires corned with a squeal and before he knew it they were on their way.

Down the hillside and away out of the fields, picking up speed silently. The rows of rust-colored plantings sped by in fanning parallels that would come together one day in infinity.

If only he could be sure.

"I must have been suffering from some kind of amnesia, Allen," he attempted measuredly. That could be it, couldn't it? "Till just now, I guess. When I saw you."

"I figured that, from your eyes." He figured that? Really? "But you can relax now. For sure. Fix yourself a drink." Allen indicated the oversized glove compartment. "Just like old times, huh, eh, Judson?"

Right, right. "Where are you taking me?"

"Home, sir."

Of course.

Allen chucked a cartridge into the tape deck, and they drove the next hour saying very little else.

Wait till I see her, he told himself.

It was as rich as they come. The very private driveway curved around a garden of manicured shrubs and as the limousine ground to an effortless halt, small white quartz stones spitting under the wheels, he stared at it, the whole picture, waiting for it to snap back into some kind of alignment for him.

Foyer.

Hall.

Den.

Lots of wood and leather. Something stirred in him, a half-remembered song.

Footsteps like the knocking of a kid glove. A striking woman, 29 going on 40, a streak bleached into her hair, *tres chic*. She crossed the white carpet, pale arms outstretched.

"Oh, darling!"

A kiss. Almonds. No, egg cream. No, almonds. He flowed with it, tasting, sifting. Her teeth remained together.

He felt the wide band of a custom bra beneath the silk blouse, saw tears dried almost before they appeared, her eyes darting like hybrid tropical fish.

"I can't believe it's really you!"

"I can hardly believe it myself," he heard himself say.

"Al told me where he found you. That horrible place! Oh, what must it have been like for you?"

"It wasn't half-bad." Over her shoulder he counted the paintings hanging on the wall, behind the couch. "Nothing like this, of course."

"Of course not." She hugged him, rocking back and forth. "Only, how did you end up in a place like that?"

"I think I had trouble with the car. Can we sit down?"

"Oh, you must be tired and hungry and, oh, my poor darling! The car, yes, of course. Were you hurt?"

"Scratched up a bit. Maybe I drove into a ditch or something. I can't be sure."

She paced around the lucite coffee table as he sat. The cushion was as soft as a bagful of kittens. "Yes, it burned, didn't it?" She eyed him peculiarly. "Why didn't you ever try to get in touch with us, to come home?"

"I didn't seem to have any ID on me."

"Yes, of course, they found your papers, and some brass buttons, I think it was, and, oh, bits and pieces. They told me you'd been burned alive!"

"Irene, I don't remember any of it. In fact—"

"*Linda*, darling. I know. Of course you don't. You couldn't. I mean . . ." She tapped her lower lip with a lacquered nail the color of a cut artery, then folded the lip under her teeth and bit at it. "Of course you couldn't be expected to remember anything. How could you?"

He wasn't sure he grasped what she was telling him. He was waiting for a message inside, and it hadn't come yet. "I want you to show me a picture of myself." She should be able to do that. "I mean, it might help me remember. Do you think so, Linda?"

She fidgeted, watching the hall.

"There's no time, darling. You're back now and you need a shower and some clothes and . . ."

He propped his feet on the coffee table. It was his, wasn't it? "I'm fine. Just let me sit here and take it all in."

She looked at him distractedly, as if she could only be satisfied at this moment by his following her lead. Perhaps she needs that, to stay ahead of whatever it is she's really feeling. Okay, I'll let her call the shots for now, he thought. He didn't want to blow all *this*. He'd pick it up, learn the ropes soon enough.

As soon as it all came back to him.

"You know," he offered, trying to make a joke, "a man could really get to like it here."

"Darling." She advanced, the walls so white behind her, light filtering through the gauzy drapes. He remembered something like that. "There'll be time later. You've been through . . ."

Such an ordeal, he finished for her. The whole thing was off-center somehow. She leaned over him, her hands like forceps on his shoulders. He smelled avocado oil in her hothouse skin. Cleavage hung dark below one breast through the vee in her blouse. She wet her lips, her tongue a small pink ferret. He felt an urge to throw her down between table and couch, her white flesh spilling out of her silk, spread her open right then and there under him so that he might know who and what she was.

He rose, one hand on her neckbone, now the other. She looked like a painted alabaster idiot, he decided. About to break under his scarred, sunburned hands.

"Judson . . ."

"Don't say any more." She expected too much. She had no right.

His hands traced the tendons of her moving throat.

"Darling," she whispered, her voice swishing like nylons, "you're hurting me."

He lowered his hands.

He allowed her to lead him down the hall. He saw a bedroom, neat as a hospital ward.

"Later, darling. It's been so long. *Hasn't it?*"

"Wait," he said. "Are my clothes in the closet, here?" He started into the room. "If they are, I'd like to have a look."

She stepped in front of him. *"No.* I mean, I burned all your things, right after we heard about the accident. I couldn't bear to see them anymore."

"Then whose clothes are they?" Another man's? Well, he thought bemusedly, maybe she isn't so glad to see me walk back into her life just now, after all.

"Allen's," she said hurriedly. "This is his room now. In fact, while you're in the tub, why don't I pick out something of his that suits you, and then . . ."

"What if it doesn't fit?"

"Oh, but it will, darling. You and he are the same size."

"I didn't remember," he said.

"That's all right." She led him to tiles and heat lamps and plush towels. They were monogrammed JB. That detail reassured him, though only slightly, "No one expects you to."

After dinner she prescribed a drink. "Scotch or Jack Daniel's, darling?"

"Don't you remember?" he asked.

She fawned over him and moused with him and handled the cord on his robe. He found her attractive in an angular, disciplined way and her fixed, controlled expression became less noticeable as the firelight waned. In the morning he would remember Allen coming into the room, her cool fingers removing the glass from his hands and the words "the drink," perhaps from his own lips. She woke him, or rather what sounded like a loud slam in another part of the house woke him, and she strung back the drapes in the bedroom and set him up for his breakfast tray.

"Allen," he struggled to say, head throbbing, "was he . . . ?"

"I've sent Allen on an errand. He'll be back with the El Dorado in a few minutes. I know what, darling. Why don't you stop by Westward Dynamics this morning?" A rat-shrewd light came into her eyes. "You might find a nice surprise waiting for you. Your office hasn't been touched, you know. I've seen to it." Had she really? Had no one taken his place, then, even after so long?

"Seeing it again might have a tonic effect," she persisted. "You might even find that you're—"

His mouth was asbestos and his head felt as it had the morning after the night before the night before, that time at Leveland's.

"Linda. Don't push me." She was watching the driveway below. Satisfied, she returned her attention to him. She was wearing a thin dressing gown. It creased familiarly down her body, clinging in a breathing vertical fold at her abdomen.

"First I've got to find a doctor," he announced. "Get me my clothes."

Hearing that, she appeared relieved, oddly enough. She shifted imperceptibly to another level.

"Why not?" she murmured.

"What?"

She trailed to the bed, where the edge of the mattress sealed the gown to her thighs like a second skin. "We'll have to hurry. Allen will be back with the car soon." She met his eyes, calculating something. Then, with mechanical decisiveness, she touched the ribbon straps at her shoulders. A moment later she lifted the sheet.

The car navigated the suburb, skirting the city. The distant layered din of freeways oppressed the roof of the car, the subsonic pressure of an avalanche building to smother him. Encapsulated in the oversized sedan, he felt shrunken to the size of a child. Uneasily he touched the great seat next to him. An envelope, by the unused safety belt; he undid the flap with one hand and withdrew the contents, riffled the edges. A stack of bills. It felt like all the money a man would ever need. Allen's? Not bloody likely. Perhaps she had placed it in the car when she opened the door for him. He recalled Allen standing there, his tie wrinkled, his face beaded, his eyes swimming with perspiration. What kind of errand had she sent him on? She had pothered the door shut after him, almost eager to see him on his way. She did not kiss him. She smiled with a model's efficiency as he drove away past the eucalyptus trees, but when he glanced back, adjusting the mirror, her face was set and waxen. Like Allen's.

Maybe they're more concerned about me than I thought.

He wheeled with mounting impatience through street after identical street, not realizing for several miles that he had forgotten to get directions. The hell with it, he thought. He would find an intersection, a sign, a way. He would get his bearings and make it one way or another now. He thought that.

He drove past a discount store, a supermarket, a mindlessly milling shopping center. The people appeared speeded up as if in a silent film. Children like deranged rabbits scattered before the wheels.

And so on and on, block after patternless block.

My God, he thought, what have I come back to?

Impulsively he wrenched the wheel, changing course. He could still make it to the freeway, watch for yesterday's landmarks.

Traffic lights, staggered in an obstacle course, batted their hooded eyes with furious indifference. He spotted an opening in the cheap circus boulevard. The freeway sign was familiar. He aimed for the on-ramp.

A woman with a pilfered shopping cart, her view blocked by the overstuffed brown bags she bussed, clacked across the pedestrian walk on the other side of his tinted windshield, her face pale as cancer.

He accelerated, shutting her out.

Brakes screamed on all sides and horns like deep-throated trumpets. He had a brief, shuddering flash of what it would mean to die here, struck like a dog and run over again and again by countless unknown assassins.

Now he heard the piercing wail of a siren, trying to lure him aground in this trashed sector.

Not on my life.

A gas station loomed ahead. He gunned the engine and the car swerved and dipped and lurched to a halt.

He slammed the steering wheel with his fists.

A boy with a rag in his pocket marched to the window and mouthed, "Fill 'er up, sir?"

Unable to make out the boy's words through the glass, he nodded him away.

A police car bumped over the curb and eased into the station.

He started the engine again.

In the police car, the officer covered his mouth with a coiled-cord microphone.

A pounding, so close it seemed to be in his head. Twisting to his left, he saw the boy knuckling the glass.

He hit a button and the window rolled down.

The boy hooked a thumb toward a sign. NO SMOKING TURN OFF YOUR ENGINE.

He glanced back and saw the pump hosed into his tank.

He cut the ignition.

He did not notice a second squad car enter the station.

He leaned into the headrest and squeezed his eyes shut until shards of light fired on the inner surfaces of his lids. When he opened them again, the boy was cleaning the windshield with a wad of blue paper toweling. At the end of one wiper blade, an old parking lot receipt clung stubbornly to the glass. LAX, it read. The boy respectfully avoided it, as if the cardboard tag were a permit of great importance.

He heard the hose jump. The boy polished off the window and circled to the rear to retract the nozzle.

"Cash or charge?"

He unpacketed one of the bills and handed it over.

"Do you know your transmission's leaking, sir?"

No, but if you hum a few bars I'll fake it. "Get me a map, will you?" he snapped.

"Sure. Lemme get your change. She's throwin' oil pretty bad. Eh, you don't have anything smaller, do you, sir?"

He glared back.

His eyes followed the boy to the office. The boy took a key from his belt and hunkered over a cash box.

The policeman entered the office.

It had been so long since he had seen a cop—how long?—that the siren and the quick black-and-white wolverine at his tail had jarred him and he had overreacted, detoured into the station. Apparently, though, he was not the target. However, the boy now glanced back curiously at the limousine, as the uniform quietly vied for his attention.

So what? he asked himself. If he's going to write me up, let him, and let's get it over with.

He pushed out of the car and headed to the office.

The uniform met him, a reflexive hand at his side.

"You give him this fifty?"

"It wasn't a tip." To the boy, "I'd like my change." He picked through the white, blue and red road maps.

"In a hurry, are you?"

He eyeballed the cop.

"That your ve-hicle?"

"It sure is. If you don't mind—"

He followed their focus to the limousine. Eight or nine police had materialized while his back was turned and were in the process of turning it inside out. He watched blankly as three more squad cars arrived, joining the four already there.

A hand between the shoulder blades.

"Put-your-hands-on-the-door-spread-your-legs-don't-move."

"What do I do with this?" asked the boy, waving the bill.

"Evidence, son."

Damning evidence, by the sound of it. But of what?

Searched, frog-marched to the car. Uniforms swarming, black shoes and white hands and shortwave radios groaning static against the grinding traffic.

"Money's there, all right." Envelope, proffered pincer-like, for Top Cop's inspection.

"Hold on, my wife gave—"

Fugitive fifty bagged with the rest. "Mister, this money was reported stolen less than an hour ago." Smirk. "Now what do you say to that?"

"License plates check out, sir. Bledsoe, Judson Stephen. 3729 Arroyo Glen. This is the car."

"Of course it checks out. If you'll take a minute to call my wife—"

"What's your name, fella?"

"Uh, Judson. Bledsoe." Painstakingly enunciated; his jaw felt wired. "What's it supposed to be?" A not-at-all insincere question, that one.

"You tell me, fella. You tell me."

"Look. This my Cadillac. I am on my way to my office at" what was it? "Westward Dynamics. Check it out. Go ahead. If you'll just let me sign your God damned ticket—"

Snickers, waggling heads, sounds like the wheezing of disappointed schoolmasters. "It never fails to amaze me, you know? In broad daylight. You would have had better luck trying to get away with stiffing a liquor store. Don't you guys ever get it? All right, you're under arrest. Just a minute and somebody will read you your rights."

"What charge, for Christ's sake?"

"You want to watch your mouth, little man. How about grand theft auto, breaking and entering, two counts of kidnap, let's see, armed robbery, assault with a deadly weapon. Attempted rape. How's that grab you, smart guy?"

"Attempted *what?*"

"We'll think up some more, don't you worry." Clipped, close-mouthed, orders to a stick, an object, a spot on the sidewalk.

"I don't get it."

"We don't have to tell you anything yet, you got that?" Then, taken in by dumbfounded lifemask but probably not, probably more out of a long-suppressed yearning to swing weight behind such words: "The lady notified us an hour ago. The story seems—" What panache on that word! "—Seems to be that you flagged down the lady's chauffeur in one of those halfway settlements, forced him to drive over the County line, that you proceeded to hold them both at gunpoint—" Again, a liquid familiarity with such a word. "—At her residence until this morning, when Mr. Bledsoe arrived home from a business trip, at which time you took him hostage and fled the premises with over ten thousand dollars in cash. And the car. Let's have a look at that coat."

Lapels flailed as if by a professional pickpocket.

Monogrammed.

JB.

"These are his clothes."

You have such a way with words, officer. And that about wraps it up. Mark it and strike it. Move 'em out.

"Just one more thing."

Yes? Yes?

"What did you do with your hostage?"

Dum-da-dum-dum.

He broke and lunged at the car for proof, papers, ID, a picture, something, anything with which to identify himself. The glove box rattled open.

In the gaping shadow, a revolver.

Struggle in handcuffs. Jerk and strain your back, raging until the blood bursts like drums in your ears over the traffic and the crackling radios.

"Sergeant, you want to take a look at this."

Bent knees, tops of caps. Trail of oil oozing from the car. Dark oil, spreading in a pool under the trunk.

"Yeah," volunteered the boy, "his transmission's throwin' oil like a sieve."

The sergeant knelt, dipped a finger, smelled. "This isn't oil, son." Dramatically. "Get that trunk open."

The trunk yawned.

Luggage, flight-tagged.

Shoe.

Foot.

Leg.

Body, contorted like an uncooked pretzel in a gray suit. Dead, of course.

Of course.

Blood from single bullet wound trickled from deathmask skull, still congealing, to asphalt.

Cop: "Well, shit." Crowded like actors silenced by an unexpected entrance, huddling for a next line. "All I can say," says one of the cops, "is I sure hope his old lady had plenty of life insurance on him."

Get it. Get it now, almost all of it, enough, enough. Too much. How they must have planned the murder, searching for someone, the only kind of fall guy who would, who *could* play along with them; at last, realizing in a cold flash the only place they could hope to find such a one. And Allen had even picked someone the right size. They were good. Oh, were they good! "You're God damned right! How right you are! Don't *you* guys get it? You can bet your asses she had plenty riding on this! Oh ho, the plan of the cen-tu-ry!" You laugh maniacally, a man who has been handled and knows it at last, set up only to be flattened again, a moment of clarity, until a club at your throat takes you out.

On the blacktop, blood melting and coagulating with spilled gasoline and motor oil, a shimmering rainbow beginning and ending in its swirling depths.

The trial: hired flagellants relive your crimes in the courtroom, pick them over as meticulously as worms spawned within the deed. (You didn't do it, the Pentothal sessions in the Medical Center prison ward prove it; such evidence is inadmissible, of course.) The defense: doctors hover, mercenary angels in metallic suits and half-boots, in conference with wire-sideburned lawyers. (The Clinic pays for them all with impotent, reluctant, constipated dedication; bad publicity, a guilty verdict could, just might, will scare potential customers.) The back story: (There was no back story until the moment you sprang up like a ripe dragon's tooth in the road, the five hundred survival dollars in fives, tens and twenties provided in a shiny new wallet; there never is.) Like any other voluntary, emphasize voluntary customer/patient at NeuAnfang Clinic, you paid, in advance, naturally, to have your memory selectively "cleared"—read: a sequence of protein injections, primarily puromycin and 8-azaguanine, into the cerebral cortex. (The cost: a basic 33 thousand dollars; more or less depending on the stipulations in each personalized contract.) You were then shoved gently, professionally out the door, pointed quite fail-safely down the only road, along which the rehabilitation communities, halfway settlements like Drop City are sown every few miles across the floor of the isolated valley; no through traffic, no campers allowed, only an occasional bus to and from the Clinic like the one on which you hitched a ride (had you stepped off the road, stumbled, fallen, panicked, waved him down?) free again to take your chances on the neurological pathway (no forks other than those you make yourself). The verdict: the Clinic must take no chances. Guilty or not, you are pled mentally incompetent to stand trial.

"You would have come to see it for what it was, by the way, sooner or later anyway, Jack. (Do you want to keep that name?) Nobody gets it right off. I don't know who discovered water, but it wasn't a fish. The answers come in their own time, and not until the questions start to pop up on their own. After all, questions come out of some kind of order in words, and the answers, I guess, have to come out of the order of your life. You wouldn't, you couldn't come looking for me until you'd already found me, in a sense. Too much in the beginning only keeps the client confused, so he starts to fall back on the great mother Clinic and all us witchdoctors. You didn't pay your money to get turned into an invalid. A new chance is what you wanted. We try to see to it that you make one for yourself. The way *you* want it.

"We're supposed to keep you under observation for ninety days. Then the court will be wanting a report on your, let's say sanity. Hah! 'Course there's nothing wrong with you now. But who'd believe it? We've had too much bad press to convince a jury that people like you come for the treatment for any reason except to hide something. Your record's clear—you weren't wanted for anything or we couldn't have taken you—but try to explain that, try to convince 'em on the stand. Every doctor on our staff could talk till he's blue in the face and it wouldn't make much difference. Far as they'd be concerned, you were running from something or other—you had to be, see?—even if the law hadn't got wind of it yet. It would have, they'd think. They don't believe in innocence, Jack. They can't. It's the way they think.

"Now, your observation can be handled in different ways. That much is left pretty much up to us, under the law. But I'll tell you something, Jack. We feel a responsibility to our clients. Yes. As much protection as the law allows, and then some; that's not altruism; it's just good business. You came over to us because you woke up one day and found you'd got turned around into something you couldn't live with anymore, a kind of person that sickness of theirs had made into a thing that only knows how to get in its own way.

"You go on, sleep, Jack. It's dark out. I'll be giving you a few more of these injections, and then you can give it another try. That's one detail they didn't specifically prohibit us from doing for you."

"No." You try to raise your head but the light is everywhere, so you can't even see Dr. Leveland. "No more injections. I—" You are struggling to make a decision, one that seems all of a sudden to be the most important you've ever made, more important even than the first one. "I already had one new deal. Nobody," you realize, startled at yourself, "promised me anything when I came along the first time, the very first time, I mean. I—I think I'd like to play this one out to the end."

You are very sensitive to the pressure of the bed supporting you, the sound of wheeled appliances carting along the halls outside your door; so many, each going as silently as possible through his appointed rounds. You hear the soft ringing of an elevator in the hospital, a sound you seem to know, people coming and going within its confines, and if stretching face muscles, the 13 steps of a grin can be heard by your human ear, then you hear that, too, there in the room close to you.

"You're going back to a place where there's just no model for the kind of behavior I was talking about. What you do after that is up to you. I can tell you, though—I guess you expect me to—that a certain young lady was knocked down a few notches when you left. Far as I know she's still waiting."

"Roland." Your mind is starting to turn over, to move like an electromagnet and you feel the energy spiraling outward from a core you weren't sure you possessed until this moment. "What about the ninety days?"

"Well, they'll want a diagnosis at that time, from me, I guess, since I'm the acting physician in town. I'll hook you up to all that mumbo jumbo and they'll get a print-out back here at the Clinic. But hell, how can I diagnose you? I open my mouth to tell you it's raining, and in the middle of the sentence the sun comes out!"

You're planning already, how to find a way to get at the truth about Linda Bledsoe and that son of a bitch Allen, how he worked it getting into the valley past the detours, just to pick up someone like you to take the rap, someone whose word, they knew, would have a value approaching absolute zero in the eyes of the law. There must be a way. Ninety days isn't going to be much time.

"Now," says Roland, "don't go too fast right off. I know you're brave enough to be scared, but you might still be a little too humble to win."

You look up. His face is completely washed out by the brightness of the light.

"On the other hand, Jack, old boy, you don't want to use Drop City to hide out. Now why did I bother to say that? I think you already know, or I wouldn't be taking a chance on you."

You make a questioning sound in your dry throat.

"Just what you already know, Jack. That a place a man

can hide in can be something else, too, when he needs it. *It can be a haven.*"

But his voice fades. His voice fades and you are already there, coming up over the reeds and sage into a wine sky, stopping on the edge where nobody ever gets off to wipe your face with your own good handkerchief before turning into it once more. Hear his words, circle his office and begin again, you are circling the town, the lights coming on over the movie marquee, it is one you have seen before but never stayed through to the end but there is no rush, it will be there tomorrow night and the night after; you are relieved that she is not yet there on her stool behind the glass, doling out tickets like brightly colored lies, ones which those who choose to enter will be happy to live by, as you cross the empty street to the bright blue sign misting in the haze of a warm day turning slowly toward evening. Inside, to the right, the fish still thriving under glass, to the left, the old dark wood and leather crescent railing, and moving somewhere in front of the jukebox that looks like nothing so much as an overstuffed chair sprung through with lights, a woman dances with herself, a coin ready for one more in an endless succession of plays, twenty-thirty pounds overweight and ready for the winter, fingers wet with beer. The door thumps securely behind you as you go to the bar and order the first in a series of very stiff drinks, and when Eleanor comes over you turn your back not unkindly on Mr. Shiply, the barkeep who is nothing of the kind but who has found a way of being that suits him well enough for the present, as he says "Well hello there, Mr., what was it?" But he is too late, Eleanor is against you and your feet are moving already to a music that seems to be playing just for you.

green, green, promenade in green

And you will not sleep in the hotel this night and you will not sleep in the boarding house, it is still too soon, it is time to lose yourself in order to come back to where you began, and as you take her arms in the dance you remember another arm, the uniform sleeve drawn up: old, almost healed, the knots of hematomas and the scar tissue where the hardening had been surgically removed, years ago, in another life long past, and mercifully so, mercifully forgotten, a life which you saw then and understand now had been tracked relentlessly by endless hypodermic needles . . . But it is too soon to think of that now, too soon.

tell me who you love,

tell me who you love

You do not try to speak to this woman of any of it. It is something too sharp and too wild. For you cannot, you know, use words to get beyond words.

THE CHAIR

"Marty," she said, "I need you."

He studied the lips. The air was opalescent with cigarette smoke, the lights too far away to make it easy. Her complexion was smooth and taut; a faint bloom of perspiration glittered in the shadows below her cheekbones. It was impossible, of course. And yet . . .

"Christy?" he said, incredulous.

He wanted to reach out and touch her to be sure. At the same time he was seized by a desperate impulse to leave his chair and run: between tables to the bar, even to the dance floor where faces he seemed to know had been grafted onto bodies he would never recognize, bodies which now gyrated feverishly to music he thought he had forgotten long ago.

"I've been looking for you all night," she said. "I—I was afraid you wouldn't come." He heard her voice masked by the noise, as though through a wind tunnel. "Can we go somewhere? We can't talk here."

Martin rose uncertainly and followed. The crowd surged. Her form grew smaller and was lost to him. He threaded a path between abandoned chairs, his arms brushing a table, upsetting a half-finished glass of wine. A red blot spread across the white linen. He righted the empty glass and tried to move on.

A powerful hand stopped his wrist.

"Didn't think you'd get away that easy, did you?"

Martin looked up. A smudged copy of a face from his childhood towered over him. Around the eyes grainy skin crinkled with amusement, emphasizing preternaturally blue contact lenses.

"Bill Crabbe," said the tall man expectantly.

Martin gaped. It was true. Crabbe, the baseball star from high school. Martin shook his hand.

"How ya doin', buddy?" Crabbe pumped his arm. "My gosh, Jerry Marber! You're sure lookin' good. What you been doin' with yourself all these years?"

Martin realized he had been mistaken for someone else. He considered correcting the tall man. At that moment there was a pause in the music and hyperventilating couples pressed back between the wooden pillars to their banquet tables. An intoxicating cloud of hair spray and cologne blew over him. He gazed through the crowd to the polished walls and round windows, searching for Christy's face. He cleared his throat.

"Excuse me, Jer," said Crabbe abruptly, "but there's Wayne Fuller. I gotta say hi. My gosh, look at him. He hasn't changed a bit, has he? Old Wayne. Hey, over here!"

Crabbe moved on, paddling against the throng with his big pitcher's hand outstretched.

Martin spotted an exit. Christy or someone very much like her was leaning against the lacquered door, trying to light a cigarette while her eyes grew whiter, sweeping the ballroom.

For me, he thought. She's waiting for me, even after so many years. I should have known. I should have kept the faith. Well, maybe I have without realizing it.

We'll find out now, won't we?

Couples swept past in a frenzied rush. The room seemed to tilt as bodies hurried to one side. The backs of men with polyester suits and indeterminate waistlines bobbed six deep in front of the cash bar. Martin took a deep breath. He felt drunk. He steadied himself against a chair and aimed for the other side.

"Jimmy!" called a booming voice.

He pressed on through the louvers of crepe paper strung from the bandstand, a wall of voices closing in. Heads streaked with graying sideburns and permanent wave curls blocked his way. When they moved aside, he noticed that Christy was gone from the doorway.

"Jimmy Madden! I knew it was you!"

The gravel voice of a bull-necked football coach boomed again. This time it jarred him to a standstill.

Martin turned and was confronted by a short-sleeved sport shirt, the same print he remembered from school. He scrutinized the face above and nodded, smiling impatiently.

What was the coach's name?

Then he realized it was not the coach's face, after all. It was Warrick. Mark Warrick, once star lineman for the Greenworth Buckskins. He had made it to the state play-offs, if Martin remembered correctly.

"Nice to see you, Mark," said Martin reflexively, "Only I'm not . . ."

A sweet-smelling woman disengaged from the pack and took possession of Martin's left arm. He felt her breast push into his side.

"Gail!" said Warrick. His lantern jaw dropped open and uneven teeth shone there wetly. "Are you still with Bob? I mean—"

"Not for a year-and-a-half," announced Gail. She kneaded Martin's forearm as if measuring it. "And how are you, Joe?"

The man in the sport shirt plowed ahead. "Guess what, Gail? I'm head coach at GHS now. Did you hear? Uh, are you, I mean, did you come alone?"

She said, "Don't I see your wife, Mark? That sweet little thing over there in the corner, waiting for someone to ask her to dance? What *was* her name?"

Martin was aware of the underwiring of her bra prying his ribs apart. She turned on him again, inches away, and blinked into his eyes from beneath lids heavy with raccoon mascara.

"Joe Ivy. Did you know that I used to have the most humongous crush on you?"

"Yes," said Martin hurriedly. "No. I didn't. I don't. That is, it isn't me. I'm not really here."

He disembraced and tripped forward, wrinkling someone's satin. The exit still appeared the length of a football field away, as if seen through the small end of a telescope. He jostled wrists and left ice cubes clinking thickly in plastic cocktail tumblers, and made a final run for the deck and the night outside.

He was chilled by the sudden touch of a harbor breeze on his neck.

He did not slow until he had gone all the way astern on the Promenade Deck, where he leaned back on his elbows and allowed the image of the Windsor Room to recede into a frame of brass portholes and freshly-painted guardrails.

The doorway to the ballroom remained open, throwing a rectangle of yellow light onto the boards below the main mast. Through the doorway he made out a hand-lettered streamer of bunting on the aft wall, above the bar. WELCOME GREENWORTH HIGH SCHOOL CLASS OF '62, it read, 20 YEAR REUNION.

She stepped in front of him, eyeing him in the old way. Behind her head a warm glow caught her hair. He tried to read her expression, but in the backlight there was no clue. He sought for the right way to begin again. He straightened, his body inching involuntarily closer to her, and the spill of warmth diminished to a sliver and faded as the exit door whispered shut. A round of whooping applause rose up inside as a toast was made onstage, and then the door sealed and there was only the rhythm of a drumroll to blend with the lapping of dark waters which rocked the bulkhead almost imperceptibly beneath his feet.

He wanted to make up for so much lost time, to force her to a confrontation so long in the coming, to send bolts of blue fire shimmering over her and down her throat. Instead he said, "Christy."

She dropped her cigarette, and a wind swirled it away in a vortex of sparks.

"I want to know," he said, "how it's been for you. I want to know it all. Or whatever you want to tell. If you can tell me. You know you can. Christy." He held out his hand.

She lowered her eyes and fumbled for another cigarette.

"I'm glad everything worked out for you and Sherman," he lied.

He almost gagged on the name. It was the first time he had said it or even allowed himself to think it for perhaps fifteen years. Sherman the loser, the guy who never had any friends. Till Martin came along and tried to help. In the end, Martin learned about helping too much. . . .

Your move, he thought, afraid to think any further. Tell me that it's dead between you, that it always was. Tell me that you haven't changed, and make me believe that I haven't, either. Do it. Do it now, or stay out of the rest of my life.

She was suddenly shy, unable to look at him. "I don't know how to—"

"Begin anywhere."

He waited.

A solitary craft passed in the bay, its running lights obscured for seconds at a time by the massive rigging of the deck upon which he and Christy stood.

"You always hated him, didn't you." She said it oddly, as if to reassure herself. As if the idea gave her some kind of satisfaction.

"What does it matter?"

"I think it does. That's why I came."

That's why? he thought, growing more disoriented by the minute. Well, if she wants to explain, she's certainly taken her time about it.

As if I care. As if it makes any difference now.

I was never angry at her. Hurt, yes. And confused. *I would have married you myself, did you know that?* But angry? I could never let myself feel that, and now it's part of another life, what happened then. One thing is certain: she can't speak for him, Iago in a crewneck sweater. She couldn't then and she can't now. He had a chance, once, to face me. He didn't. And now it's too late.

"Forget it," he said. "Things happen. Even among friends. Especially among the best of friends."

Her eyes lifted and glared, pinwheels in the centers.

"You were always so damned forgiving. Do me a favor, Marty. Stop being so understanding! You know you hate him. Admit it."

Was she daring him? He could not imagine why. What would be the point?

"Christy, I meant what I said. I want to know that you're happy. That's all. If you don't believe that, then you never really knew me."

"But I do know you. That's why, Marty. That's why I need you now."

Her voice softened and the years disappeared like wildflowers over the hills. He remembered or imagined her, he did not know which, sprawled across his lap, curled against his chest. So many nights . . .

"Marty."

Then, just as unexpectedly, he was snapped back to the present as her tone tightened again in a rising glissando of barely-suppressed emotion.

He began to doubt himself. Had it been his fault, then? Some incident he had conveniently forgotten all this time which had sent her packing and into Sherman's arms? Had he somehow misremembered for so long what happened that night? Was that possible?

Marty. Only she had ever called him that. Perhaps no one else ever would, no matter how many more years were left to him.

She moved her body until they were close enough to touch, and yet they were not touching. He was aware of the heat radiating from her skin, trembling the taut membrane of his clothing. The scent of her burned his nostrils. He forced himself to breathe.

"Marty," she said. A single strand of hair, invisible as a spider's web, touched his cheek. "Do I have to beg? *I need you.*"

She told him it was five minutes away. Whether it was more or less than that he did not notice.

Behind them the Queen Mary's raked funnels, piped in red and black and towering like the truncated stacks of a nuclear power plant, gave the converted liner an illusion of movement, as if the ship had docked there only temporarily and was even now pulling up anchor to pace the car out of the old Naval Yard and around the misty intersections of the coastline.

She looked at him once as a blurred refinery passed outside, but she was not seeing him. The plume of an endless fire licked the sky, the natural gas burnoff of a pipeline to the center of the earth. She was seeing through him, a translucent X-ray of his flesh and bones in position there against the glass where she had arranged for it to be.

A sign with the words DE LUXE APARTMENTS swam into view.

She turned past it, again, then fine-tuned the wheel at the end of a cul-de-sac behind the building and parked beneath power lines that crackled as if underwater.

It was one of those courtyard blocks that dead-end at the ocean, where accelerated disrepair is rationalized as quaint because there is nowhere left to move once one has reached the edge of the continent.

The headlights clicked off and the fog stopped swirling. A steady corona encircled a streetlamp like a halo around the moon. The pulse of the motor was replaced by the breathing of an unseen tide.

She leaned across him. Against his will his fingers curved to receive her.

"Wait," she said. "We're almost there. God, I've waited so long for this. You don't know."

She retrieved her purse from behind the seat, put away her keys and swung out of the car.

Their footsteps clacked on the sidewalk. A rusty tricycle like a twisted spider littered a shadowy yard. Somewhere television voices were muffled by flickering blue window shades. A cat cried from a hidden place with the voice of a human baby. They climbed steps to the second floor. The corroded screen door creaked with the sound of a fingernail on a blackboard. A deadbolt lock glistened under the scratchings of her key.

"Here. We won't need the lights."

She led him into darkness. A soft cushion met the backs of his legs.

The room took on dim form. Gradually black oblongs of furniture appeared around him, only to dissolve when looked at too closely. Through a doorway, in the cavern of another room, the constant eye of a pilot flame burned coolly beneath a gas appliance of unknown shape.

Seconds passed.

Stray light began to creep in from the courtyard outside, so that the indistinct plane of slatted window blinds cast the suggestion of bars over his hands.

He smelled an old perfume, and then she was gliding down and down next to him in the overstuffed chair. He heard the whisper of her stockings, her body as it moved in her clothing.

"Christy . . ."

She stopped his mouth with cold fingers. He saw the glint of her eyes as they focused past him.

"What?" he asked.

"Shh."

He followed her gaze across the room.

A thin strip of light glowed beneath a door at the end of a hallway.

Was someone else here?

Not *him*. Surely she wouldn't have—

A child, then. Why not?

Of course there would have been a child for them. It was only natural. Why hadn't he expected it?

Still the thought took him by surprise, even unnerved him. How old? he wondered. How long after she left him had—?

But no. He put that possibility from his mind.

He touched her awkwardly, unsure of the moment.

She moved her head from side to side, and her lips brushed his. They were, he thought, as cool and dry as desert flowers.

"No," she said hoarsely. "Later. I promise. But first there's something you have to do."

"Wait," he said, realizing where he was and what he was doing. "You've got me wrong. I didn't come here to . . ."

"Didn't you?" She blinked at him. Was she mocking him? She was, he decided. She was.

She rose, pulling him out of the chair. In spite of himself his body strained after her.

An afterimage of her crossed the room.

He heard a knocking.

She was standing at the end of the hall, in front of the closed door.

He followed as, on the other side, a shadow passed across the crack of light.

Something moved. Something heavy.

There was a jangling of keys, and the door opened.

Martin was momentarily blinded by a flood of light. When his eyes were able to adjust, he saw the figure of a man before him.

"Honey," she said, "I—I've brought someone home for you."

The figure stood so stiffly for so long that Martin began to wonder if it might be a manikin. Finally he detected movement in the eyes, tiny dots peering out of tunneled sockets. Then the shoulders slumped, the low bulk shuffling aside, the thinning spikes of uncombed hair vibrating in the flare of a dozen or more high-intensity light bulbs which were plugged into every corner of the small room.

She fidgeted, her tone winding up like a violin string again.

"You remember Jack, don't you?"

Her eyes darted nervously between them. The irises were closed down to pinpoints. He could not help but notice now a fine webbing of lines etched around her eyes, radiating outward, imprinted there as if by years of squinting under a merciless sun. The pupils were washed out like a faded photograph.

"Don't you, Sherm?" she said.

Martin stared at her.

What the hell is she doing? he thought. What kind of sick game is this?

The man in the bedroom smoothed his hair and rubbed his soft hands over his white face, and straightened.

Martin had no choice. He stepped over the threshold.

There was a closeness in the air, a sickly-sweet incense that was a mixture of old clothes and unchanged bedding and slow currents of exhaled air circulating and recirculating above overheated lamps. The man made an effort to draw himself up to his full height, and Martin was overcome with disbelief.

He remembered Sherman as several inches taller, his own height exactly, in fact. But it was as if the frame had contracted with time, the spine settling, the posture folding in on itself to support so much sagging flesh. Martin tried to believe his eyes.

Often lately he had found himself wondering what a man his own age was supposed to look like. As a point of reference he had hoped to identify at least one passing on the streets. But he had never been sure.

Now he knew.

A shudder crept up his spine and over his scalp.

And then something which had once seemed so important left him with an inner shrugging that was like a sea change, a great burden lifting and departing in a flash. His eyes stung.

He glanced back and saw that Christy was no longer there.

"Jack," said Sherman tightly. It was Sherman, all right. "Jack Martin. We have a lot to talk about. We must have. Sit down. Won't you. Jack."

The son of a bitch, thought Martin. The poor, tired, worn-out, sorry son of a bitch. The years with her, years that were supposed to be mine, and look, just look what they've done for him.

And, thinking that, so much hate went—somewhere. Anywhere. Receding into the white light, going, and gone. All at once he felt himself very old, like everyone else a victim of unforeseeable circumstance. Like the ones back on the hotel liner, the rest of his classmates. They were no longer so very strange, were they? And neither was this man. This old friend. It was true, wasn't it?

It was. And there was nothing he could do about it.

He sat.

"I reckon you heard. About me and Chris getting married."

"Yes," said Martin.

Sherman lowered himself gingerly into a straight-backed chair.

Martin noted that the room was nearly bare, with no concessions to comfort. Everything in sight had been painted in blacks and whites. There was a collection of FBI "wanted" posters framed plainly on the walls; he recognized the faces of a kidnapped heiress and a famous black radical teacher; another, that of a square-jawed young man with rimless glasses and a doomed, defiant expression, eluded him. Somewhere a simple electric clock ground through its endless cycle.

"So. How the hell are you, Jack?"

Spare me, he thought. Spare us both. And yet how else to get through this conversation?

"Can't complain." Quickly Martin acted to forestall the inevitable personal histories. "Say, what's with all the lights?" It was a reasonable enough question. He really did want to know. "Not running scared of the dark in your old age, are you, man?"

It was also at least half a joke, but that part of it didn't work.

Sherman regarded him with detachment, jingling an oversized keyring. On a shelf behind him two miniature armies of historical footsoldiers collected dust on a board, eternally poised to relive some long-forgotten battle.

"Yeah, well. Guess you could say I got my fill of dark places in the Corps, you know what I mean?"

At some point down the years Martin had allowed a single bit of information about Sherman to enter his consciousness: that he had served in some branch of the armed forces. Enlisted, he seemed to recall.

"Marines?" he asked.

"Army Corps of Engineers. They had me doing field work in New Mexico. You know what a spelunker is, Jack?" He said it with a trace of pride.

"I think so." Martin racked his brain. "You mean you made maps of caves, that sort of thing?"

Sherman nodded. "Carlsbad was blacker'n the place where the Devil throws his old razor blades."

"Ah." That explained it, then. After a fashion. He guessed. "So. What have you been up to since?"

"Well, there was Chris to consider, of course." Of course. "I needed something with, you know, more of an opportunity for advancement."

"Right."

What's a former spelunker to do? wondered Martin. It seemed absurd. But then what did not? For the life of him he could not think of an appropriate follow-up occupation. Indeed he could not even imagine making a living by crawling around caves with a flashlight and a notebook.

It takes all kinds, he thought. And, really, was it any more ridiculous than the way he himself had found? Yes, he thought, it takes all kinds. Any way is good enough to make what people mean when they point at something and call it a life. Who am I to judge?

"So," Sherman was saying, "I went into a career in law enforcement."

What else? thought Martin. Why not? For those who like that sort of thing, well, I'd have to say that's more or less just the sort of thing they would like. Right?

"After I graduated from Texas A & M, a buddy of mine got me an in with the Department of Corrections. I had it all planned out. I was going to work my way up through the system—they start you out as a jailer no matter where you train—and then transfer back here. It was as good a place as any to start."

"Beats Terminal Island, eh?" He didn't know what else to say.

"Yeah. That was what I thought. Till those bastards got hold of me."

Martin drew a blank.

Sherman sat forward on his chair, his eyes bulging. "They took thirteen hostages."

"They did?"

"Yeah. When it was over, two of us got out alive."

Martin shook his head. "I'm sorry," was all he could come up with. "I didn't know."

I still don't, he thought. Some kind of prison riot, was that what Sherman was talking about? There had been the one at Attica, others. Quite a few others. He couldn't remember the names of the institutions. He didn't want to ask.

"You know what those bastards did?"

Martin held up his hand. "No, I don't, but . . ."

"They did *things* to us." Sherman was shaking with rage. "Things that shouldn't happen to any man."

He was not talking it out. He was reliving it.

Martin wondered if it would ever be over for him. The answer was clear enough. It was written there in the man's twisted face.

Martin wanted to help but for some reason resisted the impulse. Besides, he asked himself, what was there to do?

"I'm not the man I was, Jack. Not the man she married. I'm just not the same. You know?"

Martin nodded, embarrassed.

"I wanted to go back in and get every one of them. With my bare hands. The State swore they'd do it for me. But they didn't do the job right."

Martin squirmed. The heavy wooden chair was beginning to wear through the seat of his pants. It certainly had not been designed for extended use.

"Things have changed a lot since then," Sherman was saying.

Martin was developing a splitting headache. The small, severe room with its pounding lights was becoming oppressive. He wished for Christy to return and lead him out. He had done what she asked. He had faced Sherman, or had allowed Sherman to face him, for whatever it was worth.

"I'll make it right again, Jack. What we're going to have is another kind of revolution in this country. And it starts right here."

"Let it go, man," said Martin gently, His throat was dry. He swallowed with pain. "Life's too short."

"Yeah." Sherman jerked his pale hand to indicate a neat stack of books next to the toy soldiers. "That's why I'm ready."

Martin sat forward, eager for an excuse to shift his weight from the punishing seat. He shielded his eyes. The titles on the nearest spines shimmered into legibility. *Crime and Punishment In America. A New Handbook of Hanging. History of the Guillotine. Executions USA.*

"They'll be out in a few years," said Sherman, "if they aren't already, I know they'll find me. They always have. And when they come for me this time, I'll be waiting."

The nearest light bulb sang with current, electrifying the air.

Martin became aware of a feeling he had suppressed all night. It was that tingling you begin to register when you know something is terribly wrong but you don't quite know what it is yet. It was here, not only inside him but all around him, prickling his legs like pins and needles. That he could not name it made it no less real. He could ignore it no longer.

He saw the other man as if for the first time.

Martin flexed his legs and started out of the chair.

The pale man was on his feet. In one quick step he was standing over Martin.

He reached around the chair.

Martin looked down.

A strap dropped from under the armrest and buckled over his wrist, cinching it to the chair. First one wrist, then the other. He watched. It might have been happening to someone else.

Sherman swayed over him, his breath sour, light coruscating through the filaments of his hair. Then he doubled over in a bowing motion. Martin heard the ringing of another buckle, another as straps closed over his ankles.

"What . . . ?" he began.

"You want to know what this is, Jack? Look over there."

The framed face of the sullen young man wavered on the wall alongside the other posters. The thick bifocals, the defiant sneer, the 'fifties haircut . . .

"That," said Sherman, "is the Bantam Red Head himself. Old Dead Eye, they called him. One of the worst bastards who ever lived. He blew away eleven people before they got him. But they got him good, didn't they? June 25th, 1959, the basement of the Nebraska State Penitentiary. It was painted white. Just for him. Charlie Starkweather. You've heard the name?"

Martin listened to Sherman's flat, expressionless voice as the blood pounded in his ears.

"And this is what they used. That buddy of mine, he let me know when they retired it. Had it shipped out piece by piece, just for me." Sherman patted the high backrest proudly, "Charlie Starkweather's chair. The same one, by God. And now it's mine."

Martin felt himself trapped in a nightmare from which he could not awaken.

"Why?"

Sherman's face split in a tortured smile. "Twenty-two hundred volts, that's why. I had to wire this room special. Still, if I don't turn off these lights, every fuse in the building will blow."

He wagged his head with satisfaction.

"I read everything there is to know about it. First the body turns red, then black. If you leave it on long enough. The brain cooks hard as an egg and the blood burns down to charcoal. Never fails. It never has yet, and they used it twelve times. Fast and clean, you know. It does the job right—takes care of a lot of paying back. In less than sixty seconds."

With a casual motion Sherman turned off the first light.

"But *why?*" said Martin. "Why are you doing this?"

Sherman shuffled to the next light.

"Who knows why anything ends up the way it does, Jack? If I'd never met you. If I'd never met Chris. If I'd never gone to work where I did. A whole lot of ifs. If you hadn't treated her like you did."

He switched off another lamp.

"If you hadn't let me marry her."

Click.

Martin strained against the straps. The leather cut into his wrists.

Click.

"You might say those are the mystery parts, I guess. But I know one thing. I'm going to start living in my own house justified. And that's a fact."

Click.

A growing darkness spread as Sherman spoke from the shrinking, impenetrable depths of the room. Martin was nearly blind, the ghosts of the lamps burned into the backs of his eyes. He arched his body and slammed his head into the backboard. But the straps held.

Sherman hesitated by the last lamp. His silhouette blazed in bas-relief.

Then he reached into a fuse box by the door.

Martin's heart was ready to burst out of his chest.

Sherman lowered his hand. He relaxed and slumped against the white wall. His eyes twinkled out of the shadows.

"Anyway. You get the picture. That's the way it'll happen. When it happens."

He wheezed, his body rocking with compressed laughter.

"See how easy it is? No matter what time of the day or night they come for me, I won't have anything to worry about. Will I, Jack?"

He lumbered back toward Martin.

With a flick of his fingers he released Martin's arms. As

he knelt before the chair and unstrapped the legs, he raised his chalky face.

"Well," he asked, "what did you think of my little demonstration?"

Slowly, very slowly Martin raised himself. Though his legs would not work properly, he dragged himself to the door. He said nothing. There was nothing to say.

One by one Sherman switched the lights back on. The bulbs shivered to life with a faint high-frequency whine.

Martin swung one foot over the threshold behind him, into the waiting blackness of the hallway.

Sherman collapsed wearily into the big chair. It was larger than Martin had realized, made of heavy boards bolted together in a grotesque, inhuman design. The weight of it, the edges and the extreme angles gave it the appearance of a malevolent throne.

Sherman rested easily in it. As if his body had molded itself to the rigid contours, the unyielding angles with years of practice. As if he belonged there.

"Anyway," he said. "It was nice to see you. Jack."

Already his voice was withdrawing, slipping away.

"Stop by again. Anytime. Bring a friend. I don't go out much anymore. Inside, outside. What's the difference? It's all the same. Isn't it."

He sighed, his cracking voice barely audible.

"They should have finished me off," he added, "when they had the chance."

On the wall, close to the door jamb, was the power box. The cover was open, a gleaming switch inside waiting to be thrown. Martin measured its proximity to his hand.

Maybe I'd be doing him a favor, he thought. Maybe I'd be doing us all a favor. I couldn't have known that until I saw. For one shining moment I actually thought that I could forgive him and everything would be right. But now that's asking too much. How can there be forgiveness for the unforgiving? His judgement will have to come from someone stronger than myself.

There was a movement behind him.

"You can do it."

The words were whispered directly into his ear by a voice at least as detached and bloodless as Sherman's.

"You know you can!" she hissed. "You've always hated him. Admit it! It will make you free. It will make us both free. You'll see! It will—"

Her tone was seductive, excessively reasonable. The sound of it was almost cruel. The words were almost kind.

Martin met her eyes.

Her face was no more than an inch away. It glimmered there, half in darkness and half in the synthetic light, a film of excitation giving off an unnatural redolence. Her breath was hot, passionate at last. A rising pulse raced through the vein at her throat.

It was, he decided, a face he no longer knew.

"I—I can't do it myself. I'm not strong enough. But you! You can. You know you can. And then—"

He lurched past her and plunged into total darkness.

As Martin stepped out of the cab, an enclosed boarding ramp pointed the way up to the Queen Mary's foredecks and tiered rooms like a tunnel leading him back into the heart of a sleeping juggernaut.

Despite the hour, the parking lot contained the cars of several hundred late visitors, scattered in irregular rows beneath the mercury vapor security lamps. Surely at least some of the cars belonged to diehard members of the reunion party.

He mounted the ramp and headed for the escalators.

The Windsor Room was deserted, the celebration's tattered paper decorations fluttering in the updraft of an unseen air conditioner. The foyer was still furnished with a makeshift horseshoe of card tables draped in white linen and marked by hand-drawn arrows and directions for registration. On the table labeled "J thru N," a stack of unclaimed name badges reclined among pencils and straight pins, already gathering dust.

A reflection of the bay outside rippled across the ornate ceiling, creating an impression that the entire deck lay submerged beneath the waters of the harbor. At the end of one of the connecting corridors an electric floor polisher whirred on through the night; the sound seemed to be coming from more than one direction at once.

Martin walked through the hall to the damp Promenade Deck, but there was no one in sight.

He turned up his collar and left the area.

He searched long passageways of locked staterooms from which no sound could be heard. An occasional room service tray blocked his path, littered with half-eaten snacks or the remains of party set-ups. Once he saw a cart loaded with dirty glasses and buckets of drained champagne bottles. He hesitated by the door. There was a DO NOT DISTURB warning hung on the knob and no light or movement was detectable within, only the low drone of a fitful snoring.

He moved on.

As he approached the lounge at the end of the ship, he heard the cacophony of cheap disco music overlaid with raucous voices and the chiming of glasses raised in desperate celebration.

He rounded the last corner and stood watching. Inside, men in wrinkle-proof suits and women in stiff gowns and uncomfortable shoes lifted a last round under the patient eyes of a half-dozen weary cocktail waitresses.

He came to the carpeted entrance.

"I'm sorry, sir," said a young woman, "but we've already had last call. The coffee shop is still open if you'd care to—"

"Hey, Macklin!"

"That's fine," said Martin. "It's all right. I'm looking for someone."

"Jim Macklin!" A man with a loose tie tipped his glass from a table by the window.

"Excuse me," Martin told the waitress. "I think I see him now."

He dodged barstools. As he neared the window, a hand from an adjoining table clamped over his wrist.

"Where you goin', Jer?" It was Crabbe, the baseball star. "Take a load off and pull up a chair."

"Thanks, I . . ."

"Bill, I think you've had one too many," said the woman with a beehive hairdo. "This here's Dave McClay. I'd know him anywhere."

The man at the window table leaned close. "Aren't you Jim Macklin? I could've sworn—"

"What are you talking about?" said a man with thinning hair. "I'd know my old friend Marston anywhere! Remember how we used to go toolin' around at night, up by the graveyard where—"

"Hello," said Martin. "I don't mean to intrude on your party."

A waitress appeared carrying the bar tab on a platter.

"What are you drinkin'?" asked Crabbe.

"Sorry, folks, the bar's closed."

"Boo!"

"What time is it? It can't be that—"

"Come up to my room," said the man at the window table. "I got a suite for the weekend. Had to fly all the way from Salt Lake City and—"

"And boy are your arms tired!" said the woman with the beehive hairdo.

They all had a good laugh over that.

On the way out, Martin said to the baseball player, "Do you remember a guy in our class named Sherman?"

"Sherman," said Crabbe. He navigated the barstools uncertainly. "Oh, sure! That jack-off? Everybody on the team hated his guts. Aw, is he here tonight?"

"Not exactly," said Martin.

They arrived at the elevator.

"Let's have a *real* party," said one of the women. She tried to punch the call button and missed.

"Old Sherman," said Crabbe thoughtfully. "Christ, the only party he ever got invited to was on April Fool's Day." He shook his head. "What a dork!"

"Where?" said the woman.

"He couldn't make it tonight," said Martin.

The elevator opened and the others maneuvered to find places inside. Martin took Crabbe's arm and held him aside.

"He wanted to come," said Martin, "but he's got a bit of a problem. At home. You know? I was thinking. You might be able to do something for him. Kind of lend him a hand, so to speak."

"That creep." Crabbe spat on the floor. "I always wanted to kick that son of a bitch's ass around the corner."

"Believe me," said Martin, "I know what you mean."

The elevator door was closing.

"Are you guys coming with us or not?" asked the drunken woman.

"We'll be up later," said Martin, "to celebrate."

"Don't start without me!" yelled Crabbe.

He was too far gone to resist. Martin steered him toward the lobby, measuring his words.

"It's not far," he said. "I stopped by myself a little while ago."

They were coming up on the main exit, the ramp to the parking lot and the profound darkness outside.

"He's just the same as he used to be," Martin was saying, "only worse. If you know what I mean."

They stood together on the doormat and the panels slid away before them onto the waiting night.

"Say, listen, Bill. I really think you might be able to do him a big favor. Not to mention me. And yourself. If you've got a few minutes. I can show you the way."

A line of cabs hovered at the curb.

"I was wondering. Do you feel like driving? Or," suggested Martin, "would it be quicker to take a cab?"

Crabbe regained his footing and weaved forward, allowing Martin to let him continue.

A moment later they were speeding away, red taillights disappearing in the mist, and the fog settled like rain all around where they had been, closing over the lot and the ship and the rest of the world.

NOT FROM AROUND HERE

ON
(Black)
(Sound: Clatter)
10
9
8
7
6 . . .

There was a restless passage of footsteps on the other side of the wall as Joe Ivy peeled off his white gloves and leaned forward over the console—expectantly, even after so long. *They actually pay me for this?* Then he remembered: *They don't, really.* Still. It was worth it, wasn't it? All he needed to make the moment perfect was a tub of popcorn and some Junior Mints. Did they even make Junior Mints anymore?

5
4
3
2
1 . . .

The old tingle started. I hope I never lose that, he thought. Then what would be the point? Without the tingle you might as well lie down and begin clawing the dirt in on top of you.

The first frames steadied in the ground glass: the old UA logo, scratched but unbroken. Could this be the film he'd been looking for? If he could find the scene . . .

The image was nostalgic, warm—and getting warmer. Too warm. Orange and puce with an overlay of magenta.

He groaned.

Well, what else could you expect? It was nearly all Eastman negative film back then, whether they called it Warner or Metro or Pathe or "blazing" or "gorgeous" or "fiery" color: dye-coupled stock, the cheapest way for the studios to go, from the mid-fifties through the sixties and seventies, even most of the way through the eighties. Prints and negatives alike guaranteed to fade before you could see a kid through grade school, and what of it? Color was color, right? That was what they thought.

The clatter of the Moviola seemed to recede as the opening measures of a waltz lilted out of the tiny speaker.

FADE IN:

Robert Mitchum

in . . .

The door opened behind him.

"Joe," said Roger. Joe did not look up. "Guess what the old Jumping Bean's 'gramming for lunch? All the nachos you can stomach for nine ninety-nine! Is that radical? 'Course, if Rose Marie's coming by. . . . What's this one?"

Roger leaned over Joe's shoulder as the title came up.

THE WONDERFUL COUNTRY

"Never heard of it," said Roger.

Joe laughed shortly. "What does that prove? You ought to—"

"How old *is* this flick, anyway?"

"Here comes the copyright. You ought to check—"

Roger squinted into the viewer. " 'M-C-M-L-V-I-X.' That really tells me a lot. Hmm, let's see . . ."

"You ought to check this out, anyway," said Joe. "Hear that score? It's by Alex North."

"Who?"

"Ask Tom and Denny," Joe snapped. "They're selling a used copy of the soundtrack album. For six hundred dollars."

Give the guy a break, Joe reminded himself. He's your friend. More than that. Without him you wouldn't be able to do any of this, and we'd all be stuck sucking the Big Tube night and day. And then you'd never find your precious scene. You'd have to give it up. Anyway. Not everybody grew up in a movie theater. Maybe he's better off, who knows?

Joe kicked back from the machine, eased his neck muscles. "I was seventeen when I saw it. Drove my Ford Fairlane down to Long Beach, caught it on a triple bill at the old Art Theater. Remember the Art, Rog? It was on Cherry, I think, just south of—"

"Looks older," said Roger with the authority of the casually informed. "What'd they shoot it on, infrared film?"

"Yeah, well, I have to take what I can get. It's from another private collection. Where else? This one's seen some heat and humidity, all right. But it's the only thirty-five millimeter I can find. For Larry's Mitchum festival."

"Don't tell me. It was Yaeger. You got this one from Yaeger, didn't you? The guy who stores his prints in the back of a laundromat?"

"Actually it's his mother's garage in the Valley."

"Uh, maybe you should tell him about refrigeration."

"He'd have to rent a meat locker. You see the size of these cans? His 'comb's full. He sleeps in his car." God help him, thought Joe. And God bless him.

"Can you do anything with it?"

"I've seen worse," said Joe bravely. "Remember *Johnny Guitar*? Or *An Affair to Remember*, with Cary Grant and—?"

"No."

Joe sighed. "Well, it's the same process. Tape transfer, computer enhancement."

"What's left to enhance?"

"I can restore it if the emulsion's intact. Then UCLA runs off a 'gram from our tape, same as always, charges it to the copyright owner—MGM now; I looked it up. They'll pay for the thirty-five printback, too, as long as they get to keep it. There's an AFI tribute to Mitchum coming up, which ought to make it worth something. Anyway, Larry should have it in plenty of time for his festival."

Roger smiled down indulgently at his partner. "Guess what? We're out of blank tape."

"Then open a factory cassette. One of those Betas that never sold. *A Chorus Line, Thirty Years of the Tonight Show,* Stallone in *Streetcar*—you know, dust collectors. I'll erase it and—"

"Then we won't be able to return it for credit."

"Screw the credit."

"It takes money to run a business," said Roger slowly, as if explaining to a child. "It takes inventory on the shelves to generate cashflow, to balance our expenses, Joey, our *hobbies.* You understand that, do you?"

Joe swiveled his chair around. The film continued to clatter through the Moviola, Alex North's theme to *The Wonderful Country* continued to lilt sweetly out of the speaker at his back, violins trilling through the distortion like drowning canaries.

"Do *you* understand, Roger? This is not anybody's God damned hobby. Let's not even talk art. Let's talk money. You want to talk money? I have a deal with the Twenty-in-One. *We* have a deal. We split fifty cents on every dollar that comes through the boxoffice, after they make back their nut. No distributor fees to pay, as long as it's a one-shot and the studio gets back a new print. That means—"

He cut himself off. He listened to what he was spouting; it grabbed him by the short hairs.

So this is how it started for Mayer and Cohn, he thought, for Jack Warner and Adolph Zukor and Dino De Laurentiis. Once upon a time they were probably in love with movies, too, with the way it feels to be part of a light show seance in an auditorium full of buttered popcorn dreamers. Until the day somebody gave them a long, cold look at the ledger. A wave of self-loathing passed through him. He shook his head and shuddered.

He shut off the film transport. The strings wound down and died on an extended chord. Let it go, he thought, as the sound of footsteps began again on the other side of the wall.

"Sorry," he said.

"Forget it," said Roger, vaguely embarrassed. "We've had this conversation before. I know what you're saying. Don't worry about it." Roger stopped in the doorway. "Anyhow, let me know about lunch. This might be a good time. There's nobody up front. But," he added gently, "it'll pick up this afternoon. You'll see." He winked.

With great care he closed the door behind him.

My God, thought Joe. The way he respects something that doesn't even matter to him personally; if that isn't a virtue I don't know what is.

He deserves better from this business. He's put a hell of a lot more into the Video Pit than I have. I'm pulling him down—pulling us both down. But my part of it will pay off, I swear it will. I'll put in more hours, find some killer prints nobody's seen in forty years, not even on TV. There have got to be enough people who care out there to support what I'm doing. It's just a matter of reaching them.

"Yeah," he said to the closed door. His face was burning and his neck throbbing. "We'll see."

He turned back to the bench and touched the power switch that would shut down the entire mechanism.

The projection gate was frozen on a single frame of film: a medium close-up of a woman with red hair. That would be Julie London. She was a kind of predecessor, he realized, to the great award-winning actress Annette O'Toole. Beautiful, he thought. Not the scene he had hoped to find, but a nice one in its own right.

He could not remember much about Julie London's acting; all that remained of her in his memory was a sequence of strong two-shots against a richly-saturated Western sky, her hair swept away from her white forehead as she lowered her eyes from a laconic Mitchum. Beautiful, and a face worth preserving. If he didn't, who would? Chances were none of her other films, a small, undistinguished handful, had been deemed worth saving by any collector. Look at that face, he thought, even as her hair appeared to fade into the muddy film base, more like an old dog's now than a woman's. Who cares? he thought wretchedly. *Color is color, right?*

He sat there with his finger on the switch, imagining the money boys, ex-agents and accountants and conglomerate sharks in three-piece suits, hustling figures like pimps. How much had they thought they were saving in the long run by using cheap film stock? Twenty thousand a picture? Thirty? One percent of the budget; less than that.

The long run. How long? A few weeks? A few months at most? Then burn the prints. Save one or two to work from, to copy in sixteen millimeter for TV or onto tape and discs, if they even thought of video then. Then burn the negative. What's the point of preserving it, with the silver in the film worth a hundred bucks an ounce or whatever it was worth back then? After all, who would ever want another theatre print? Let's be realistic. What's the future of movie houses? He could hear their cynical voices. Old wave, new wave, cinema noir or cinema verite, the handwriting on the wallpaper or the shadow in the corner, it was all the same now: video graffiti. A pitiless joke plyed on us while we were sleeping off the last few years, like those plastic hubcaps on the new Mini Mercedes he had seen cruising the Mall this morning. Too damned late, and what of it? And so on. In this way he allowed himself to slip deeper and deeper into introspection—until he remembered Rose Marie.

What had Roger said? That she was coming here? He knows more than I do, Joe thought. She could have called the store and I was busy. Or she said something about it over breakfast, and I forgot. It's possible. I've been working so many hours . . .

He reached for the phone, punched his home number.

After ten rings he gave up. Not home. She forgot. Or I

forgot—same thing. Or she's on her way here to meet me. That must be it.

"Roger?" he yelled.

As he stood, the frame he had stopped in the film gate warped, crinkled like cellophane and burned through.

This, he thought, is impossible. It had never happened before. In fact, the machine was designed specifically to prevent just such an occurrence.

"Shit," he observed.

He killed the power and wound back the reel by hand. Now he would have to splice it before making his video copy. There were probably other breaks in the film already, it seemed so dry and brittle. Well, it's only a frame. But what a frame. Probably the best close-up in the whole picture.

Roger knocked softly before entering.

Joe removed the film from the head and made the cut at once, while it was on his mind. The frame dropped out cleanly. He had caught it in time. One lousy frame. "Did Rose call?"

"When, today? I don't think so. Why?"

"I thought you said she was coming by for lunch."

"You know better than I would," said Roger. "Give her a call."

"She hasn't come by the store in six months."

"She doesn't like me," said Roger. "I knew it. Wives never like their husbands' friends. It's a principle."

"Bullshit," said Joe.

"Maybe you should call her anyway. Does she like nachos? We can smuggle her a plate on the same check."

"I already called. She's not home."

"Oh."

Joe dropped the melted frame of film onto the bench. It rocked there in the draft from the open door, crisp as a burnt tortilla chip. "Anyway. It's about time for you and me to lay down a liter of Margaritas." Joe wiped his hands and headed into the store. "Say good-by to Julie, Roger."

"Who? Oh, I get it. Is that her name? Okay. Good-by, Julie."

They walked through the store. Roger got his keys and made for the glass doors, where outside hundreds of overexposed, pastel shoppers milled about like extras on their way to or from their honeycomb apartments, endless as the constant procession of footsteps on the other side of the thin walls, wandering in and out of every shop but this one.

Joe passed racks of videocassettes. One whole wall was the Universal-MCA library, on sale. *Pillow Talk, Thoroughly Modern Millie, Lover Come Back, Earthquake, Airport* et al., *Space Shuttle '90, Space Shuttle '91*, etc.

He touched *Pillow Talk.* It had gathered a layer of dust you could spread with a butter knife.

"Take it easy, Doris," he said. "Try to be good while we're gone."

"Who?"

"Doris Day. If you can't be good, be bad."

Roger turned the sign around in the window. "Well, don't forget Mary Tyler Moore while you're at it," he said, playing along. "Ever since that nude scene in *The Rosy Crucifixion* . . ."

"Good-by, Mary," said Joe. "*Auf Wiedersehen.*"

"And how about Sylvia Kristel in, what was it, *Airport '79*? I hope she can score some business while we're out."

"Good-by, Sylvia." Joe lingered over the tapes, cutting dust with his finger. "Good-by, Victoria Principal in *Earthquake*. Stay away from that Marjoe what's-his-name. He's no good."

"Victoria Principal," said Roger nostalgically. "She was definitely not from around here."

"And good-by, Jean Simmons in *Spartacus*," Joe said, "the bathing scene . . ."

"Was she in that? I remember Laurence Olivier. . . ."

"Fuck Laurence Olivier. Good-by, Julie Andrews in *Torn Curtain*, under the sheets with Paul Newman!"

"Hitchcock, eh? I remember Hitchcock. Well then, good-by, Tippi Hedren!"

"In *The Birds*? Aw, man, what about Suzanne Pleshette?"

"I was thinking *Marnie*. The honeymoon. I saw that one."

"You got it. Good-by, Marnie."

"Good-by, Raquel Welch in, let's see, how about *Indira*?"

"That was Zoetrope. I'm only up to Universal."

"So?"

"All right, good-by, Teri Garr in *One From the Heart*! Good-by, Nastassia Kinski in *Unfaithfully Yours*! Good-by Patti Hanson—and Dorothy Stratton—in *They All Laughed*! Good-by, Genie Francis in *General Emergency*! Good-by, Goldie Hawn in *So Cute, So Dead*! Good-by, Lisa Marie Presley in *The Priscilla Presley Story*! Good-by to all of you! Good-by—"

Roger opened his mouth wide and let out a monstrous belch. "Good-by, stomach and intestines," he said, grinning dopily, "if we don't get over to the Jumping Bean pronto!"

"Let's go."

They hit the sidewalk in front and started around the fountain to the Mexican restaurant.

"Hold up," said Joe. "I want to check the 'gram next door."

"What for?" Roger shaded his eyes in the bright white sun and considered Joe nervously. All around them impatient shoppers elbowed past, loaded down with VisaMall purchases. "You don't take that stuff seriously, do you?"

A teenage couple whizzed past, jerking to the beat of taped music from their shuttle shoes. The beat faded with them as they zigzagged away through the crowd, to be replaced by the piped-in dreck of middle-aged golden oldie seventies disco Muzak. "It's not that I take it seriously," said Joe. "It's just that—never mind." He backtracked to the Indects, Inc. storefront next door.

Today's message shimmered in the air in front of the window: another selected quotation from the pages of THE WAY OF THE WACH, copies of which were, of course, available inside. Joe centered his head to read it.

At that moment a careless pedestrian bumped into him, shoving Joe into the display so that the message field blurred around him. Joe regained his balance and pulled out of it as a precocious, ectomorphic boy wearing collector's item antique horn-rimmed glasses, his face buried in a printout, stepped around him and through the hologram.

" 'Scuse me," muttered the boy without raising his eyes. He was reading the July issue of a science fiction magazine, MECHANICAL ADVENTURES. He was in a hurry. Obviously an intellectual, thought Joe; you don't see many of those around here.

"All right, all right, what's the word for the day?" Roger positioned himself reluctantly next to Joe. With unconcealed derision he read, " 'Today is the . . .' "

"It's not that I believe it," said Joe. "But I got in the habit of checking it out every morning, on the way in, you know? Don't you do that?"

"Waste of time," said Roger. "Like horoscopes, biorhythms, cookies with fortunes inside. They're selling fancy answers to people who can't eat it plain. Look what this one says. If that isn't—"

"I know. But have you ever noticed how it's always right? I mean, whatever it says each day seems to fit."

"It's an illusion, Joe, a projection. Let's get gone."

As far as he could see in either direction, the merchants of Mile Long Mall offered up the usual holograms of their wares. Within this window, a waiting room half-full of weary and curious shoppers reclined, their eyes lost in the oversized pages of Indects' own recruitment text, THE WAY OF THE WACH. A chance to rest your feet for free. At least they don't buttonhole you on the sidewalk and argue you to death like the Scientologists and cult evangelists. It's more like a Christian Science Reading Room, very low-key. Which is, I suppose, the way it should be—the Way of the Wach, whatever that is.

Before he left he got a good look at the day's message. It read: "TODAY YOU ARE ONE DAY CLOSER TO YOUR MEANINGLESS IMPENDING DEATH."

"Very nice," said Joe dubiously. A tremor passed between his shoulder blades. "I never noticed anything like *that* before. Wonder what it means?"

"Take my advice," said Roger. "Don't ask."

"Why not? *You* don't take that stuff seriously, do you?"

"I don't like the way some of them look when they come out of there. Their eyes are, well . . ."

"What?"

"It's bad for business, right next door."

"You never know," said Joe. "Nothing sells like disaster movies, for instance."

"What are you talking about?" Roger's face was incomprehending. He gave up trying to understand his friend and looked ahead. "You're living in the past. Irwin Allen is dead. Come on. We need to lay up and talk."

"About what?"

"Nothing. Come on."

They threaded a path through the noontime foot traffic.

There was Larry, gawking from the entrance to the Tiffany Twenty-in-One. He was standing beneath the marquee that advertised this week's fare. Theaters One and Two were showing *Monkeyshine Memories* with Sondra Locke, and a new Paul Schrader melodrama, *You Can't Hide;* Three and Four a pair of horror films, Wes Craven's execrable *Don't Make Me Hurt You*, and David Cronenberg's *They*. Five and Six had foreign films for the wine-and-tofu set—Bresson's uncompleted *The Good Thief*, and Tavernier's *The Running of Beasts*. Seven had Peter Fonda's *They Couldn't Believe Their Eyes*, Eight another crowd-pleaser, Stephen King's comedy, *The Hoagy Man*. Nine through Twenty were presently empty, having been recently recombined to accommodate the anticipated larger crowds for the next revival booking, which would be the ten-day Mitchum festival. Kicking off, Joe thought proudly, with *The Wonderful Country* and *Fire Down Below*, which he had finished restoring just last week. It was exciting. He waved.

"Hi, Lare!"

But Larry ignored him, gazing over his head to the

parking lot. Joe crossed and sidled up under the awning of Moony Cob's Outback Smoking Shop.

"Something's going on out there." Larry strained his eyes. "Commotion, people yelling. Then some guy went tearing off like he had a rocket up his ass."

Roger joined them. "Must be that kid again."

"What kid?" said Joe.

"You know, the kid. He's always hanging around the crash-pad. I see him from a distance when I drive in. Never could figure what he was up to."

"Looked like he was ripping somebody off," Larry said, "the way he was shuttling ass."

"The shops, you mean?" asked Joe. "How would he get past the security tapes?"

"Cars," said Roger. "Don't ever leave your keys in the ignition."

"What would be the point?" said Joe. "He couldn't drive them out without the right Visa. If the card he sticks in the slot doesn't match, the gate won't open."

"I don't think it was a car," said Larry.

"Stuff *in* the cars, then," said Roger.

"Why would he be hanging around the crash-pad, in that case?" said Joe. "It won't take anything but automotive material. So he couldn't even be ripping off what people leave in their cars and selling it for scrap. Hell, that wouldn't be worth the effort, unless he's really desperate; the compactor doesn't pay jack shit. If it would take it, which it won't. It won't even take metal shopping carts. The Mall got wise to that little scam the first year, and GM reprogrammed the sensors."

"So he carries stuff out on foot," said Larry.

"I don't see how. Not with the COPters. Not if he's done it before. They would have caught him by now."

Roger was right. Already a whirling COPter had appeared in the bleached summer sky over the mirage of parking spaces. As they watched, an LAPD officer touched down on the blacktop, lowered his arm and began folding the spinning blades back into the handle of his nightstick.

Baton, thought Joe. That's what they call them on TV, on *T.H.U.G.S.*

"He's had," said Larry.

"I can't believe I never saw him," said Joe.

"I can," said Roger. "You're always holed-up in back, playing with—working on your films."

"Speaking of which . . ." began Larry.

"You'll have it by the nineteenth," said Joe, "don't worry."

"I'm not worried about that. But I've been meaning to talk to you. You know, the gate wasn't up to par the last time, for the horror festival."

"You're telling me?" said Roger. "I put our cut in the bank. The autoteller flagged the account, the amount was so small. Something about a minimum balance or they cancel our VisaMall credit. Anyhow. We gotta go."

"It was the subject matter," suggested Joe. "I should have known that. But I honestly thought that there were enough people out there—"

"It's not your fault. I went along with it. But, shit, I just made the same mistake again with new product! Now I'm going to have to pull Three and Four before the week's up, guarantee or no guarantee, Golan's losing a bundle everywhere. You'd think they'd get it—you'd think *I'd* get it. That kind of picture's about as appealing anymore as dead babies on a stick. People want to see—"

"Right," said Roger. "Larry, we'll catch you on the way back."

"I would have booked *They*," said Joe.

"I know you would," said Roger.

"Who wouldn't?" said Larry. "After the Academy Awards—"

"Later," said Roger. "Lunch is only till one."

They left Larry babbling about the fickleness of the public, the unwillingness of people to leave their 'combs at night, even for a movie—especially for a movie—and so on in that vein. The last they saw of him he was climbing a stepladder to change the marquee, his head still wagging, as if trying to talk himself out of jumping.

Joe wished him luck. If he goes under, where does that leave the rest of us? The next nearest revival house was all the way out by MacArthur Park; word had it that that one was about to be subdivided into a Spanish-language multiple. Is it really so futile? wondered Joe. Do people forget so fast—*all* the people, everywhere in the greater L.A. basin and, one might infer, since this is the number one film market in the U.S., the whole plugged-in country? And on and on. Lately there was no end for him to this kind of thinking.

They turned in at the plate of steaming nachos, between Vitamin City and The Rubber Bisquit. You could almost smell the aroma. Roger passed his hand through the 'gram, winked and pantomimed sniffing his fingers. Joe's gut did a belly flop with a half gainer twist, righted itself and bobbed along on a tide of nausea. It was the processed cheese they used, he decided. It looked pale and stringy, like . . . what?

The Jumping Bean's lounge was dark. The waitresses wore imitation space stewardess uniforms and Aztec headbands which glittered in the strobing of a TV screen above the bar, between black velvet paintings of South American Indians in full feathered regalia. The Indians were pictured pointing solemnly toward what was supposed to be the Enterprise taking off or landing, one or the other, over Lake Titicaca. Roger led the way to a table in front, next to a window that faced the fountain.

Joe noticed the silhouette of a woman who was just now entering Indects, Inc. across the way. She was wearing the identical yellow silk blouse he had bought Rose Marie for her birthday. Probably got it at The Body Shot around the corner, he thought, same as I did. Seeing the woman, he felt his taste confirmed.

"I'm worried," said Roger, sliding over tuck-and-roll leatherette.

"So am I. The horror festival just wasn't fashionable. In fact it was distinctly unfashionable—that's the point. I understand now. People want to see what they can talk about at cocktail parties. It's that simple. And horror doesn't make for amusing conversation, apparently. Even if they're drinking Bloody Marys."

"Two Bloody Marys?" said their stewardess-waitress.

"No, no," said Roger. "Pitcher of Margaritas, two glasses. And two Specials. You serve food here in the bar, do you?"

"Yes, sir."

"As I was saying," Joe continued. "Not even Cronenberg's Oscar for *Cities of the Red Night* was enough to draw them in. They'd rather see more of the same. The triangular family, 'comb cohab, the ninety percent divorce rate, the Kiddie Lib Amendment—you know, stuff they can relate to without straining their imaginations. In other words, stories about themselves."

"That's not what worries me."

"Well, it should. It's as if they're all part of some big, incestuous family, connected by cable so they can talk to each other about their own lives. Why should they want anything different in the theatres? Even as damned few of those as there are now. That's what I'm telling you! Maybe I've been wrong all along. Maybe there's no market for revivals of *any* kind. You've been letting me kid myself. So I'll never find that so-called famous scene I've been looking for for ten years, which is probably the real reason I've been doing this for so long. Maybe I'm not supposed to find it. I appreciate it, man, but it's a dream. There's no—"

"Listen to me."

Roger reached across the table and gripped Joe's arm. At the same time the waitress reappeared and slipped two huge platters under their sleeves, effectively cutting Joe off.

"Careful, fellas. Hot plates."

Roger locked eyes with Joe as she poured the first two drinks from the carafe. When he finally took his arm away, there was melted cheese on his cuff. It stretched out in a strand from the flour tortillas, which were mashed flat and grilled, about as Mexican as matzos. Like . . . something, thought Joe, and ground his teeth together, chewing salt.

"You can do it. If not with Larry, then try some other theaters. We have enough money to keep going. It's not as bad as you think. But Joe." Roger glanced out the window again, toward the shop. "You've been working too hard. I think you should take some time off. In fact, why don't you start this afternoon? Besides, you—you ought to spend more time with Rose Marie."

"You're crazy."

"I can handle the store. What's to handle? They come in, pick out their tapes, I ring it up. Big deal."

"I can't. I'm obligated to get the print ready. And then I'd better rethink this whole arrangement. Because if all I'm doing is throwing good money after bad . . ."

"You never get to see her anymore, isn't that true? Admit it. You need time together, time to—"

"Why do you keep saying that?"

Roger glanced outside one more time and then lowered his eyes, as if about to perform an unpleasant duty. There was a beat of silence between them. Across the bar, someone slugged a dollar into the jukebox and Blind Boy Ruff's recording of "The Incoherent Blues" began to throb out of hidden speakers. Roger bit into a nacho, put it aside. He cleared his palate with drink. He blinked coolly across the table at his friend. "It's none of my business. But why the hell did you let her start going there in the first place?"

"Who? Where?"

"I've heard stories. After that *Sixty Minutes* piece last weekend . . ." Roger's face fell. "Don't tell me you didn't watch it."

"I was working till midnight, you know that."

"Christ." Roger's lips tightened. "They sent a video crew in there with Connie Chung last month. I guess you didn't notice. I didn't want to say anything at the time. But now—you better talk to her."

"Talk to Rose?"

"It's not all sweetness-and-light and Jesus washing away

your sins, according to Connie Chung. It's king-sized elephant shit. 'Today is the first day of your newborn independent life.' What in the holy hell does that mean?"

"You mean the quote in the Indects window? That's not what it said. It said—"

"I read it. I was standing right next to you." A peculiar reflection of fear and concern appeared in Roger's eyes. Joe had never seen it there before. It was kind, almost patronizing. "Never mind. It doesn't matter. What matters is that she's throwing your money away. You can't have that much left on your card. At least you should be worried about that. It's none of my business but . . ."

"You're right. It's not."

Roger fell silent and plunged into his nachos.

On the television screen above the bar a promo flashed for the next NBC Big Event, Melissa Gilbert starring in *Shelley Winters: A Life*, to be followed by the premiere of something called *Lee Vaunce and the Smoker* with Gary Coleman and Redd Foxx. Momentarily distracted, Joe wondered whether both would be over by the time he finished up tonight. He hoped so.

"God damn it, Rog, I don't have any idea what you're talking about." Was Roger saying that Rose had joined Indects? That she'd been going there, right next door, without even bothering to say hello? "You expect me to believe that? You think I don't know my own wife after fifteen years?"

Joe threw his nacho down.

It was why Roger had thought she might be stopping by for lunch; Roger thought Joe already knew. It could be the reason for the new chill, the way she kept her distance at home now. Whenever he did manage to see her. A long time since they had talked. She was usually asleep by the time he got back, still in bed when he left in the mornings. Because of his work. It fit.

He couldn't eat. He rolled cheese off his fingers with distaste. Like an afterbirth, that was it, he thought morbidly. He finished his drink and poured another.

"I wouldn't have brought it up," said Roger. "Except that you're my friend."

Roger averted his eyes. Outside, the boy with the horn-rimmed glasses passed. Joe continued to dispose of Margaritas. Roger did not stop him.

"I better get back," said Roger finally.

"I'll take care of it," said Joe.

Roger took out his VisaMall card.

Joe held his palms up and shook his head stubbornly until Roger took the card back. "Did you hear what I said? I said I'll take care of it."

He waited until Roger had gone. Then he got up and went to the pay phone. He put in his card and punched his home number. A song called "Running In Darkness" was playing on the jukebox. It was loud. He almost couldn't hear. But there was definitely no answer. He returned to his seat and stared out at Indects, Inc. as Roger crossed and reopened the store.

Someone came into the bar and started a mild argument with a waitress. Joe did not look up. Outside, a bell of spray from the fountain began to blur his view of the reading room. The Margaritas were doing their job.

"Check the card," said a thin, intelligent voice.

"I don't need to check your card," said the waitress. "You were in here this morning. You don't have enough credit for a book of matches."

"Check it again. There's credit on it now."

The waitress inserted a card into the register. "Nine dollars and some change," she read sarcastically. "Am I supposed to be impressed? What are you gonna get in here for nine bucks?"

Joe realized he had nearly a whole plate of untouched nachos in front of him. He glanced up. It was the boy with horn-rimmed glasses, and he looked hungry.

"It's all right," Joe said to the waitress. "He's with me."

"Suit yourself," she said.

"I can't eat any of these," said Joe, pushing his plate across the table. "You're welcome to them."

The boy shrugged and slid into the booth, flopping his copy of MECHANICAL ADVENTURES onto the tabletop, cover up. The lead story was entitled *Escape From Uranus*.

"I have to get back to work in a minute, anyway."

"Me, too." The boy reached for the salt shaker and dug in.

"You like machines, huh?" said Joe. "Computer technology, things like that?"

The boy made a noncommittal gesture. "What else is there?"

"I don't know about that."

"Well, I do," said the boy, chewing thoughtfully. "You have to. To survive."

"I'll have to think about that one. My name's Joe Ivy, by the way." Joe extended his hand but the boy had a fistful of grease and cheese. "That's my shop over there, the one—"

"I know. I saw you in front of the reading room."

On impulse, Joe played a wild card. "Ever been in there?"

"Sure."

Joe caught the waitress's eye. "Refill here," he called, positioning the plate between them.

"And a machaca burrito," added the boy. To Joe he said, "Don't worry. I have credit."

"What exactly do you know about the reading room? How it works, what they do in there? It's for my wife. She's been asking me to find out."

The boy studied him, swallowing.

"I guess I could stop in and ask them myself." If you won't tell me, he thought. Snot-nosed bastard.

"They don't tell you much. But I figured out how it works."

Joe waited. His teeth were aching. "It's a self-improvement course, is it? Some new kind of religion?"

"It's whatever you want it to be."

"How do you mean?"

"It's the books."

"THE WAY OF THE WACH? I should pick up a copy. You've read it?"

"They won't let you take it. You have to read it there."

"Why?"

"Because. They don't want you to grok how it works. I know, though. The secret's in the pages. They're plastic—that's why they're so big. Each page is two sheets laminated together, with ink in the middle. Only it's not ink. It's a colloid of telepathic bacteria of extra-terrestrial origin, brought back from orbit by the Enterprise II in '93. They like to say the message of the Way was discovered by their founder, Mason Flowers, on his private space probe, but that's part of the hustle. Crusty Havoline wrote it up in his MECH AD Science Fact Column. I guess they figure we're too dumb to make the connection. It wasn't on TV. Not even Connie Chung knew about it. But I bet Flowers has an in with NASA. He got a few cc.'s from somebody on the Enterprise, and now he grows his own in the Indects labs. It's easy. All you need is a biologically neutral culture medium . . ."

"Excuse me," said Joe, "but are you out of your mind? I hope you don't mind my asking."

The waitress brought a new platter of nachos and a machaca burrito. The burrito had obviously been microwaved; the outer layer of tortilla was dry and flaking—not very appetizing. But the boy accepted his lot, spooned on salsa and inserted one end of it into his mouth.

"I got credit on my card, didn't I?" he said around squirting bites. "You tell me how I did that if I'm crazy."

That was a point, Joe supposed, albeit a stupefyingly tenuous one. Or was it? Across the Mall, an elderly woman in a mock-Enterprise jumpsuit shuffled into the Indects, Inc. storefront. Keeping up with the times, he thought, such as they are. Even on her last legs. He wished he were outside so he could hold the door for her.

"How much do they charge for—for this self-improvement course?"

"That I couldn't tell you. But it doesn't come cheap."

"That part I can believe."

As the jukebox began playing "I Love You, Honey, But the Season's Over," Joe found the waitress, let her deduct the meals from his card and left.

He waited outside by the fountain.

More people came and went through the door to the reading room. No one he recognized.

He realized that Roger could see him clearly from inside the Pit. It would be easy to tell Roger that he'd decided to take his advice, but like pulling teeth to give him the satisfaction. He backed off casually, checking his watch as if on a last-minute errand, and made his way to the edge of the parking lot.

It took him a few minutes to spot Rose Marie's car.

As he neared it, heat waves from the summer sun glanced off the yellow selenium top and rose skyward, distorting the surrounding cars and the buildings in the distance so that the stamping machines on the skyline, unmanned while their crews took time off for lunch, appeared to waver and begin to melt over the newest row of unfinished honeycombs.

He came up to the car, which was his car as well, and was aware of an unaccountable but overwhelming feeling: as if one of his best friends, someone he loved, perhaps, had taken from him something unique and irreplaceably valuable. The trouble was, he couldn't remember precisely what it was. So he knew that whoever it was would be unlikely to admit it. This feeling grew as he stepped close enough to touch the burning metal, to see the familiar upholstery and objects on the other side of the rolled-up windows, the souvenirs and residue of the years they had used and driven and maintained it together as a part of their lives. A great sadness passed through his chest then like an unexpected wind from somewhere out on the edges of the world or of space. He felt ridiculous; he did not know why; and he was not sure what to do about it.

Suddenly he heard a clanking sound.

It was too soon for the stamping machines to restart their relentless building work. From morning till night he could not escape their booming and grinding rhythm, not even in the back room of the shop, except during the early afternoon break. It was still early afternoon, wasn't it?

He took a few steps and peered into the next aisle of cars.

And saw the boy, he of the science fiction magazine and horn-rimmed glasses, crouched behind an 89 Toyota Corolla Shuttleback. Next to him, in the shade of the car, was a stack of silver saucers. They were, he noted as he drew closer, not exactly silver saucers. They were hubcaps.

As he watched, the young man pried off the Toyota's right rear hubcap and piled it with the others.

Joe hid behind the yellow car and followed the boy's movements through the dirty safety glass of the windshield. He saw him lift an armload and hurry away through the rows, routinely checking each car he passed and rejecting the smaller baby moons and snap-on wire wheel covers as if they were too much trouble to bother with. Then, in the clear, he hunched over and duck-walked quickly to the gate. To the crash-pad.

Joe trailed him, staying out of sight.

No car was entering the gate just now, so it was easy. Drop the hubcaps on the compactor scale. Insert your card, tucked away in your back pocket with the July issue of MECH AD. Wait a few seconds for the machine to ring up your credit based on today's price for automotive alloy. No need to establish vehicle ownership, since so light a weight obviously doesn't involve an engine block—it could as easily be a creased fender, a dented hood; hence no serial number to match. Withdraw the card, pocket it, smile with satisfaction as the compactor does its job, and move on. That's all there is to it.

Joe was astounded. It was so brilliantly simple. The crash-pads, mostly located along freeways and busy city routes, were provided for instant disposal of wrecked or disabled cars. With the growing traffic in and out of Mile Long Mall, one had naturally been installed here for the convenience of shoppers. There was even a new car dealership, Mies Fiodur's Mini-Track City, located at the South

Lot exit. Joe knew him. In fact, it was where he had purchased Rose's car. The dealer was prepared to give on-the-spot trade-in credit against a replacement, minus a cartage fee for towing to the nearest compactor, if the customer hadn't made it that far. But surely no one at GM had anticipated the uses to which their recycling machines could be put, given a little resourcefulness. Leave it to the kids, he thought. They always find a way.

Joe tipped an invisible hat to the boy, saluting him, and started back.

Well, bless his mercenary heart, he thought. The Kid. He's found a way to beat them at their own game. I wonder what he does the rest of the day, after boosting enough credit to scrape by, just enough to pay for his beloved science fiction printouts and something to eat? Dealing directly with the public with no middleman involved. He's licking the game on its own terms. There is a way, after all, to turn the system back on itself, to make it feed off itself and pay out the right to survive for another day in spite of its demands. True symbiosis between man and machine, or something like it; close enough so that the difference is academic. If only I had that much energy and ingenuity.

When he got back to Rose's car, the hubcaps were missing. Of course.

He threw back his head to laugh.

The woman he had seen earlier, the one in the yellow silk blouse, was walking this way. With the sun at such an angle, he had trouble getting a clear look at her. It was like a certain flaring, backlighted shot he had seen in a movie once. She reminded him of . . .

It was Rose Marie.

He ran to meet her. "Hey, Rosie! Hi, honey. I saw your car. What're you . . . ?"

His relief was short-lived. She walked right past him, holding tight to her purse.

"Honey?"

She blinked fast and bore down on the car, taking those

fast, short steps that always threatened to topple her from her heels if she wasn't careful.

"Are you pissed off at me or something?"

Rose Marie fumbled with her keys, missing the lock and scratching the paint on the door. Oh, well. She was shaking, actually shaking.

"What is it?" He rushed up and reached out to help her. "Here. Let me."

"Keep your hands off!"

He backed away, shocked.

"Rose? Don't you know me? Who do you think I am, sweetheart? Rosie?"

"I most certainly *don't* know who you are. And if you don't get away from here fast, buddy, I'm going to start screaming!"

There was a wild look in her eyes. Like a trapped animal willing to do anything, including biting off a part of itself, to escape. He considered. Either she's about to crack. Or it's the best act she's ever put on, bar none.

I better not come any closer, he thought. She's on the edge, about to flip out. I've seen it before. But not like this.

Calm her down first. Find out what's wrong. One step at a time.

"Rose, I'm sorry. Whatever it is, I'm sorry. Now let's talk this out. You tell me what it is and I'll try to make it right. I guess it's my fault. It *is* my fault, okay? We don't even have to talk here. I was about to take the afternoon off. Honestly. We can talk at home. I'll drive. Or you can drive. I don't care. But whatever it is—"

"Help!"

"What are you doing? Rose, honey, I didn't mean it, whatever it was! I love you. I'd never do anything to hurt you. I—"

She turned on him, her lips trembling and her teeth bared, suddenly become like some kind of jungle wild woman. "If you don't keep away from me, mister, I'll—I'll call—"

"Call who? Your husband?" He tried a placating grin,

but it had no effect. "I *am* your husband, for God's sake!"

"I," she said, spitting syllables, "do not have any husband. I am not married now, nor have I ever been. And if I were, it certainly would not be to you! Now I'm going to get in my car and drive straight to the gate. I don't know what you want, fella, but if you try anything funny I'll honk my horn so hard and so loud that every COPter in this neighborhood will be on you faster—faster than—" She groped for a simile, red-faced.

Dumbfounded he stood aside and let her open the car door, close it, lock it, start the engine, pop into reverse and shoot back. She braked with a screech one inch from the taillight of a new Datsun Tapir. He closed his eyes. They were expensive assemblies, at least seven or eight hundred to replace. Apiece.

She rolled down her window.

"And you better give me back my hubcaps, fuckface, or I'll have you busted for theft! Didn't think I noticed, did you? I know your type! Creep!"

She flashed her eyes at him in the blazing sun, a spark of contemptuous pity shining there. An instant. Then she roared off.

His eyes stinging in a cloud of exhaust, he felt his legs carrying him slowly backwards into the empty parking space, withdrawing by inches between the narrow boundary lines etched like scrimshaw on the melting pavement. He was, in his way and as best he could, trying to understand.

He sat in The Video Pit, his head in his hands.

It was now early evening. The telephone was still before him. Was there any point to trying one more time?

She had meant business out in the lot. Before he slipped away, COPters came down out of the sky to surround her car and its blinking emergency signal. They found the boy almost at once, only to release him when they brought him to her for identification. From Joe's vantage point she was so small, even the violent shaking of her head and the pointing of her slender arm, like a bit player in a second unit long shot. They found nothing to incriminate the boy, of course. His steals had already been eaten by the machine, the same machine that would later extrude them re-formed as factory replacement parts, or perhaps an entire new car to be offered for sale in a GM showroom somewhere. Had the boy been arrested, he would have stepped forward. But now Joe had only Rose to deal with, and himself.

He knew this call would be like the others. Still, what else was there to do? If he drove home in his own car, she wouldn't let him in. If he forced his way in, she would scream bloody murder and call the police. He didn't want to face that.

He reached for the phone. Punched his number. Counted the rings, waiting for her to answer.

There was a clattering in the receiver as she picked it up.

ROSE: Hello?

JOE: Please don't hang up. I'm not harrassing you. I only want to—

ROSE: Now you listen to me. For the last time. If you do this again I'll have the police trace the call. They can do that, you know. They'll throw you in jail so fast—

JOE: You don't need to do that. I mean you no harm. This is all a misunderstanding. Your name is Rose, isn't it?

(SILENCE.)

JOE: Rose Marie Ivy. You live at—

ROSE: My name's not Ivy.

JOE: Sanchez, then. Rose Marie Sanchez, your maiden name. You live at 3944 Via de la Carcel, around the corner from the old AMF Profile Shop. There's a—

ROSE: How do you know that?

JOE: From the bedroom window you can see a pepper tree. We've lived there for twelve years.

ROSE: What do you mean "we"? I live alone. I've always lived alone! Who is this? I—I don't have to tell you anything!

JOE: Honey, this is Joe. Do you hear that? My clothes

are in the closet, my toothbrush is over the sink. Remember me? My—

ROSE: I don't know what your game is, but you've got a sick sense of humor, did anybody ever tell you that?

JOE: Yes. You did. Many times. Only I'm not joking. Believe me. Something's happened. I don't know what but—

ROSE: I'm not joking, either! Why should I believe you? You're a sick, sick . . .

JOE: Give me a chance to—

ROSE: To what? Drive me out of my mind? First you follow me, try to mug me, then you make threatening calls. Well, this is the last time! There are laws against people like you! If you call again you'll be talking to the LAPD! Now *good-by!*

The line went dead.

Good old Rose, he thought. Never a dull moment. If you don't see it her way, she won't play.

Hold tight. There's an edge creeping up on you, only a thin line, but if you allow yourself to slip over it now you're through.

He picked up the phone and dialed Roger.

ROGER: Hello?

JOE: Rog, has—has anyone called since you've been home?

ROGER: Not till now. Where are you? You're not still at the shop! My God. You had me worried, buddy. I tried to get you at home.

JOE: You called the house? Did Rose say anything?

ROGER: She hung up on me. I figured you had a fight.

JOE: Yeah, a fight. That's it. Roger, you—you do know me, then?

ROGER: Well, you don't sound too happy, naturally. But I always know your voice, man. You do sound wiped-out, though. Not that I blame you.

JOE: Then everything's the same?

ROGER: It'll be fine. You'll see. I'll move your stuff into the spare room. Don't even unpack. I'm sure Rose'll come around.

JOE: What are you talking about?

ROGER: The stuff that—oh, Jesus, haven't you been home yet? The least she could have done was tell you. It's none of my business but . . . Joey, she must have moved your things out while you were at work, your clothes, books, everything. It was on the front porch when I got here. Sharon almost shat a brick sideways when the movers came with it. But don't you worry. Leave it like it is, except for underwear, toothbrush, the bare essentials. You'll be back home before you know it. These things blow over. Take my word for it.

JOE: I'm trying to, Roger. I'm honest to God trying to.

He set the phone down gently.

She must have planned this whole thing, then. Moved me out of the house and out of her life before it happened. Whatever it was. She was ready for it. I don't know how, but she was. Score one for her.

He got up from his workbench, paced the store, away from the light. On the other side of the glass doors a scattering of indefatigable shoppers pressed on to their last rounds, ignoring the darkened glass and his face behind it.

He counted his steps, idly touching display racks of videocassettes.

It all started with the store, he thought. Business was never good enough. Because I talked Roger into stocking too much of the wrong inventory. Look at the titles. Favorites of mine, a drug on the market. Too many genre movies, like Franju's *The Forbidden Door*, Lieberman's *The Shudder*, Sole's *Cabin One*, Romero's *The Dark Tower*, Carpenter's *El Diablo*, Argento's *The Fear Threshold*, Hill's *Clue*, De Palma's *The Grassy Knoll*, Cohen's *Blood*, Dante's *No Survivors*, Hooper's *The Black Fear*, Spielberg's *Talking in the Dark*. Plus the old-time libraries from the majors. All of limited appeal. One might think I consciously set it up that way, so that I'd be forced to turn to restorations as a way of bringing in more money. So that I'd have to spend so many, many hours here instead of at home. One might think so.

Well, to hell with all of it now.

He pushed the door open on darkness. As far as the eye could see up and down the Mall, colorful signs were blinking off, holograms flickering out, glass doors locking, merchants and shoppers departing for the night. The imposing facades of Bullock's, Buffum's, Robinson's, alongside the smaller, independent businesses like Moony Cob's, Victor's Barbecue, Tom and Denny's Two Guys From Lynwood—all were shutting down. Soon they would be home to dinner and family, or to leftovers and video; it was all the same after the lights go out and the cast withdraws to its honeycombs.

I wonder where the kid sleeps? In between the buildings, at the back of the shop, probably, if he can't afford an apartment of his own. I could get Larry to let him into the theater at night. It's cool and dark in there and the seats are comfortable. I could even give him a job here, rent him the workroom and let him take over for me when I'm gone. If he cares that much about real movies, if he ever groks that there's a difference between movies and video.

Next door the reading room, too, was closing down for the night. While he stood there the 'gram with its mysterious, all-purpose message dimmed and cut off. He walked outside, locking the Pit behind him, and stood in the space where the message had been.

A clerk was totaling up the register and rearranging books next to the lounge chairs. He was a pale but healthy-looking young man with a shirt that was too tight and shoes designed for running rather than standing all day on synthetic carpeting. Joe tapped on the glass with his ring finger.

The young man saw him and made a referee's *out* signal with his arms. Joe persisted. The young man came to the door, unkeyed it.

"Sorry, mister, we're closed."

"It's important."

"We'll be open again at nine a.m."

"I can't wait."

Grudgingly the clerk let him in and returned to his

closing ritual. "I can give you one of our brochures, I guess. Read it over, and if you need any more information—"

"What does—did—that quotation mean?"

The clerk was bemused. "Which one?"

"The one in the window this afternoon."

"What did it mean to you?"

"I don't know. That's why I'm asking."

"I couldn't answer that. Everyone finds exactly what he seeks."

"What does that mean?"

"It speaks to you personally. The Way has many faces. All are equal to the Wach."

Joe tried to remember what the kid had told him. Mind-reading bacteria, for God's sake; science fiction. "You mean it's different for everyone, that no two people see the same thing? Like an optical illusion?"

"There are no illusions here. You check those at the door."

Roger had seen a different message, or so he claimed. Why would he lie? He wouldn't, Joe decided, not to me. That's not his style.

Joe leaned into the window enclosure. The laser and mirrors were angled to reflect an open page of THE WAY OF THE WACH.

"Don't touch that," said the young man.

"Why not?"

"It's a bitch to align."

Joe peered down at the book. It was open to a thick page. Plastic, as the kid had described. And dusty. Even though the quotations changed every day, the page had not been turned in a long time.

He tried to read it upside down. But there was nothing on the page except for a blot of black ink in the center. As he leaned over it, he saw that the blot was actually composed of millions of tiny specks, trapped between two layers of transparent laminated vinyl. He leaned closer. It was getting late and he was tired. Very tired, apparently.

Because as he got closer the specks seemed to move, subtly rearranging themselves into rows of printed lettering.

"Let me see that," he said.

The clerk handed him a copy of THE WAY OF THE WACH from the counter. "Try this one. They're all the same."

Joe took the book from him.

"You can start while I'm finishing up. If you're sincere. It'll take me a few more minutes. You won't have enough time to really get into it, though, not tonight. It's heavy."

Joe held the unwieldy volume in his hands and opened the cover awkwardly. The young man spoke the truth. It was heavy, all right.

He was suddenly afraid to open it completely. He had an intense premonition about what he might find inside.

"Let me ask you another question."

"Yeah?"

"If I read this, what will it do for me?"

"Are you confused, no place left to turn? Are you searching for the Way?"

"Who isn't?"

"Then this will enable you to find it. It will make you free and allow you to begin again. You'll be born all over. But only if that is what you truly desire. The Kingdom of Heaven—"

"Does it do that for all your customers?"

"Why don't you ask them?"

"Did it do that for my wife?"

The clerk hesitated, then smiled oleaginously. "Ask her. Or better yet, trust in the evidence of your own senses. Isn't she a happier person now, without the guilt of past mistakes to weigh her down? Isn't she—"

"How much did it cost her?"

"It's in the brochure."

Joe waited.

"Okay. For each Step of the Way, we ask a donation of a mere three hundred dollars. To help cover our administrative costs."

Holy shit, thought Joe. "How many Steps are there?"

"Volumes I through IX, plus whatever you decide the Final Step, the one that makes you clean, is worth." The young man turned a clear eye on Joe for a second, as if seeing him for the first time. "That's straight, friend. There's no way it has to cost anybody more than three thousand. That's all we ask. I don't think it's unreasonable. The final Volume, Step X, is purely optional. That means it's up to you. You don't even have to pay until you've read the first nine. It's kind of like a money-back guarantee. If you don't think it's the best thing you've ever read, you don't have to pay. Nobody's refused yet, though. Ninety-nine percent—"

Joe took out his wallet, removed his VisaMall card. "Deal me in."

"I told you, we're closed. I'm only talking to you out of the goodness of my heart. In the morning we'll be happy to—"

"I can't wait till morning. I—I promised my wife. I'll pay whatever you want. How long does it take?"

"We encourage you to proceed at your own pace." The young man eyed the door nervously.

"I want all ten Steps. Right now."

"All at once?!"

"I'll take full responsibility."

"You'd have to sign the consent forms, anyway. . . ." The young man chewed his lip. "I'm closed up now, though, see? I cleared the register. I'd have to—"

"Just give me the books, Steps, whatever they are. Do I go back there?" Joe pointed to a curtain.

"Yes, but I couldn't even ring up your card. I told you, the terminal's down for the night. How do I know you've got enough credit?"

That was the ace Joe had been counting on, in the event Rose Marie had charged it on his card instead of her own and cleaned him out. There was no way the clerk could check now.

"Say, you look familiar," said the young man. "Don't you work in the Video Pit with that other guy, what's his name?"

"It's my store. Our store." He flipped open a line of credit cards and ID. "See there? My business address, resale number, everything. Tell you what. If my account's not good for it, you can have my share in the store. I'll write you a promissory note. Fifty percent, in exchange for the course."

"Jesus Christ, what would you want to do that for? The Video Pit must be worth a hell of a lot more than three grand."

"Take it or leave it. But only if I can do it now."

"Look, I only work on commission."

"Then no one will know about this but the two of us. Put it in your own account at the bank in the morning. Keep my card until then. As far as Indects is concerned, you went home. I'm not even here. You're not here. This is between you and me. Right?"

"I don't know," said the young man. But he moved to lock the door.

"I want the same thing my wife got."

"Our records are strictly confidential."

"Hey." Joe grabbed an application form and wrote out a quick but binding promissory note on the back. He signed his name to it with a final flourish. Then he inked his thumb and printed that next to the signature. "See this, asshole? What more do you want from me?"

The young man stared at Joe, a silly expression on his lips, as if unable to decide whether to embrace him or bite his nose off and run for cover. Maintaining this expression he pulled out a drawer and riffled through the files. "What was the name?"

"The woman in the yellow blouse."

"Oh, Rosie! I know Rosie."

Rosie, he thought. Rosie, your ass.

"She's been coming here for three months. I remember. She took the Final Step this afternoon."

"That's what I want."

"I can't stay here while you wade through ten books. I've got to get home. What if the security tapes do a sweep, it gets to be midnight, I'm still sitting here . . . ?"

"Then just give me the Final Step."

"Two hours and that's it."

The young man pushed aside the curtain and set a stack of nine volumes on the reading stand beside Joe's recliner chair.

"Do up as much as you can to prepare. Then, when you want to go all the way—" He pulled down a single-book-sized sealed carton from the storage shelf. "—Finish up with this. It's the big one. Volume X."

Joe adjusted the reading lamp over his head. "Why is that one brand-new?"

"Volume X's can only be used once. It's a specification of the manufacturer. The directions are on the cover. Follow them exactly."

"Why can't you give me the same one you gave my wife?"

"It's a personal directive from Dr. Flowers." The young man's eyes wandered to the storage shelf, where a used Volume X carton addressed back to Indects, Inc. headquarters lay open and waiting to be resealed.

Joe said nothing.

"I'll be over at the Weenie Wigwam for as long as I can stretch it. I wanted to catch the NBC Big Event, anyway. My VCR's jammed. I may as well watch it there. I'm going to lock the door behind me, so you'll have to wait here till I come back. And stay out of sight. Got it?"

"Got it," said Joe. "I'm on my own now."

"Right. And remember—two hours. Three hours absolutely max. It's the best I can do. Okay?"

"Okay."

He waited for the young man to leave him.

He lifted Volume I gingerly from the top of the stack. The book was broad but surprisingly thin, with only a few dozen hefty pages within. The washable imitation-leather cover was well used. Comfortable. Almost inviting.

A strange calm fell over him. He thought:

It's as if I've been waiting year after year for everything, including my life, to get underway. When I was twelve I was sure it would all happen once I finished high school. At eighteen, after college. Then Rose Marie came along. There seemed to be so much of it written there in her face and in her eyes, so many things worth knowing. Beautiful things. Things she never told me.

Once again, somehow, it got pushed back.

Thirty, thirty-five. . . . I began to wonder whether it would ever happen. When? At fifty, sixty, seventy? When would I know? It's been a long, slow preparation. But that was the flaw in my thinking as long as I can remember. There will never come a day when the time is right for it to begin. I will never be ready. For this waiting, the dogged hours and decades of it, is in fact my life, the very stuff and substance of it. This is, in a word, It. The real McCoy and the genuine article. The which than which there is no whicher. It always has been. It always will be. That's all there is. There ain't no more.

He focused his attention. Time was passing even now, as inexorably as the falling of a scythe.

He opened the book. He began to read.

What he experienced during the next few minutes was simple but exquisite, as unexpected as a kiss in the middle of a fight to the death. So pure and direct, such a pleasant escape that Joe only wished he had read it when he was a boy. It was exactly what he needed, though he could not have realized that until now. The more he read the more familiar it became. It contained all of his favorite story elements, arranged and combined in perfect proportion. There was even a timeless yet unpretentious moral for him to ponder at the end. By the time he finished he was almost certain he *had* read it before, a long time ago, just out of reach of memory. *I would have thought of it myself, if it had occurred to me. If I were a writer, of course.* He could not find the name of an author or copyright owner anywhere in the book. It was without a doubt one of the best stories he had ever read in his life.

He closed the book, amazed.

No wonder the reading room is so popular, he thought. If everything is as perfectly written as that. So this is why

Rose fell for their line. How could she not? If all the books are this good—if the introductory book in the lobby is half as good—then it's inconceivable that anyone could resist.

He reached for the second volume, opened it and scanned a few lines.

Unbelievably, it was even better than the first. Richer, more detailed, more psychological in its approach. It cut closer and closer to what was truly on his mind. The answers seemed to have been laid out for him in a neat progression, one step ahead of his own thinking.

But there was no time.

He flipped ahead through the laminated pages.

Well, he thought, either my problems are more universal than I supposed, or else Mason Flowers has achieved a level of insight into the human condition that Freud only strived for. If this pseudo-scientific religion—or pseudo-religious science—is being franchised in every mall in every city across the country, there's no stopping it. The potential is awesome.

But hold on. Hold on a minute.

He closed the book and set it back on the stand. He leaned away from it. He watched as it appeared to flatten and become thinner, as the padded cover settled back into place.

He counted off a few seconds to be sure. Then he reached for the third volume, flicking its cover open with his fingernail and quickly withdrawing his hand.

The print inside was moving.

It could have been an optical illusion, a trick of the lighting.

But no.

As he leaned out of its field the lines froze, half-formed, and then slowly proceeded to melt back into the center of the page.

These books, he realized, are reading me.

That's it. The books in the lobby are teasers, able to provide just enough of what you want to know in the middle of a hot afternoon to make you feel refreshed and renewed. And to be sure you come back for more.

Of course you would want to go on to the first Step. How could you resist? The books are picking your brain, taking their cues from your own mind, replicating and mimicking and giving back what you want to hear but can't formulate consciously for yourself. Each person who handles Volume I thinks it's the best book he or she has ever read. How could it be otherwise? The volumes become progressively more sophisticated, and you're hooked. The ink, whatever it is—telepathic bacteria, if that can be believed; have mercy—is produced in strains of increasing sensitivity, so that the Final Step . . .

He grabbed the carton and took out Volume X.

I want to go all the way, he thought. I want the Big One, the full treatment, same as Rose. So I can know. So I can understand what's happened to her.

Telepathic bacteria. What a concept. From where? From space, the kid said. From somewhere in orbit. How long have they been there? If that's the case, they could be out there forming and re-forming themselves into anything the world wants to see. Flying saucers. Invaders from Mars. Spurious television signals, maybe. Who knows? Escapees from Uranus. A message from the archetypal God of our dreams. The Living Word.

That, he thought, is the Way of the Wach.

The final volume was bound on a grand scale, huge and ribbed and weighty. To befit that last, Really Big Donation. Of course. He scanned the instructions on the cover.

Do not hold in hands until ready to use.

Place fingers in hand grips before opening.

Wait ten seconds.

Do not set book down until you are finished.

Wait ten seconds before closing cover.

You may feel slightly drowsy. Do not attempt to operate heavy machinery.

Thank you.

His hands were shaking.

He balanced the heavy book. The hand grips were two sets of finger moldings embossed into the front and back covers. In order to use it, you had to insert your hands into the spaces. It was the only way you could get the book open without losing your grip.

With difficulty he tipped the edge to the light and examined the openings. There was a tiny silver point at the end of each thumb space.

He drew up his legs and supported the book on his knees. Touching only a corner, he raised the front cover an inch, two inches.

The small silver point within, a needle, flashed in the lamplight as it extended a few millimeters.

Enough to break the skin, he realized, and get inside you, into your bloodstream and so into your brain, to get to the thoughts that are most deeply hidden. The pain, the repressed memories. To seek them out and absorb them and take them away. To eat them, like bacteria. Yes. That is why each Volume X can only be used once. It feeds; it fills up. After it has cleansed you and made you free.

I'm ready, he thought. Oh God, am I. Lift the scales from my eyes and the burden from my soul. *Do it.*

He hesitated. He stopped himself. He put the book down.

He climbed out of the chair and went to the shelf. There. Another recently-used Volume X lying in its carton, waiting to be resealed and returned for purging. Was it the one administered to Rose Marie this afternoon?

It has to be, he thought. What it took from her is still trapped there between its bloated covers. I need to know what it was. The suffering she carried with her so quietly for so long until it became too much for her to bear. The pain of the last fifteen years. The pain of her life with me, which I never knew anything about, which I was too blind to see. Let me take it into myself, all of it, and if need be let it do to me what it did to her, if that is the only way. But let me know it before the last evidence of our life together is erased forever from the universe.

He took the used copy of Volume X down from the shelf. He leaned back. He inserted his fingers. Into these poor hands, he thought. With a rush he opened the cover.

His eyelids feathered shut. Darkness swirled around him.

It was so easy and yet so hard to let go. Going away, he thought. Going. Gone.

As this comes in, so much pain will go anywhere.

Good-by to all I loved. Good-by to my years of idle dreaming, the minutiae which adds up to the definition of a human life. Good-by to those I never forgot. . . .

Good-by, at last, Julie London. You might as well go now. Good-by, Shirley MacLaine in *Artists and Models*, Patricia Smith in *The Bachelor Party* and Beatrice Pearson in *Force of Evil* and Barbara Ruick in *Carousel*. . . . Good-by, Pat Crowley in *Money From Home* and Marge Champion in *Showboat* and Janet Leigh in *Houdini* and Barbara Rush in *When Worlds Collide*. Audrey Hepburn in *Roman Holiday* and Leslie Caron in *Lili*, Kay Kendall in *Genevieve* and Joan Collins in *Sea Wife* and Terry Moore in *Beneath the 12-mile Reef* and Sophia Loren in *Houseboat* and Gloria Grahame in *The Man Who Never Was* . . . you lived on unchanged for a time in me. Debra Paget in *Birds of Paradise* and little Debbie Reynolds *Singin' In the Rain*, Sherry Jackson in *Come Next Spring* and Susannah York in *The Greengage Summer*. Sarah Miles in *Time Lost and Time Remembered*. Luanna Anders and Daria Halprin. Janet Margolin. Elizabeth Taylor in *A Place in the Sun*. Young Lana Turner. Ingrid Bergman in *For Whom the Bell Tolls*. Claire Bloom in *Limelight*. Jean Simmons in *The Blue Lagoon*. Grace Kelly in *To Catch a Thief* and Ida Lupino and Marilyn Monroe, and Brenda Scott and Annie Helm and Annie Ditchburn. Brenda Vacarro in *Summertree*. Jean Seberg and Jeanne Crain and Jessica Harper and Jessica Lange, Donna Mills and Donna Loren, Susan Penhaligon and Susan George, Barbara Carrera and Barbara Steele. Joan Goodfellow in *Buster and Billie*. Mariette Hartley. Senta Berger. Maria Schneider and Maria Schell. Catherine Deneuve. Monica Vitti. Joanna Pettet and Joanna Cameron and Joanna Lumley and Joanna Cassidy. Ursula Andress. Margot Kidder. Jane Seymour. Caroline Munro. Kathleen Beller and Kathleen Quinlan, Roseanna

Arquette and Pamela Ludwig and Pamela Franklin and Bonnie Bedelia and P.J. Soles. . . . Too many to name. And to the frame I never found, the most beautiful I've ever seen from a movie I can't remember, a girl surrounded by flowers with the sun at her back, burning her image into my brain, whose face I cannot see. Good-by to you all.

He felt a cool jet of antiseptic spray on his thumbs, and then the images flowed in.

His life—or was it Rose Marie's—flashed before his eyes, moments that became feelings, summers that went on forever, instants that flew past in the blinking of an eye. Days longer than any nights, nights that never ended. Every bit, every scrap and every second and the shadow of every move and the shape of every feature and the whorls of her skin and the contour of every touch, and the whispering away and the squandering of it all, second by second, the good and the bad thrown out together, as if none of it had mattered more than the flickering of a wing across the sun. All speeding backwards to the first, the second in time when it began, every breath of it back to the beginning.

He felt it eddy around him, and clear.

He was sitting. Only it was not he. It was she, Rose Marie. Someone was walking this way across the grass, an expanse of electric green spread like a bright carpet as far as the eye could see. A man, a young man, the sun flashing his hair into the brilliance of flames, behind him the forgotten buildings of a college campus.

He looked down at his hands. She looked down at her hands, folded in her lap against the sparkling yellow dress. It was the first of May and there were flowers everywhere.

He stopped in front of her. She looked up. In his eyes she saw herself reflected, beautiful for the first time. The flowers were all around, trembling behind her, the blazing sun coruscating through them and through her with a great and mighty light.

He was, she thought, the most handsome boy she had ever seen.

"Hello," he said, his voice vibrating the air.

"Hello," she said, afraid that her own voice would not be heard for the pounding. "W-who are you?"

Joe Ivy held to this image for as long as he could, until it flared out and burned through his eyelids. Then there was only the marking of his own pulse, alone in darkness.

And:

OFF.